D0006937

# THE
# *STALKING*
# HORSE

*By the same author*

THE THOUSAND DOORS

THE HEIRS OF CAIN

THE SONG OF DAVID FREED

THE OTHER MAN'S SHOES

THE SWORD OF THE GOLEM

# THE
# *STALKING*
# HORSE

*Abraham Rothberg*

SATURDAY REVIEW PRESS
*New York*

11-76·77-

*Copyright © 1972 by Abraham Rothberg*

All rights reserved. No part of this work may be reproduced or transmitted in any form or by any means, electronic or mechanical, including photocopy, recording, or any information storage retrieval system, without permission in writing from the publisher.

Published simultaneously in Canada
by Doubleday Canada Ltd., Toronto

Library of Congress Catalog Number:
ISBN 0-8415-0209-9

*Saturday Review Press*
*230 Park Avenue*
*New York, New York 10017*

PRINTED IN THE UNITED STATES OF AMERICA
Design by Margaret F. Plympton

For *David* and *Dody Westheimer*
the Texas branch

56037

*stalking horse,*     n. 1. a horse, which a hunter may conceal himself behind in stalking game; 2. hence, a pretense; a blind.


*All ideologies are relative; the only absolute is the torment that men inflict on one another*

Evgenia Ginzburg

# THE
# *STALKING*
# HORSE

# 1

# A Classical Education

Their gray Lincoln materialized out of the morning mist like something on the hunt. It came up the long straight road too fast, flashing predatory in the alternating slashes of shade and early sun, the tires screeching like an animal. Watching through the binoculars Nathaniel Chapman brought their faces into sharp focus, Gordon Hauser driving and Andrew Wheelwright in the death seat. When the car turned into the yard and parked, its nose headed away from the house, ready for a swift getaway, Chapman put the glasses down and came out of the sun porch on to the veranda. Andrew Wheelwright's New England face was almost a caricature of Franklin D. Roosevelt's newspaper photos, the pince-nez glasses clipped on his long aristocratic nose, the meerschaum cigarette holder rakishly held in his strong even white teeth. He waved the holder and called, "Hey there, Nathaniel, getting much?" When Hauser got out, Wheelwright asked if he remembered Hauser.

"Hauser stays where he is," Chapman called back.

"Come off it, Nathaniel!"

"You want to come on up, Andrew, okay. But not Hauser. If you don't like that, take off."

Hauser's handsome face, with its Adolf Menjou mustache and elegance, darkened, but he only looked down at his shoes. Wheelwright patted his shoulder, then strode up on to the veranda, hand outstretched, but Chapman didn't shake it. "Not very hospitable," Wheelwright remarked.

"I don't take this as a friendly social call."

"But it is, it is. Just two old friends getting together after a long absence for a talk. Calls for a little *politesse*, don't you think?"

"You always said I had bad manners."

"So you do, Nathaniel, so you do." Wheelwright turned, stretched, and looked back down the road. "Beautiful *allée* those elms make. Someone must have planted them a long time ago so that we—you—could enjoy them now." Wreathed in smoke, his face was sibylline. "Always liked elms. Tough, hard, long-lasting wood. Hate to see us losing so many of them, and to a lousy fungus. *Ceratostomella ulmi*. Carried from one tree to another by bark beetles. Causes Dutch elm disease. Nearly wiped all the elms out of New England." His eyes still raking the long line of trees, he asked, "English or American elm?"

"*Ulmus Americana*, of course." Chapman's smile was forced. Wheelwright was disconcerting because he had all sorts of odd information, the kind you didn't expect him to have, like *Ceratostomella ulmi* and bark beetles. "You know I'm a patriot."

Wheelwright didn't rise to the bait. "You *are*, Nathaniel, more than you realize." He turned on his heel, his smile natural. "Even in New Jersey I prefer English elms. The snob in me."

In the sun porch Wheelwright went to the windows to look at the elms once more. "Going to offer me a drink, or doesn't your hospitality extend that far?"

"Not now. Ordinarily, yes."

"You're making this harder than it has to be."

"I told you."

"You told me and I remember."

"I'm telling you again, then. I'm out. Finished. Through. I'm not cooperating."

"Or cooperative. You're repeating yourself, Nathaniel. You said that on the phone when you asked me, ordered me, not to come up here from Washington." Deliberately, Wheelwright came over to the desk and flicked ashes on the binoculars. "Watching for me?"

Chapman blew the ashes off the binoculars and put them into a desk drawer. "I use those for birdwatching," he explained. The moment I'm in the same room with him, he thought, I begin to feel the necessity for explanation, and then the necessity for deception, as if only by lying can I protect myself from losing to Wheelwright something I mean desperately to maintain. No wonder I was afraid to let him come up here. The moment he arrives, everything I've put together to make a new life, teaching, leave from the university, working on the book, seems jerry-built and unimportant. Only what *he* does, what *he* wants, seems infused with urgency and importance. The intrusion into his precariously built and balanced peace Chapman resented bitterly. No matter where you go, they don't let you be.

"Birdwatching," Wheelwright repeated neutrally. Slowly, he surveyed the room, his blue eyes cold and enlarged behind pince-nez lenses taking in the wicker furniture, the old rolltop desk, the typewriter, the bookcases, with what might be fastidious distaste or contempt. Before asking, "How much of all this is yours, Nathaniel?" he had already turned his glance outdoors again, to the elms.

"About a hundred and thirty acres."

"Water on the property?"

"A little stream that sometimes dries up. Small pond you can actually swim in. Couple of wells for drinking water and the like. Why, Andrew, you looking for some real estate? I didn't think you were ready to quit yet."

"I'm not ready to quit," he said without emphasis. "Tell me, though, why didn't you ever invite me up here when we were at school? You know, for vacations? Or with Phyliss afterward? Your parents lived here, didn't they?"

"I grew up here."

"Then why?"

"I always thought it wasn't grand enough for you," Chapman confessed. He was ashamed, because he had also thought that Wheelwright might look down on his parents. What could the sophisticated Andrew Wheelwright, Skull and Bones, left halfback, with money and connections, find to interest him on a New Jersey doctor's farm? The farm had even less to offer Wheelwright now. Out of the way, virtually isolated, almost no one ever came there except Helga, the cleaning woman, and an occasional repairman.

"A shame you and Betsy didn't have kids while you were still together. This farm's a great place for kids to grow up," Wheelwright observed.

Chapman ran a finger silently over the typewriter keys. "Why don't you tell me what's on your mind?"

Wheelwright chose his words. "We've had a Russian defector under wraps. Came over in London. We're not ready to surface him yet, but we want him out of Washington. He's been cooped up in one place or another for a long time, so he's depressed and angry."

"Understandable," Chapman murmured, but Wheelwright ignored him.

"Stale. Won't give us much more. Says he didn't defect to exchange one prison for another." He added ironically, "Says he *chose freedom!*"

"Didn't he?"

"Chose? He ran." Wheelwright sucked noisily on his cigarette holder. "We want to give him some tether, not quite turn him loose, but leave him looser."

"And you want me to be the tether?"

Wheelwright nodded.

"The answer is no."

"This is a very special man."

"Defectors from over there are—by definition—all special men."

"He's someone you know—knew—Nathaniel."

Chapman felt the sweat sudden on his palms. "Where?" he asked. "In Russia?"

"There and elsewhere."

"Someone I knew well?"

"Aleksei Mikhailovich Fedorov."

"You son-of-a-bitch!" Chapman said, the words escaping from between his teeth like steam under pressure.

"Let Fedorov stay with you for a couple of months, maybe only a couple of weeks, until we decide what to do with him."

The only sound was Chapman's fingernail on the typewriter keys until he asked, "Did Alek ask you to come talk to me?"

"He said you were the only American he trusted."

"Ha! Did he *send* you?"

"The idea was ours. He only said he wanted to talk to you."

"Why didn't you let him?"

"He was under wraps."

"That the only reason?"

"No."

"He's in danger."

"They're after anyone who comes over, especially if he was KGB." Wheelwright shrugged. "They tried to kill him twice."

"Even under wraps?"

"What better time?"

"If you knew about Alek and me, They'll know too. Their dossiers are as good as ours, their memories too. Maybe better." Wheelwright's wince pleased him. "They'll come after him here."

"We'd keep an eye on you, if that's what you're afraid of."

"I'm afraid all right, of Them and of you." Wheelwright was setting out the lures: curiosity, danger, the chance for revenge—worse—perhaps the chance for forgiveness or for being forgiven. Next would come the offer of cash. He no longer needed Wheelwright's cash, but there had been all those times at college and afterward, when Wheelwright's picking up the check meant the crucial difference.

"We'll pick up the tab for expenses, of course."

"Of course," Chapman acknowledged sarcastically, "and a little extra, eh?"

"Too rich to need the money, or too proud to take it?"

"Your boys ran a check on me before you came up here, Andrew, so you probably know what I own and what I owe to the penny."

"You exaggerate our efficiency."

"In technical matters, you're efficiency itself."

"You do stay sore for a long time, Nathaniel."

"I'm sore because I hurt all over—still."

"Sore at the Agency, or Aleksei Mikhailovich, or the whole beautiful world as it is, Pangloss?"

"All of them."

"So you're up here in New Jersey tilling your own garden, or your old man's garden."

"Voltaire was wise."

"You've even got a maid to take into the bushes to teach the elementary laws of physics."

"Wheelwright!" Chapman sounded a warning.

"What, and prim too! Where's the old swordsman I used to know?" Wheelwright remarked mildly. He walked to a chair and sat, his shoulders slumped, looking like those photographs of Roosevelt after the Yalta Conference, old and tired, the cigarette holder no longer jaunty but depressed from the side of his mouth.

Another ploy . . . another way of doing his job. . . . I'm not going to feel sorry for him, Chapman told himself. He's a thoroughgoing bastard doing a gangster's job. I've seen him use that ploy a hundred times before. If you won't help your country, help me. More personal, immediate, concrete; for some people much more effective. But he felt a pang of pity nonetheless. "You're looking a little piqued, Andrew, the old golden-boy luster rubbed off a little?"

"Not a little, Nathaniel, a lot, if that makes you any happier."

"It does, it does," he said, mimicking Wheelwright's repetitions.

"I thought it might."

Chapman rose and started to pace. "Why park Fedorov with me? Why park him at all? Your people have been at him for months, probably squeezed him dry. Why not just give him a ticket and some money and let him start clean? Just because he was KGB?"

"Only *co-opted*, Fedorov would note, not really *recruited*. Essential difference. God, they make Jesuitical distinctions there!" Wheelwright exclaimed.

"Wrong religion. Not Jesuitical, Leninist. Though maybe the roots are the same. The 'opposition's' not that different from us, we've got ones who 'cooperate' too but don't actually 'belong,' who don't sign on with the Company," Chapman reminded him.

"Co-opted or not, he's ex-KGB, and I'm not sure he's ex," Wheelwright asserted. "Is he bona fide or are They planting him to play back? Who is trying to kill him? Why? And were the attempts for real?"

"Too bad They didn't get him."

Wheelwright was startled. "That bad?"

"Better men have died—and for worse reasons."

"Better men than thee and me, too, Nathaniel."

Chapman's pacing grew more emphatic, rhythmical. "The problem is whether Fedorov's another joker who got tired of the muck over there and decided to come over here, or if he's still working a double, a sleeper. Somebody takes a potshot at him—was it that way, Andrew, a shot?—

and then he tells you I'm the only one of two hundred million Americans he trusts . . . and you buy that. So you play it just the way I would, if I were in your shoes. You want to bring him up here, plant him with me, which means that I'll be his 'collar,' and you'll be staking him out like a nanny goat for a tiger, so you can discover who's hunting him and for what.

"Fedorov asked about me? Maybe. More likely, someone —you?—remembered that Fedorov and I'd been friends. The rest was logical. Chapman's got an out-of-the-way place where the 'opposition's' supposed to be off-limits. Good, we'll stick Fedorov up there. We'll send Wheelwright up to talk to Chapman. They went to school together, so Andrew's the right man to talk to him, old-school tie and all that. If Chapman's peeve against the Department hasn't faded, old Andrew can persuade him. After all, this is the Agency not the Department. He cooperated with us before, he'll cooperate again. Just in case, though, let's run a check on his friends, finances, professional life, to see if there's another way to get to him." Chapman's words were swift, as if he were reciting an overlearned lesson.

A smile spread across Wheelwright's face. "We didn't teach you too badly, did we now?"

"When you live with ferrets long enough, you get to think like one. And, of course, you brought Gordon Hauser up with you to plant a couple of 'bugs' so you could keep track of how things were going."

"Is that why you wouldn't let Gordon into the house? For shame! You're behind the times, Nathaniel. If we want to listen, we don't even have to get inside your bloody house, not even close. We can sit out there half a mile away and listen to every squeak of the bedsprings. But"—he tapped his cigarette holder against his temple mockingly—"good thinking."

"I can still think clearly enough not to get involved in this. I'm not cooperating any more. I don't like this kind of deception. And there are few people in the world I care to see less than Aleksei Mikhailovich Fedorov."

"Once, in your salad days, old buddy, you said, *'It is more shameful to distrust one's friends than to be deceived by them.'* "

"So you remember that?"

"I have prized the Duc as I have prized Niccolo. Must I remind you that you introduced me to both?"

"We helped in each other's education, Andrew, more than we should have. But the virtue of a classical education is that it gives a man the means of being a scoundrel and defending his scurrilousness. I wish I'd learned to distrust my friends earlier, and more. I might have been less betrayed."

"Everyone gets betrayed, one way or another." Wheelwright was impatient. "Yet Rochefoucauld was right."

"Aleksei Mikhailovich Fedorov set me up for the KGB."

"You set yourselves up, you and your lady. You both should have known better. Moscow's no place for romance."

Chapman heard his own breathing, "Nor for love," he remarked.

"Love's a mania. They taught us that at Yale—the virtues of a classical education—and you should have learned it."

"Do you see Phyliss and the boys?" Chapman asked abruptly, enjoying the pain on Wheelwright's face.

Wheelwright ran his hand through his thinning, graying blond hair, his headshake despairing.

"Not the boys either?"

"Won't speak to me on the telephone when I call."

"But you *do* call?"

"Oh, sure, Phyliss and I are civilized enough."

"Unlike me. Betsy and I haven't talked or seen each other in almost five years—and glad of it."

"Unlike you, my friend. Do you realize it's two years since I've seen you? Phyliss, at least, knows that sometimes you do everything you can and it's not enough." He stood up and looked out at the elms and Chapman knew he would bring their talk back to what he'd come for. He was a dogged man. "That's over now," Wheelwright said, "my Phyliss and your Betsy, and your Valentina Andreyevna, so let's get down to cases. Will you let us park Fedorov here?"

"There are hundreds of places you could squirrel him away. Why here? Why me?"

Wheelwright was still staring at the glistening elms, the shadows in the *allée* beneath them almost evaporated in the morning sunshine. "We're not sure he's genuine," he said. "We think he's holding back. We want an eye on him and to know he's in safe hands."

"You think he's really a plant?"

"He should have been dead, twice. They tried with a rifle and a scope—and missed. Then with a grenade in an automobile—and it misfired."

"Too coincidental? Maybe They're just as big fumblers as we are."

Irritably, Wheelwright turned from the window and asked, "Do you have a gun?"

"A shotgun, a couple of hunting rifles. One even has a scope, but I don't hunt any more. Not animals. Not men. Not even Alek Fedorov. You think I tried to murder him?"

Wheelwright grimaced. "You've got the training, the weapons, the motive."

"I didn't know he was within six thousand miles of here until you told me."

"You keep them oiled and cleaned?"

"My revenges and hatreds?"

Wheelwright laughed coldly. "No, the guns."

"Too puritan to let them rust."

From his jacket pocket Wheelwright took a Walther automatic, two clips, and a box of ammunition. He dropped them into the drawer with the binoculars. "Keep that handy, and loaded. Whoever's been after Fedorov may have figured out that you have some connection. You might have visitors."

"That gun official?" Chapman pointed at it, not letting him shut the drawer.

"No."

"Should I say thanks?"

"You still have bad manners. When things sort themselves out—if they do—I'll come back and take it away from you." Chapman let him shut the drawer. He put his hand out and this time Chapman shook it. "Good-bye, Nathaniel," Wheelwright said, "if you change your mind about Fedorov, you know where to reach me."

They left the way they'd come, careening down the road under the elms in the Lincoln, while Chapman followed them with the binoculars until they disappeared on to the high road. Only seconds later, before he had put the glasses down on the desk, a dull roar shook the air and a column of flame and thick oily smoke shot up. Chapman grabbed the Walther from the drawer, checked the clip and the safety, stuck the gun into his waistband, and ran for his own car.

# 2

# Tryst in Moscow

Valentina held his genitals prayerfully, as if in some rite of worship. Examining them, she whispered, "How sad they look."

"*Post coitum triste*," Nathaniel responded, half-embarrassed by the close, admiring scrutiny, still full of her presence, the grace of her bent head, the beauty of her legs as she sat on the bed in the lotus position.

"Are you Jewish?" she asked.

"Because I'm circumcized? No, in America, most male children are circumcized."

"What do they call them in American?" she asked.

"Penis and testicles," he replied, hesitating only for a second.

Valentina shook her head, her long blond hair rippling like cloth of gold over her shoulders. "Not those names they give in biology courses. What *people* call these. People's words."

People's words, he thought, are what most people call dirty words. He told her.

"Prick, Nathaniel?" she repeated, holding it questioningly on her fingers. "And balls?" cupping them gently on her palm. The Russian accent made the English words strangely humorous so that in spite of her serious and tender mien he burst into uproarious laughter.

"Is not prick to puncture with a pin or a needle?" she asked, puzzled.

"That, too, Valya."

"Is it because it sometimes draws blood?" she inquired.

By way of explanation he told her about the time when he was a small boy and another boy called him a prick. Afraid to ask his parents what the word meant, because, although he didn't know its meaning, he knew from the way the boy had used the word that it was a "bad" word, he'd gone to the large dictionary his father kept on a lectern in his waiting room and which, at that point, he still had to stand on a chair to read. He'd looked the word up, read the definition carefully, and though he knew all the explanatory meanings, not until he was at Yale did he understand how much the *people's words* embodied the wisdom of time and human experience. To explain, though, one had to know that the word had different facets from which its jeweled meanings shone. It meant to pierce slightly with a sharp point, or mark by means of a small puncture; it also meant to ride with spurs or urge on with spurs; and, simultaneously, to affect with anguish or remorse; finally, it also meant to remove a young seedling from its bed to another seedbed suitable for further growth.

"The word includes all those things?" she marveled, "from being deflowered through being ridden into ecstasy and later filled with pain and disappointment, and finally being filled with child. All the understanding of what this lovely root of flesh does," she said in Russian. Her fingers held him fast, stroked and raised him up.

"*In the beginning was the word,*" Nathaniel intoned, "and this the word made flesh," grinning as he watched himself grow.

"You are sacrilegious," Valya responded, letting him go, though by then success was in her grasp.

"Between us, Valentina Andreyevna, nothing can be sacrilege," he asserted, and drew her over him like a down quilt.

"How lucky for us that Aleksei Mikhailovich was lent such a splendid flat," he reminded her, lying back on the pillows. At the small dressing table she sat brushing her heavy hair away from her forehead, over her ears and down in front of her breasts. "High ceilings, old Italian furniture, and this veritable stadium of a bed." He bounced up and down on it, demonstrating again the springiness of the mattress.

The electric crackling of her hair stopped and her hand, the brush in it, hung over her head like a threat. She half-turned to him, her profile sharp even in that dim light, repeated shiveringly in the dressing-table mirror as in water. "Valya, are you sorry?"

"We waited so long, but . . . " Once more she began the regular brush strokes, her hair catching and reflecting the light as she continued in silence. Chapman sprang out of bed and, standing behind her, lightly touched her breasts. She went on brushing, more slowly now, languidly, her head thrown back, lips parted. "But what?" he asked. Her upper teeth caught and held his lower one and he was moved to kiss her lips apart. As he did, she answered, so close to him that he breathed in her breath. "Whose flat is this? Why does Aleksei Mikhailovich have access to it?"

"Belongs to a friend of his named Kornilov, a camera-man who's off on location in Pamir," Nathaniel explained.

"Are you sure?"

"If Alek said so I believe him. He's my friend."

"In this country we do not have such friends any more. That time is past. It has been dangerous too long for such friends."

"You think this was 'arranged,' Valya?" His hands slipped from her breasts.

"What people have flats like this?" she asked, her voice hidden, her eyes darting as if they were already trapped. "Only Them. Only theirs."

"Your flat is as grand as this," he protested.

"I am Them too. Fyodor Vyacheslovich is a Stalin Prize winner. You do not win the Stalin Prize unless you belong to them, heart and soul, and our flat is his reward for belonging to them. Like the devil, they pay well for a soul. Aleksei Mikhailovich is a journalist, a writer, a scenarist. He belongs to them too, or else he couldn't publish a line."

"Are you sure?"

Valya shook her head. "There is talk that he cooperates with them. Other writers are careful with him—too careful —too much backslapping, too many vodkas, too much drinking *Brüderschaft* with him. Even my husband does not trust him, although they have been acquainted for years." Her eyebrows arched. "But then, Fyodor Vyacheslovich trusts no one. Perhaps not himself."

"Not even you?"

The brush stopped and she swiveled from the waist to face him. "Especially not me," she replied.

"Is that why you came?"

Her laughter was soundless, sardonic. "If only things were that simple, Nathaniel. A husband doesn't trust his wife, so she gives him cause not to trust her. She presents him with the traditional—the comic? the tragic?—set of horns." Valentina shook herself, turned back to the dressing-table mirror, and resumed brushing her hair.

Chapman massaged her shoulders, gently kneading her flesh. Again she threw her head back. "When you do that, it's as if you'd taken my heart in your hands and were molding my soul, shaping my destiny."

"Would you want that, Valya?"

Her eyes opened and stared into his. "Whether I want that or not, it has already happened."

"Because you're here?"

"Because I let us become entangled, let us go beyond 'permitted' contacts."

"Because we became lovers?"

"No, because we became—we are—friends."

"That *is* a crime."

"You laugh. But you know it *is* a crime here. Every foreigner is an enemy. An American especially. You're the enemy, and we're supposed to watch you"—she winked mischievously, in spite of her anxiety, then was serious again—"and report on you to Them."

"The authorities would like to think—or perhaps like others to think—that every citizen is a Chekist at heart, but you know that isn't true."

"In this one thing, they may be closer to the truth than you imagine," Valya maintained.

"Then why did you let me arrange it?" Chapman asked, now genuinely perturbed.

"I didn't know it would be here, until this morning."

"And once you knew?"

"You didn't tell me Aleksei Mikhailovich had arranged it until I arrived. Perhaps, if I had known . . ."

"I'm sorry," he said, knowing what a lame apology that was, the two most useless words in the language.

"Probably I'd have come anyway. If we'd had to walk once more in Gorki Park, or talk casually and briefly at another official reception, afraid to touch or linger a moment too long because eyes and tongues were everywhere, or pretend still another time that we'd met at the Bolshoi by accident, I'd have screamed, or thrown myself on you and bitten your lips till they bled."

Chapman touched his mouth. "You did well enough in that department."

"I tried to persuade you to come to our flat when Fyodor was out, or away on a lecture tour, but you wouldn't."

"I thought it was too dangerous for you . . . and there's something distasteful about cuckolding a man in his own bed."

"You think this less dangerous? Oh, Nathaniel, you *are* a fool! If you're going to make love to a woman, to another man's wife, what difference where? That is a peculiarly bourgeois fastidiousness."

"I cannot believe . . ."

"You cannot believe! Here, everything is believable, especially the unbelievable. What's more incredible than that the Chief Cultural Affairs officer of the American Embassy and one of the leading actresses of the Maly and Moscow Art Theaters should be making love in what is probably a KGB flat?"

"I'm not a trusting man by nature or training, Valya. We Americans are not altogether fools. We know we're watched, bugged, followed. We know about being compromised and trapped, but I also know Aleksei Fedorov. I don't trust many people, especially here, but I do trust you, and Aleksei Mikhailovich."

"Your trust may be only fifty percent justified. Here and now, that's not enough."

"I helped Alek, I saved his life," Chapman said, hesitated, and then continued, "He knows and is grateful. He wouldn't betray me. He wouldn't betray you."

"Did you tell him it was I who was meeting you here?"

Chapman smiled. "Not gentlemanly. Bourgeois fastidiousness."

She gave no answering smile. "It doesn't matter," she said. She laid her hairbrush down on the dressing table, rose, and began to don her brassiere.

"Don't go," he said, reaching out his hand, but not touching her.

"It's hard to make love, to enjoy, when you're frightened. See." She pointed to him, trying to make a joke of it. "Don't your people warn you about us seductive Russian Mata Haris?"

"We get some training in such matters."

This time her smile was broad and genuine. "Doubtless."

"Let me have a look around," he suggested, more to set her mind at rest than because he thought he could find anything. Without the proper electronic equipment it was almost useless.

She shrugged her other breast into the brassiere, and said, "Look."

Methodically, he went over the room, bed, lamps, tables, doorframes, even the old copy of Levitan's *Quiet Haven* in its nineteenth-century gilt frame that hung over the bed; but he found nothing. If it was a KGB flat, someone there who'd put that painting over the headboard had an ironic sense of humor.

Having watched his every move, Valya said finally, "You won't find a thing. They prepare these places years in advance, before the buildings are constructed. They're very thorough. They had forty microphones in the walls of the American Embassy for more than ten years before your people discovered them."

"Back in the fifties they even managed a transmitter in the United States' Great Seal in the Ambassador's office." He laughed. "Some KGB electronics expert has a sense of humor."

"To find such things you'd have to take an ax to the walls."

*An ax to the walls.* That was what he'd wanted to do so often here, pull down the very walls, level them, and start anew. But he knew such things were impossible. She continued to dress, and again he asked her to stay.

"It's been a wonderful afternoon, Nathaniel, one I'll remember for a very long time, longer than I'd like to, longer than I should, but now I can't contain my fear." She shivered, straightened her stockings, and stepped into her shoes. "It is dark enough to leave now and not be seen. Besides, Fyodor Vyacheslovich will be home for dinner tonight—important guests—and I must be there. The perfect hostess and attentive wife."

Not until she was ready to leave—an elegantly groomed woman who would have looked at home on Fifth Avenue or the rue Saint Honoré, and who therefore looked out of place in Moscow—did he ask a final time, "Stay, please."

Tears started in her eyes. "When I want to cry on stage

next time, I'll think of this," she whispered. "I'll think of you sitting here on the bed, your"—she switched to English —"prick and balls"—then went back to Russian, "sadly mourning, asking me to stay. And I'll remember how I had to go, how I was afraid to stay, how for only a few hours, for one of the few times in my life, there"—she pointed to the bed—"I was free of fear. You were"—she caught herself up—"you *are* an oasis in my desert, full of figs and cool shade and fresh water. Whatever happens, it was worthwhile."

Chapman embraced her, the rough tweed of her suit a hair shirt against his flesh. "Nothing will happen, Valya."

She hid her face against his chest. "I can hear your heart beating," she cried out.

He kissed her hair, tasted its fragrance. "Much worse if you couldn't hear it beating. *Swan Lake*'s at the Bolshoi two nights from now. Meet you during the intermission?"

She agreed.

"Aleksei told me I could have the keys to this flat whenever I wanted, at least until his Kornilov returns from Pamir."

"Not here, please," Valya pleaded.

"Where then?"

"I don't know."

Brushing her lips against his, not saying good-bye, Valya pulled herself together in a single, shuddering movement, like a soldier coming to attention but not quite so stiffly. She looked poised and serene, a lovely woman returning from a satisfactory afternoon's shopping. She closed the door softly when she left the flat, but Chapman heard it as loudly as if it had been slammed.

# 3

# *Dacha*

The Martynov dacha was not far outside Moscow, but just beyond the radius of "permitted" journeys from the capital. He had been to the village several times in the past to speak to various writers and artists who lived there, always asking for and receiving official permission; but now, because of the trial and sentencing of Sinyavsky and Daniel earlier in the year, official permission for contact with writers had dried up. Chapman had debated with himself whether to go by electric train from Moscow—making it more complicated for Them to follow him without being obvious—or to drive up in his own car, which might make it simpler for them to keep an eye on him, and might even give him the chance of eluding observation altogether. Ever since he'd come to Russia he'd always assumed that he was under surveillance, yet he thought they watched him only sporadically, spot-checking his activities as they did most of the other foreigners in Moscow in whom they had a passing—but no particular—interest. Now he was not so certain. Perhaps they *had* some special interest in him. Yet, if Valya had been willing to risk meeting him in an apartment she thought was theirs, he could risk what could only be the minor problem of being turned back on the road to the writers' colony where Fyodor Vyacheslovich had their dacha.

For three weeks after their tryst at Kornilov's apartment Chapman had not seen Valya. She had not met him at the Bolshoi, nor had he been able to reach her on the telephone to arrange another meeting. At the theater they told him she was in rehearsal and not taking calls, and at her apartment the maid said Madame was at the theater rehearsing, but when they both asked him to leave his name or a message so that Valentina Andreyevna could return his call, Chapman had cautiously and politely refused. At the embassy he'd gone about his duties so dispiritedly that the Ambassador himself had seen fit to rebuke him. "You're only going into your third Russian winter, Nathaniel, and you're beginning to behave as if it were your fifth. You look like you need a couple of weeks in London or Paris, or even Helsinki," the Ambassador commented, but he took no administrative measures to implement his suggestions.

Despite the mornings when he awoke in a panic that he would never see Valya again, the nights when, in despair, he drank more than he should so he could sleep, Chapman went about keeping up his connections with the dissidents involved in protesting the Sinyavsky-Daniel trial and the trials in its aftermath. Because he had government permission to take his courses in Russian history at Moscow University, he was able to remain in touch with students, teachers, writers, and intellectuals from whose ranks the dissidents were chiefly recruited. He collected their protest letters, their "white books," their pleas to "world public opinion," their verbatim accounts of trials closed to the foreign community, which they had smuggled out of the courtrooms. Just as previously he had collected their underground poems, essays, and short stories, Chapman now assembled the new *samizdat* publications—religious, literary, nationalist, and political protests—especially the underground newspaper *Chronicle of Current Events*, which—in a sober documentary way—reported the continuing repressions and miscarriages of justice throughout the Soviet Union. Chapman was proud to have been the first foreigner to lay hands on a copy of the underground journal before any member of other foreign embassies, or any of the foreign press—even foreign Communist newsmen—a copy he'd been given by a young student he'd known for some time at the university. They arranged to meet under the great clock on Kirov Street during the rush hours, a street so crowded that no one could see that when the young man jostled him, as if by accident, he also shoved the *Chronicle* copy under Chapman's coat.

Chapman even managed to wangle official permission for a long weekend trip to Kiev, ostensibly—for the Russians—as a student interested in "the mother of cities" and its historic role in Russian history, and—for the Americans —as a change of pace from being locked up in Moscow, a poor substitute for a trip to Paris or even Helsinki, his embassy colleages observed. He had returned with half a suitcase full of Ukrainian underground publications. All the materials had been duly copied, analyzed, and sent on by diplomatic pouch to Washington, and some "leaked" to several reliable British and American correspondents.

But the achievement he was proudest of was a full-hour film that Aleksei Mikhailovich had helped him make the arrangements for, in which he had secretly interviewed ten of the leading dissidents. In a few days now that film would also be on its way to Washington, and when it was he would heave a sigh of relief.

His daily routine had gone unchanged until yesterday, when Valya had called him to say that her husband had summarily been dispatched to the Caucasus by the Writers' Union to deliver a series of lectures and would not return for a fortnight. "I have the whole day off," Valya reported on the telephone, "so please come up to the dacha and we'll spend it together." Not wishing to be accused once more of displaying bourgeois fastidiousness or unbecoming diplomatic reluctance, Chapman decided to take the risk and drive up to the dacha.

No one had followed him. Of that he was certain. In fact, almost no automobiles were driving from Moscow that morning although many trucks were on the road going the other way, bringing produce into the city. None of the militiamen directing traffic bothered to stop him either, so that he arrived at the dacha without incident on a sunny cool spring day that still had a hint in the air that winter snows were not long gone.

An old frame house set back from the dirt road on a slight rise in the meadow, the dacha was shaded by huge oaks and willows, and there—under the trees—Valya waited for him. She wore a pair of tightly fitted blue jeans and a short-sleeved, open-throated white shirt that made her look like an Iowa farm girl just back from the state fair. When he got out of the car, she stood still until he came up the path and across the grass to meet her. At first they shook hands— almost formally—before she said shyly, "I'm so happy you could take the day." She seized his hand, kissed it, dropped it, and pirouetted away, arms raised, hair flying, chanting, "What a lovely day we have! All to ourselves. Look, Na-thaniel, isn't it beautiful here?"

It was. Beyond the dacha stretched a meadow dotted with trees, a thicket of red cedar here, a clump of paper birch beyond, scattered oaks, serene and massive, and on the left, just beyond the house, an orchard of neatly planted frail-looking cherry trees. In the distance a brown stream tumbled through the meadow until it broadened and deepened into a green pond, then broke out brown again beyond, to thread its serpentine way into a dark stand of towering larches where it was lost to view. Yet the landscape was melancholy; spring, the flash of a yellow bird; summer, a brief passionate heat; autumn, the swift rush of only a few days, green disappearing as if burned, the seared leaves dropping heavily to the ground as if slashed from the branch. An old peasant cart, wooden sides worn and broken, had been left among the cherry trees—useless— crying out for horses in its shafts, for people in its seats, for grain or fruit in its hold, and its emptiness was full of foreboding.

Valya called for him to follow and led him on muddy paths to higher, dryer ground, then through the underbrush where they startled flights of birds from the bushes into wild gyrations in the air, the birds rising so swiftly that he couldn't even identify them. They came to the green pond he had seen and Valya asked if he'd brought swimming clothes. When he said no, she suggested cheerfully, "We can swim in the raw. Fyodor and I often . . ." before she caught herself and went ahead to a rise in the ground where slabs of flat rock emerged obliquely from the earth. There she slipped quickly out of her clothing, holding her arms crossed over her breasts, rubbing her flesh. "The air is chilly, but the water makes you feel newborn." They stood naked next to the puddles of their clothes until she took his hand and guided him silently down to the pond. When they waded in, the water was so cold it took his breath away and not until he felt the earth slip out from under his feet, until he was floating free, did the dead weight begin to lift from his heart.

They swam and splashed, carefully avoiding touching, until—lips blue and teeth chattering—Valya howled that she had had enough. Chapman followed her out of the pond, admiring her slim white body, her flesh stippled with cold, her nipples dark and stiff, until she lay back on the sunwarmed rocks and wordlessly opened herself to him. He moved into her, as into water, buoyed up, the weight lifting from him altogether, his heart soaring. He felt her soar with him, her cry echoing from some remote place, the small darkness blotting out sight and sound and leaving him altogether in the grip of blind, dumb touch.

The first thing he was sure he heard sensibly again was birdsong, the second, Valya joyously proclaiming, "A nightingale! Usually it sings only at night."

Remembering her own night song, Chapman said sympathetically, "And then only during the breeding season, but it is the male's melody."

Valya understood. He liked never having to belabor a

point for her. "Where did you learn about nightingales?"
she asked.

"A friend, a very good and strange friend."

"Russian?"

"No, American." But Chapman did not mention Andrew Wheelwright's name, nor his work, nor his stock of
such odd information as the nightingale's sexual habits,
though he did tell her how, in English, the word *nightingale* was used for a nightclub singer.

Inside the dacha someone had set out to re-create the
atmosphere of a peasant hut of a century earlier. Furnished with crude, hand-carved stools, chairs, chests,
and tables, the room also contained a great faience-tiled
stove—taller than a man—on whose brightly colored
tiles were crude caricatures of Russian country faces, the
only cheerful note in an otherwise dour room. The
weathered wooden walls were bare, except for a single
magnificent ikon—a traditional Madonna and Child, almost surely from the fourteenth or fifteenth century—
which shone like a patch of sunlight. The Madonna's
love was luminous in her mien, her cheek pressed
against the Child's, the Child's eyes turned up toward
hers, his clasping fingers stiffly reaching for her breast
while the Madonna's head inclined toward him in recognition of their mutual suffering. Framed in Byzantine
gold haloes, their faces were dark as polished wood,
their formalized almond-shaped eyes, ancient and knowing, stared out of pouches of pained flesh lined with
weariness yet refulgent with fervor. The Madonna's nimbus reminded him of Valya's hair which she was now
drying and fluffing out with a towel. A slight breeze carried the acrid smells of red and yellow marigolds and
purple and pink geraniums from the window boxes into
the room, a reminder that the outside world could never
be kept altogether from entering the household, or the
present time. Everything there looked and felt as if

someone was, nonetheless, desperate to hold on to the simplicities of the Russian past.

Valya began to set out the lunch she'd prepared: borscht, pirogi, cucumber salad, black bread. Chapman remembered the French armagnac he'd left in the car and went to get it. Outside, the sun, higher and hotter, had warmed the fields to steaming. It was unnaturally quiet. All the birds seemed to have been silenced. The peasant cart beneath the cherry trees cast a sharp black shadow on the ground. After he had the bottle, Chapman slammed the car door just to hear the sound, and, as if in echo, the boom of aircraft motors thundered down on his head and he saw the white surf of jet trails in the cloudless sky overhead. He hastened back to the dacha as if trying to outrun his shadow. He opened the armagnac, poured two tumblers half-full, and toasted, "To nightingales!"

Valya's eyes shone with tears when she drank, and he felt a similar sense of desolation in her.

The food was delicious, yet reminded him how little they knew of one another. He didn't even know she could cook, didn't know where she was born, had never seen a photograph of her as a child or young girl. What had she looked like as a bride? "How did you come to marry him?" he blurted.

Her fork poised over the pirogi, her head bent, her turquoise eyes ineffably sad, Valya said, "Sometimes, at night, when I can't sleep I lie rigid next to him and ask myself the same questions. I think I know the answers, but they don't satisfy me. They're too logical. They make too much sense. Everything is too neat, so something must be missing that I do not see, that I do not know. Like having a role in a play where something in the character eludes you, some source of passion, some mystery . . . though you think you know the character like your own brother." Silently, she put the fork down on her plate.

"How did you meet him?" Chapman persisted.

"I had a part in a play of his. I was a student at the

conservatory. Everyone made a great fuss because the famous Fyodor Martynov had agreed to come and watch us perform his play, but I didn't care. I didn't like his play and I didn't think I'd like the man."

"But you did?"

Valya hesitated for a long time. "I don't know, you see. He singled me out . . . from all the others . . . said I was exceptionally talented and had a great career ahead of me. And he invited me to dinner. *Now* I think I didn't believe a word he told me *then*. He was pompous and affected, and had opinions about everything: the directing, the acting, the costumes, even the lighting. *Now* I think that I believed *then* that he just wanted to go to bed with me. But then? What did I feel, think? I don't know any more. It's a lifetime ago, Nathaniel, ten years. I was studying for what I really wanted to do. I knew I was talented, so perhaps it was I who really wanted to use him, not the other way round. Partly I went to dinner with him because the others were envious, partly because I just wanted to dress up and have an evening out on the town.

"He took me to the Lastochka, and we had caviar and champagne, and sat and looked at the river and the Krimsky Bridge. It was all very romantic. I felt grownup and sophisticated. There I was, twenty, but really younger than that, starry-eyed and so naïve! A country cousin. I'd come from Novgorod only two years before and I was in Moscow —Moscow!—and dining with a famous playwright by the dark waters of the Moskva.

"Fyodor was another man there, altogether unlike the 'great writer' visiting the conservatory. He was simple and unassuming, told me how he mourned his wife, who died the year I came to Moscow, about his two daughters, only a few years younger than I and at school. They were giving him trouble and he was concerned about them. And he questioned me about myself, my parents, my home, my schooldays, my ambitions."

"How old is Fyodor Vyacheslovich?" Chapman asked.

"Forty-seven."

"Not much older than I, Valya."

"I always preferred older men," she said, with forced yet piquant flirtatiousness. She groped for her Yunosts and Chapman gave her one of his Parliaments. Breathing smoke with her words, she remarked, "I trusted him and him alone as I had trusted no one since my father. And he has never betrayed that trust, Nathaniel, not even when I betrayed him." She flushed. "Which I did often enough. That's something you must understand about him."

"Why must *I* understand in particular?"

"Because he already suspects you."

"Did he suspect the others?" Chapman asked, hurting himself with the question more—he knew—than he was hurting her.

Her eyes went flat and distant, like those of the Madonna of Tenderness on the wall, turquoise ikon screens, guarding the sacred mysteries—or profane—of her marriage, from his or anyone's view.

"Did he give you that?" Chapman pointed the armagnac glass at the ikon.

"My wedding gift." She blinked, and the expression in her eyes changed. "Fyodor gave it to me because it was an old Novgorod ikon, and he insisted that some early ancestor of mine there had modeled for the Madonna, for whichever follower of Andrei Rublyov had painted it. And," she added, "he gave it to me because I believed, and he couldn't."

Chapman touched her cheek, ran his fingers along the strong jaw. "I want you to tell me so much, to hurry our intimacy, though I know intimacy cannot be hurried."

"And I want to tell you so much," she responded.

"Have you lived here long?"

"In the dacha? Five or six years. They gave it to Fyodor after he won the Stalin Prize, but we come only for weekends and vacations. Yet I think of this as my home, not the flat in town."

"Was it like this before?" He waved around the room.

"No. Fyodor furnished it."

"Why with these things?"

"He loves old Mother Russia. These peasant creations carved by hands long dead touch his heart in a way that few living people do."

"Perhaps it reassures him that art endures, that craft lives on even after the hands that created are dead. If he doesn't believe, that may be his idea of immortality."

Valya considered that. "It's an explanation," she agreed, but it was clear she didn't accept it.

She didn't finish eating, but put her hand out for another cigarette. "Maybe it was only my fear and ambition, so it was just another 'permit marriage,'" she continued. "Now, it's hard for me to accept that I behaved like a cliché, like all the other shameless hussies who wanted to marry to remain in Moscow. I had no permanent residence and if I married him I knew I'd be able to live in the city and not have to return to Novgorod. My career was here where I wanted to be on the stage, and Fyodor Vyacheslovich Martynov knew everyone in the Moscow theater and everyone knew him. He would help me."

"Didn't you have family in Novgorod?"

"By then, no one was left. My father brought me up, but he was taken in '48. He was a geneticist who studied and worked with Vavilov, which was enough to doom him. He died in a camp on the Sea of Okhotsk eighteen months after they arrested him. My brother was killed in 1944, during the battle of Kursk. He was nineteen and in the tanks."

"You don't mention your mother at all."

"Ah, my mother, my beautiful mother. . . . If you saw her, you'd say *she* was the one who really looked like that Madonna. Or so my father said. I sometimes think I remember her, but mostly it is what people told me later, my father or my aunt, or old photos I saw. She ran off with another man when I was four years old. She was an actress, and she and my father couldn't live in the same house.

"After my father was taken, I stayed with his elder sister, who hated my mother and, I think, also hated me a little because she said I looked like my mother, all golden and angelic-looking, but a very she-devil. The year after I came to Moscow, she died too. During the war we were evacuated to Sverdlovsk so what friends I had in Novgorod were lost, though now and then people I went to school with there come backstage to ask if I remember them. Usually I say I do, because I'm ashamed that I don't."

Chapman said nothing. Everyone you got to know in Russia was "walking wounded" so much more than in other places where he had lived. Fathers, mothers, sisters, brothers, husbands, children, colleagues, friends—killed during collectivization, or the Purges, or in the war, starved, executed, disappeared. Whenever you touched anyone, he bled. And Valya was no exception.

"Nathaniel, tell me about you."

"What would you like to know?" he inquired, trying to stem the powerful current of feeling that drew him to her, so he could define it, contain it.

"Are you married? Do you have children?"

"*Yes, tell us about yourself,*" a rich baritone voice called from the doorway. He was dark—Georgian or Armenian—with a thick mustache of the old Stalin variety and very white teeth. He had a smile on his face, but his expression was stony. Two thugs stood behind him and two others were at the windows. Chapman stood, feigning outrage, hoping that the few minutes of stalling would give him an idea of how to behave. "Perhaps," he said, "you'll tell us who you are first and what you're doing here."

The burnished arrogance of the face, the knife-edged smile, did not change at all. "Saribekyan, Tigran Anastasovich, Captain in the State Security Police," he introduced himself, the click of heels in his voice.

"Your identification, please," Chapman requested.

Derisively, Saribekyan showed his KGB card, then retaliated, "And who are you?" though obviously he knew the answer.

"Nathaniel Chapman, Second Secretary of the United States Embassy."

"Your passport, please," Saribekyan commanded, imitating and mocking him.

Chapman showed his diplomatic passport, permitted Saribekyan to verify the name and picture, but refused to let the passport leave his hands. It was cat and mouse all the way. What They wanted in playing this game still was to be revealed, but Chapman knew that he and Valya were in trouble, especially Valya.

"You realize, Mr. Chapman, that this area is out of bounds unless you have a special pass?" Saribekyan noted.

"Is it, Captain? I'm sorry. I thought it well within the permitted range or I'd have asked for official permission."

"Too bad you didn't. You've been to this village before, so you should have known. Now I must take you back to Moscow on charges."

So they not only knew who he was, they'd known where he was going. No wonder they hadn't bothered to follow him; they didn't have to: they could, and did, come at any time that was convenient to pick him up. His phone was bugged and Valya had given them the necessary information.

"And who is this?" Saribekyan inquired, pointing to Valya, who sat, head bowed, expressionless.

When she did not speak, Chapman introduced her, "This is Valentina Andreyevna Martynova, owner of this dacha."

"The woman must answer for herself."

Slowly, Valya stubbed her cigarette out in the remains of the cucumber salad, then faced Saribekyan, saying, "I am Valentina Martynova."

"The actress? The wife of the Stalin Prize-winning playwright, Fyodor Vyacheslovich Martynov?" Saribekyan's dark eyes glowed, his smile was whiter, he sounded as if at any moment he might ask for her autograph.

"The same," Valya replied, her face grim.

"The one who fucks foreigners in strange apartments, and swims naked with them, who defiles both her country and her husband's bed?" Saribekyan asked in exactly the same soft voice now charged with menace and contempt.

Valya stood up and curtsied. "The same, Captain, the same."

The look on her face and on Saribekyan's sent a pang through him, and Chapman knew their time had run out.

# 4

# Interrogation

The apartment house was new, and by Soviet standards quite modern, but the elevator rose with disconcerting jerks, and in the lobby, jagged cracks split the walls and plaster peeled from the ceiling where a crystal chandelier, many of its pendants broken or missing, was hung askew. Chapman imagined they were somewhere near Herzen Street and the zoo, but once they approached the city, Saribekyan had drawn the black Chaika's curtains, side and rear and over the glass partition which separated them from the two thugs in the front: it made him feel as though they were in a hearse. Saribekyan had seated himself between them so that there was no talk on the trip in. By the time they arrived it was dark, and Saribekyan and his toughs hustled them out of the car toward the apartment-house entrance. When Chapman turned to look down the street, one of the hoods barked, "Eyes front!" shoving him forward so abruptly that he almost fell, but Saribekyan helped him keep his feet. Several passersby deliberately looked the other way and, heads down, hurried on. But one thing Chapman had seen; the other two KGB thugs had driven up in his car and parked just down the street.

On the fourteenth floor they were ushered into an apartment living room, furnished tastefully in Danish modern

rosewood, glass, and bright orange upholstery. The toughs
left them, but he noticed they were gone only after Saribekyan had motioned them to separate orange chairs and
gone into another room. Chapman was halfway across to
her when Valya made two muffled warning movements, a
finger across the lips that might have been scratching her
nose and a stiffly outstretched palm from her extended arm
which might have been part of a yawn, both cautioning him
to sit still and be silent. In spite of her warnings and the
alarm in her eyes, Chapman went to her and touched her
cheek. She turned her face to kiss his palm, whispering,
"Ours is a truly Russian love, Nathaniel, passionately grand
—and doomed." It was like a line from *Anna Karenina*, and
he bent and kissed her fair hair for it.

That They had not separated them, not taken them directly to the Lubianka, was good; that they had driven his
car in showed that they had other plans for both of them.

Saribekyan returned, accompanied by a short, stocky
balding man, with long powerful arms, a badly pockmarked
face, and eyes like shards of gray slate. He was impeccably
dressed in a formal blue chalk-striped suit of English cut
and manufacture, and Saribekyan introduced him as Colonel Nikolai Maksimovich Abrasov. The Colonel indicated a
darkened room behind him. Hand in hand, Chapman and
Valya walked into a small moving-picture theater where a
large white screen was on one wall and a projection booth
in the wall opposite with four rows of six chairs each between. "Sit!" the Colonel commanded, but when they
chose adjoining seats, he and Saribekyan insinuated themselves between them. Abrasov snapped his fingers, a camera whirred into life, a beam of white light slashed the
darkness, and abruptly they were in the bedroom of Kornilov's flat, where they had made love. Valya had been
right; it *was* a KGB flat. Aleksei Mikhailovich had betrayed
them, set them up for a rendezvous in which they were
conducted and manipulated by the KGB in a blue film,
whose purposes and outcome were not yet clear.

The camera explored their intimacy, spying on their movements and expressing them in lingering pornographic closeups that made Chapman sick. He wanted to throw himself at the screen to tear the image off it, or turn and smash the projector, but he forced himself to sit still. What was there in lovemaking—he asked himself—which was so fine, yet so frail, that it became degrading when watched and recorded? Every movement seemed unclean, every caress depraved, every endearment an obscenity. Yet the camera was faithful to their coupling; it was what happened, yet not at all the way it had happened. The sound track distorted their voices so that their words sounded like those of other people, tinny and choked, as if transmitted over long-distance telephone. Valya said, again: *"Oh, Nathaniel, you* are *a fool! If you're going to make love to a woman, to another man's wife, what difference where? That is a peculiarly bourgeois fastidiousness."*

He heard himself stupidly proclaiming once more: *"I'm not a trusting man by nature or training, Valya. We Americans are not altogether fools. We know we're watched, bugged, followed; we know about being compromised and trapped"*—next to him Saribekyan snickered—*"but I also know Aleksei Fedorov. I don't trust many people, especially here, but I do trust you, and Aleksei Mikhailovich."*

And Valya's cautionary, *"Your trust may be only fifty percent justified. Here and now, that's not enough."*

Valya's sobbing drowned out the sound-track voices, rose to an anguished cry, then fell to furious retching, and Chapman barked, "Enough! Enough!"

Abrasov's fingers snapped again, the screen images faded away, the sounds of the words they had once spoken stopped, and the lights came on. Valya's face was in her hands, her shoulders heaving. With that sight the gnawing suspicion that she might have been a partner in the scheme was purged. He tried to get past Saribekyan to comfort her, but Saribekyan wouldn't move.

"Shall we talk now, Mr. Chapman?" Abrasov asked.

"That's a command not an invitation, Colonel. I don't have much choice in the matter now, do I?"

"No, you don't and as long as you understand that, we may be able to avoid further unpleasantness." The pockmarks on Abrasov's skin shone in the light, his face a *pointillisme* horror. At the other end of the aisle he stood between Chapman and Valya so that they could not exchange a word or touch, but before they left the projection room the Colonel sent Saribekyan to get Valya something to drink.Once they were seated in the orange chairs, Abrasov began to address them like an *Izvestia* editorial: "You have violated the rules of hospitality in our country. You have seduced the wife of one of our outstanding writers, herself a well-known people's artist. You have gone outside the permitted travel zone without official sanction," and then he finally got to the point he wanted to make, "and you have been carrying out antigovernment agitation among Soviet citizens, soliciting Soviet artists and intellectuals to defect, recruiting them for American intelligence, and meeting various people whose activities are under the scrutiny of our investigative and judicial organs." From the tone, Chapman was sure the rooms must be wired for sound and that Abrasov, too, had superiors to whom he had to convey his orthodoxy and persistence.

"And who might those be?" Chapman inquired.

"We have many films of you, Mr. Chapman," Abrasov replied mildly. "Not just your efforts in the bedroom. All would prove embarrassing to you should we make them public or show them to your ambassador. For example, we have photographs of your meeting with an anti-Soviet scum on Kirov Street to acquire a copy of the underground rag they call *Chronicle of Current Events*. We have others of you at various demonstrations—on Mayakovsky and Pushkin squares, for instance—where you were collecting various decadent verses and pornographic writings. We have excellent pictures of you stamping your feet in the snow outside the courtroom building where we tried the slanderers Sinyavsky and Daniel. You were also observed acquiring an illegal transcript of the trial proceedings there. We have other snapshots of you at such splendid historical sights in Kiev as the Church of Saint Andrew, the Perchersky Monastery, and on the Dnepr Embankment receiving copies of the poisonous writings of various Ukrainian bourgeois-nationalists and deviationists. You have even had illegal contact with those insane Jehovah's Witnesses and those kike Zionists who want to run off to their Mediterannean paradise to fight the Arabs.

"You're not a Jew, by any chance? Chapman isn't a Jewish name, but you never can tell," Abrasov remarked, his question intentionally echoing Valya's in the bedroom talk recorded on the sound track of the film they'd just witnessed. It all suddenly seemed so ridiculous that Chapman smiled.

"Do you think this is funny?"

"No, Colonel, it's not funny, and no I am *not* a Jew— though I have been circumcized," Chapman replied seriously. The Colonel had not told him all those things for nothing; he wanted something, and what it was would be revealed now.

"We have moving-picture closeups of your efforts this afternoon at the pond too," Abrasov said stiffly, "and as soon as they are developed, they'll make beautiful gifts for your wife."

"She's familiar with most of what you have there on film," Chapman responded, yet wondered what Betsy would have thought of those films if they were still married. Even the KGB had difficulty keeping its dossiers up-to-date, and evidently They didn't know he was divorced. The small chink in their armor heartened him.

The Colonel feigned consternation. "Don't you care if we show them?"

"I'd prefer that you did *not* show them, but clearly the choice is not in my hands." That should open the way to the bargaining.

"We shall also be forced to send a copy to Valentina Andreyevna's husband," he warned.

"Don't," Chapman requested, but he was not pleading.

"A bit late for gallantry, don't you think?" Abrasov remarked.

"Never too late for gallantry, Colonel."

"Since Fyodor Vyacheslovich is a leading Soviet writer and Party comrade, and also a war hero, how could we, in good conscience, keep from revealing to him how his wife has betrayed him—and with an American agent?"

"What's to be gained?"

"Your cooperation."

"In exchange for which, I assume you'll give me the negatives of the films taken today at the dacha, and the others we saw in there?" Chapman asked.

"Correct."

"How do I know you'll give me all the copies of the film, Colonel?"

"You don't. You must rely on my word."

"The price?"

"You have a film of some of our loudmouthed malcontents, those you choose to call our dissidents, and we believe you have not yet sent it out of the country. For that one film we'll give you the two of ours. A fair trade, no?"

"Why is the film worth it? Most of what they say in it is being said and written by other Soviet citizens every day, and much of it has already been published abroad."

Abrasov nodded his agreement. "Of course. But few people read books. Millions watch films and television. This year is the fiftieth anniversary of the Revolution. We do not want our achievements sullied abroad just now."

"In principle, I agree, but suppose I can't manage it? The decision is not in my hands alone now."

"No film from you—no films from us. Your ambassador and poor Fyodor Vyacheslovich must then receive the films of your sexual exertions. The other photographs we shall keep in our files in order to find something nastier for your strenuous anti-Soviet efforts—and for dealing with Valentina Andreyevna," the Colonel promised.

Chapman stood up and paced. He saw that he had no other choice, but some delay and the appearance of indecision and agitation were essential. He knew that They might, in fact, want that dissidents' film suppressed, but that would only be the first step. Once he agreed to that, they would press him further; for them nothing would suffice until he turned. Amused and contemptuous, Abrasov watched him as if he were an insect, all the while exploring pockmarks on his face with his fingertips, like a blind man reading a singularly difficult braille. Chapman agreed at last, having wrung his hands for effect, and discovered to his consternation that he really meant it.

Abrasov's fingers left his pockmark explorations, snapped an imperious sound, like breaking bone, and Saribekyan brought Valya in from the other room. Her eyes gazing at the ground, her walk a shuffle, as if already she were a prisoner in lockstep, her face had the severity of the Madonna of Tenderness ikon in the dacha. "Valya!" Chapman cried out, calling to her as if from a great distance, as if to bring her back from another country. She looked right through him, lips bloodless and pursed, then chanted:

God give me fever, sleeplessness, shortness of breath,
Bitter years of sickness—and long.
Take my own child away and my lover
And the secret, divine gift of poetry.

During Thy Liturgy, Lord, I pray that
After so many heartrending days
The clouds which darken Russia
Will turn white in an explosion of sunlight.

"The whore masquerading as a virgin," Saribekyan commented uneasily.

"The traitor playing the patriot," Abrasov added unctuously. Both were moved in spite of themselves, but Chapman was overwhelmed by bitterness and impotence. He had done nothing, he could do nothing, to help her. Biting back words, grief, he wondered how, before he was imprisoned or expelled from the country, he could find and kill Aleksei Mikhailovich Fedorov.

# 5

# *Alek*

Chapman had known they would come back, but—he thought, as he watched the brand new green Oldsmobile in the late afternoon shade beneath the elms —not after only five weeks. In the yard Hauser pulled the car close to the veranda steps and Wheelwright emerged, yelling, "Hey, Nathaniel! Get your ass down here! We've arrived." When Chapman stepped out on the veranda, Hauser, his head swathed in bandages, and Wheelwright, his left arm in a cast and a sling, were helping a third man out of the back seat of the car, a thin, old man, whose uncertain legs seemed to have difficulty keeping him erect. Though the weather was mild, he was bundled up in a heavy mackinaw, collar turned up, and a black fedora, the brim turned down all around and pulled low over his face, so that his brows were hidden. The russet beard spattered with swatches of white was too luxuriant and colorful for the ema-ciated face, out of which pale blue eyes looked at the house, the meadows, the elms. With his sleeves flapping on his arms, he was a tweed scarecrow celebrating na-ture—his voice, sounding untried, an unruly cackle—as he raised his arms to the sky and exulted in Russian, "Earth and trees and fresh air!" Wheelwright and

Hauser stood a little back, as if reluctant to intrude on the swaying man's reverie, yet ready to leap to his aid if he should fall.

The man reached both hands up to remove his fedora, baring his head and ashen face to the sun, and then— though the man he had known was clean-shaven and without a single white hair, a burly man who moved with the power and assurance of an athlete—Chapman understood that the frail creature before him who looked like a prisoner just returned from Norilsk or Magadan was, indeed, Aleksei Fedorov. Valya's face flashed before him, between them, mixed up with the face of the sorrowing Madonna of the ikon, her voice keening, *"Take my own child away and my lover."* His body crouched like a stranger to throw itself at this erstwhile friend he had promised himself to murder if they ever met again, yet the man's strangeness and infirmity held him back. Leaping down the veranda steps, aware that Wheelwright and Hauser had edged protectively closer to the Russian, that Hauser's hand was groping under his coat, Chapman wasn't sure himself what he was going to do.

Only then did Fedorov notice him. He dropped his hat, opened his arms wide, and tottered toward Chapman, his tired gray face incandescent with recognition, and as Chapman was about to slug him, Fedorov stumbled and fell into his arms, embracing him. "Nathaniel," he whispered, "oh, my God, Nathaniel!" He buried his head in Chapman's shoulder and Chapman held him until his shuddering died away. Wheelwright's disdainful smirk and Hauser's touchy alertness irked him. Had they really expected him to kill Fedorov?

"Come on, Alek," Chapman said gruffly. Leaning heavily on him, Fedorov staggered up the steps and into the sun porch before collapsing into an armchair, his eyes pinched shut, his chest heaving. A few moments later Wheelwright followed, carrying a valise with his good arm. "Let Hauser do that," Chapman advised.

"Oh, can he enter these sacred portals?" Wheelwright inquired.

"Don't be a damn fool!"

Hauser brought another valise in and Chapman asked if that was all. Wheelwright kicked the two battered, belted-around-the-middle leather suitcases, and said, "Enough, isn't it?" Chapman neither liked nor understood the curtness and intensity of the remark, but he let it pass and set about pouring drinks. "Still bourbon?" he asked. Wheelwright nodded. Hauser did too, then sat off in a corner. "For you and me, Aleksei Mikhailovich," Chapman said in Russian, "vodka."

Fedorov's eyes blinked open and he nodded weakly.

"Go easy on the sauce," Wheelwright cautioned. "He's not been eating and we've been keeping him on tranquilizers."

Fedorov took his glass with both hands, held it up, and in a faint echo of his once vibrant bass voice, said, "Peace and freedom." They glared at one another before repeating the slogan, then raised their glasses and drank, but they had barely finished their drinks before Wheelwright said they had to be going.

Chapman took them out to the car. "You look like you've been to the wars," he told Wheelwright.

"You might say we've been under fire," Wheelwright replied.

Remembering it even after more than a month made him dizzy. Chapman could still see their Lincoln lying on its side just off the road, burning like a stricken animal, the charred-bone skeleton of the chassis stark and black in the leaping blue flames. After he had pulled them both clear, he had to roll Hauser in the dirt to put out the fire eating at his hair and clothes. And then, when Wheelwright, scorched, his arm obviously broken, had once more pleaded for him to take Fedorov off his hands, to guard him, he had consented. Against his better judgment. Hoping that Wheelwright wouldn't hold him to his word, a

word extorted in such circumstances, yet knowing hopelessly that Wheelwright would do just that. How could I be
so stupid? he asked himself, recalling a dozen other similar
ways in which Wheelwright had pressured him when they
were students. But now, looking at the bandages, at Wheelwright's pallor and immobilized arm, he felt mean and
petty.

"I owe you one for that," Wheelwright declared, as if
he'd read Chapman's thoughts.

"You owe more than you can repay."

"I brought your old buddy back, didn't I?"

"Hauser?"

"You always were a smartass, Chappie," Wheelwright
said. He got back into the Oldsmobile.

"Ever dig out what happened?"

"Plastique," Hauser answered. "Very professional. Why
we weren't killed I don't know."

"Don't be puzzled, just grateful," Wheelwright remarked.

"Maybe They didn't want to kill you," Chapman hazarded, "only warn you."

"One hell of a warning!" Hauser muttered.

"They'd have killed us all right," Wheelwright insisted,
"if you hadn't hustled your ass down and dragged us
clear."

"If you were burned up, it *would* look more like an accident," Chapman admitted.

"The boys would know. Gordon used to race."

"A gifted man, our friend Hauser," Chapman noted.

"A Promethean, Renaissance sort of man," Wheelwright
chortled. "What would we do without him?"

Hauser squirmed and raced the car engine.

Though he disliked Hauser, Chapman changed the subject. "You ever see Logan Pearsall?" he asked.

"He's my boss," Wheelwright said shortly.

"They promoted him over your head?"

"Cold-cock Boston bastard, with his Old Boy connections."

"You said Pearsall was pretty good."

"He is." Wheelwright grinned. "Very good. That's why I like him even less."

"I knew him a little, in Berlin and Vienna. Some liaison, a couple of lunches. In fact, I once had dinner with him and his wife at their house in Georgetown. Thought he was one of the better intelligence types, decent, and short on cloak and dagger. Give him my regards when you see him."

The remarks evidently displeased Wheelwright. "Sure, sure," he said, "but I still hate that son-of-a-bitch." His face grew grimmer. "You have the Walther I gave you?"

"I never give presents away, Andrew."

"Keep it handy. Never know, when Hauser's taken as much riding as he can he might come back and"—he made a gun of his thumb and forefinger, thrust it through the window—"pop you off—boom! boom! just like that!"

"I'll keep it in mind."

"And keep an eye on Fedorov. We don't want him straying." Wheelwright raised his arm, peremptory dismissal and good-bye, and Hauser, alerted, spun the Oldsmobile screechingly out of the yard, roaring down under the elms toward the road. Chapman watched until the car was out of sight, turned and kicked Fedorov's hat along the ground, then picked it up, brushed the brim and crown clean with his sleeve, and carried it into the house.

Fedorov sat where he had left him, chin on chest, eyes shut, the vodka glass on the carpet in front of his scuffed, pointed Italian shoes. The changes that only a few years had wrought were remarkable, a once powerful, vigorous trunk of a man, shaved down to a pale fragile twig. His chapped lips parted and drawn thin in a grimace, his square, tobacco-stained teeth clenched, Fedorov seemed to be holding himself together by an act of will. He conveyed extraordinary exhaustion as if in crossing sides he had expended almost all his vital energies and was crouching over the flickering candleflame of his spirit, guarding it with cupped hands so that it should not be snuffed out. Chapman had seen that same exhaustion in other defectors, in prisoners, in soldiers returning from the front, in intelligence agents coming in after long, hazardous assignments. The resonance rang within him and Chapman knew it for the same disease he had been suffering since he returned from Moscow, and he felt a pang of pity for him. He tried to summon up the murderous rage he had felt, the rage he had fulfilled in a hundred homicidal dreams since he'd left Moscow, but his anger was directed against another figure —another face—perhaps altogether another man.

He dropped Fedorov's fedora on his desk, poked it back into shape with his finger, then poured another vodka. Behind him, the man's hoarse breathing was louder. When he turned, Fedorov's eyes were open and fixed on him. "Wheelwright told me you wanted to murder me, Nathaniel—why?"

"Didn't he tell you why?"

Fedorov shook his head.

"You set me up. And you handed Valentina Andreyevna over to Them."

"The apartment?"

"You couldn't have done better if you'd taken us to a cinema studio."

"Kornilov lent me the flat. He told me it was his, gave me the keys, made a thing about having to go to Pamir and wanting someone to look in and water his plants while he was gone. And he thought I could enjoy the flat. I didn't know it was Theirs, that they were using Kornilov to get to you."

"You were one of theirs. They could have ordered you straight out."

"I would have refused. They knew that."

"You couldn't refuse. You belonged to them."

"Only as far as my conscience allowed. Co-opted, remember? Not recruited."

"Hairsplitting, Alek, you're deceiving yourself and me. You were a KGB officer."

"I wouldn't have done it, Nathaniel."

"I don't believe it for a minute."

"Believe what you will then," Fedorov replied. "They outsmarted us both. They judged our characters, our friendships, our women. They knew me better than I knew myself. If I had the keys to an apartment, they knew that in time you and your Valentina Andreyevna would need a place, and that you would come to me."

"Who else was there to go to?"

"Exactly."

"So they were informed about Valya and me?"

Fedorov looked pitying. "They threw you together quite deliberately."

"Always They, never you."

"They asked me to arrange your meeting and I did that. I'm responsible for that. Does that make me your enemy?"

Chapman managed a bleak smile. "For that, Alek, I can only be grateful."

Fedorov smiled back. "So you should be. Valentina Andreyevna never betrayed you."

"There wasn't enough time."

"If you must be cynical, at least don't be a fool! They made approaches to her a dozen times to compromise you. They threatened her. We'll take your job away, send you back to Novgorod, tell Fyodor Vyacheslovich. They even brought pressure to bear on him."

"So he did know?"

Again the pitying look. "Martynov has been a KGB officer since the war."

"You mean he'd let them use his wife as a 'swallow?' "

"If They ordered him to, of course. His first wife was one of the *mozhnos,* and one of the most effective 'swallows' they had."

"Did Valya know?"

"Who knows who knows what about whom? Only those with the dossiers and computers and the memory banks. Maybe not even them. But I understand that the daughters suspected and repaid their father a hundredfold. The elder one has twice been apprehended in student groups organizing demonstrations or publishing underground literature. The younger one has been an occasional 'swallow' without her father's permission, and has already successfully compromised a Swedish military attaché for them."

Everywhere, Chapman reflected, the sins of the fathers burdened the children, a weight that could neither be shifted nor thrown off, only—if anything—accommodated and endured. But what kind of man allowed his wife to be one of those *mozhnos* the KGB used to seduce members of the foreign colony, to report on their pillow talk and compromise them? What kind of man allowed the same thing to happen to his daughter and the same pressures to be exerted on his second wife? Chapman shook himself. *Allowed?* Ridiculous. He was thinking like a schoolboy. What moved Fyodor Vyacheslovich Martynov he didn't know, but if one allowed such things to happen to those one loved, one was either crushed or deadened, or belonged to Them so irretrievably that no further motivation was required: one simply didn't love anyone enough to care, not even oneself. *All things were justified, all things allowed.*

Wheelwright had had his own way of saying it. "What difference does it make if you're not in the greased slide and someone else is? It doesn't get used up, and it might even learn something and improve its performance." But he said that only after he learned about Phyliss, and perhaps it was his way of dealing with her lovers, as her lovers were Phyliss's way of dealing with Wheelwright's long absences and impossible assignments. And his character? A five-year period in Moscow by itself was enough to produce claustrophobia and nymphomaniacal restlessness in any woman, and screaming paranoia to boot. Phyliss had managed somehow to stand three years of it before she'd thrown up the sponge, taken the boys, and gone back to the States to file for divorce. When Wheelwright had told him the story, he'd been crying drunk, tears running off his features like rain off a rockface. "I had so many horns,

Chappie, I could've qualified as a thirty-second degree
Moose . . . or is it Elk? By the time Phyliss took off, she'd
screwed everything in pants over sixteen and under seventy
among the Westerners in the diplomatic colony and was
about to make an opening to the East with the First Secretary of the Indian Embassy. And—of course—it was all my
fault."

"Well, wasn't it?" Chapman said, refusing to indulge his
self-pity, but pouring the last of his Helsinki-bought and
cherished Scotch whiskey.

Fedorov's light snore startled him. He was asleep once
more, chin on his chest, but when Chapman poured another drink the clink of bottle against glass awoke him.
"Sorry, Nathaniel. Happens to me all the time now. I drift
off. I'm always half-asleep. I think it's the medicine they
give me to 'calm my nerves.' " He reached down, retrieved
his glass, and wordlessly held it out. Chapman poured, and
Fedorov, sipping the vodka, began to talk. "Valentina Andreyevna was far worse off than you were. They put you on
an airplane and flew you out of Moscow and out of the
glorious Soviet motherland. And you were, in a way, a hero.
Twenty-four hours later you were in London, on your way
home, but Valya had to remain. That was *her* home and
there she was a traitor. She'd been threatened. She could
have cooperated, and They would have attempted to try
you as a spy and put you in prison for anti-Soviet activities
if she'd been willing. But she wasn't.

"She'd been threatened before, but now she was in an
impossible position. Your embassy saw that the dissidents'
film was shown all over Western Europe and in America,
and on the fiftieth anniversary too, and They were furious.
Another scandal to mar the anniversary. First, Stalin's
daughter defecting, then your dissidents telling the world
on television that the regime was corrupt, and especially
Them. You were out of their hands by then, but Valentina
Andreyevna was not."

"I thought I'd protected her," Chapman explained. "But

there wasn't enough time to make sure. That same night that I reported my 'interview' with Abrasov and Saribekyan, the decision was made. The next morning they flew me out, standard operating procedure in the circumstances. The Ambassador and Wheelwright promised that they'd trade the film to Abrasov for the films of Valya and me, and for Valya's being left off. By the time I got back to Washington —I was officially encouraged to take a recuperation leave en route—the films had already been shown on television."

"You have your They too," Fedorov reminded him. "In this case, though, they were right. Giving Abrasov the film wouldn't have helped Valentina Andreyevna. They would have promised, but their promises mean nothing. They might have given you a copy of the films they took of the two of you, but not the original, and they'd have used that against her later, whenever the necessity arose. Besides," he added meditatively, "I'm not sure that they didn't really want that film shown abroad."

"Why would they want that?"

"Shows what a poor, small, and powerless group the dissidents really are at home. And it permits the KGB to use the foreign interview against them in the future when they are ready to bring the dissenters to trial."

"Always good *raisons d' état.* For foreign consumption, the dissenters are weak and unimportant. For domestic purposes, they're threatening and subversive," Chapman interpreted. He went to the window to stare out at the comforting presence of the elms in the gathering dusk. "We live in a world where everything is double-edged—like a razor blade—subterfuge and deception."

"You still don't believe what I told you about Kornilov's flat, do you?"

"Would you, if you were in my place?"

"I think so."

Chapman turned from the window. "Why, Alek, because of Vienna?"

"Yes, partly because of Vienna," Fedorov affirmed, "and partly because I trust you."

"Trust!" Chapman snorted.

"Yes, trust. If I didn't trust you, I wouldn't be here. I am in your hands, Nathaniel, so weak and sick and tired that you could kill me like that." He snapped his fingers. "Wheelwright warned me that you might try, but when I insisted that I wanted to come here anyway, he gave in."

Wheelwright gave in! Chapman knew that Wheelwright never gave in, or gave up. That must have been what he wanted all the time and poor fool Alek thought he'd conceded something. A way of keeping an eye on Fedorov without seeming to, but what was it Wheelwright wanted an eye kept on him for? What did Alek have that Wheelwright needed or wanted? And why had Alek chosen to come to his house? Because he trusted him? A good enough reason for anyone—particularly a defector and ex-KGB officer— but there must be more to it.

"You knew I wouldn't kill you, Alek, didn't you?" Chapman countered.

"Knew?" Fedorov's blue eyes were cool, calculating. "No, I didn't know, but I didn't think you would. You're a reasonable man and you pride yourself on that."

"Those who love madly, Russian-style, can kill madly, Russian-style too."

"You might be a Vronsky," Fedorov joked, "but you're no Raskolnikov, Nathaniel."

No, Chapman thought, nor was meant to be. But Alek underestimated the violence of the American soul, just as he overestimated the violence of the Slavic.

Without replying, Chapman poured Fedorov another vodka, picked up the two valises, and took them to the back bedroom he'd prepared. He threw one on the bed, but when he opened it to unpack he saw the Luger, blue metal barrel and brown wooden butt, both polished to a high sheen. Promptly, he closed the bag, then set it and its mate in the closet. He turned the bed down, put the bedlamp on, and returned to the sun porch. Fedorov was asleep, the glass in his fist empty.

"Alek?" he called softly.

Fedorov started awake, blue eyes wild and fearful, then squinting and controlled. "Still dozing off, am I?" he declared. "Give me another vodka and I'll go to bed." He bolted the drink in a single swallow, then pushed himself to his feet and stood, swaying. "I think you'll have to give me a hand, Nathaniel, I don't feel very steady."

"Half-dozen vodkas on an empty stomach will do that almost everytime. Maybe you ought to have some scrambled eggs and a cup of coffee."

Fedorov drew himself up to his full height. "In my time I've drunk vodka by the liter and been able to dance the *gopak*."

"I know, I know," Chapman assured him, not pointing out that he'd been younger and stronger then. He drew Alek's arm over his shoulders and together they went staggering through the living room and kitchen, down the long hall.

Fedorov sat on the edge of the bed, his head in his hands, rocking himself back and forth, crooning the melody of "Moscow Nights."

"Homesick?" Chapman asked.

"Home—sick? Where is my home?" he wanted to know. "Tell me, where?" He lay back, rolled on his side, and pulled his legs up on the bed, trying to kick off his shoes. Chapman loosened the shoe buckles so he was able to. Fedorov drew his knees up to his chest, hugged his legs, pressed his eyes closed, and breathed a deep sigh.

As Chapman was closing the door behind him, Fedorov called, somnolently, "Why don't you go to see her, Nathaniel?"

"Who?"

"Valentina Andreyevna."

"Go to sleep, Alek."

"Why?"

"Because your KGB colleagues still have some small objections to me for *systematically violating the norms of behavior for diplomatic representatives* and would not welcome me to the Soviet motherland."

"The Soviet motherland!" Fedorov jerked himself awake, strove to sit up, but fell back. "Didn't Wheelwright tell you? Valentina Andreyevna is *here*, in New York. Fyodor Vyacheslovich was posted to the United Nations and she is with him!"

# 6

# Helga

"Were you expecting him?" Helga asked, her silvery mouth snappish, her green eyes so sharply defined by black pencil and green eyeshadow that her face had the imperious occult quality of an Egyptian princess, though her fingernails were bitten down to the nailbed.

"I knew he was coming here, but not when, or for how long," Chapman told her, deliberately evasive. He confided in Helga only with the greatest reluctance.

"Why did you let him?"

Chapman shrugged and stirred his coffee. "Because he had nowhere else to go."

"But you told me he was the man who did you and your precious Valentina Andreyevna in. If it had been me, I'd've killed him."

"Not so easy to kill a man as to say it."

"You ought to reread a little modern—or ancient—history," she rebuked him. She dropped the pork chop she was gnawing and pointed a greasy index finger at the windows, a red-nailed thumb at the door. "*Links. Rechts.* All you need. Left to the gas chambers. Right to life."

"Well, right to the concentration camp anyway," Chapman agreed. "Cheery little beast, aren't you?"

"I'm not uncheerful," Helga replied, gnawing the last

shreds off the pork chop bone. "You just bring out the gloom in me."

"Nathaniel Chapman—Gloomsday machine. Why do you come here then, Helga?"

Her look was withering. "Gallant as ever."

"Your bitchiness is showing, Helga."

"I don't mind being a bitch. I rather enjoy it."

"So you do, and so do I."

Her face fell. "Why do you have to put me down, Nathaniel, and make me feel like dirt? Do gentlemen do that?"

"Fedorov assured me this afternoon that I was the very model of a rational Anglo-Saxon gentleman."

"What the hell does a Russian know about Anglo-Saxon gentlemen? You're a WASP all right—and you haven't lost your sting—but you're no gentleman."

"A man who has lost his sting is not a man."

"But a man with *only* a sting left is not much of a man either. Did you treat your Russian tea rose to those thorns too?"

Angrily Chapman left her, and strode out on to the sun porch. Why did he let her come here? A part of him hated that Germanic intrusiveness, with its direct questions and metaphysical speculations about love, friendship, and destiny, that way of being at your throat or your feet. Yet she attracted him powerfully, the hood of heavy black hair, the flaxen skin, the chemistry of green eyes, the hard jut of breast and the wetness, the willingness, eagerness, to let him do as he wished with her. If anything could make him lose the memory of Valya, bring him some respite, it was that. Valya the golden and Helga the powerful darkness; Valya the Slav, Helga the Teuton. He was as torn by his passions for them both as his country was. Valya. . . . Had Alek been dreaming when he said she was there, in the States, in New York, only a few hours away, an easy telephone call?

The moon was low over the tops of the elms, casting their shadows on the ground, two columns of gaunt infantrymen on their way up the road to the front, with camouflage clumps of leaves and branches over their packs and helmets. ". . . till Birnam Wood do come to Dunsinane"? . . .That they were all in the States now—Valya, Fyodor Vyacheslovich, Wheelwright, Fedorov, Phyliss, Betsy, even the Ambassador, now in Washington waiting for reassignment—disconcerted him. Too much coincidence. It made him uneasy. All of it felt like walking through a dark room into a spider's web across the face, which, try as he would, he couldn't wipe away. It meant something, but what?

Helga's nose burrowed between his shoulder blades, her breasts, belly, and thighs adjusted themselves tightly against his back, and her arms went around his waist. He saw her fingers still greasy with meat, the nails chewed to the nub, clasping at his navel, and he snarled, "Why don't you go and wash your hands?" For an instant her fingers were still, then untwined, her whole body drawing back from his as if pulling against some powerful adhesive. Her bare feet shuffled back into the house.

Helga brought out all his cruelty, the cruelty that he had to admit always lurked there, but why did Valya seem only to evoke gentleness and warmth from him? Yet both had their own particular excitements for him. Even now, having hurt Helga, he felt the tremor of intent in his loins, the undecided hardening. Had he insulted her because Fedorov had so suddenly put Valya within reach, or because she'd spoken disparagingly of Valentina Andreyevna, or because cruelty was the aphrodisiac he required to screw his passion to the sticking place? And why hadn't Wheelwright told him that Valya was in New York with her husband?

In the kitchen, Helga was wiping the table, bent over, all solid breasts and buttocks accentuated by the clinging green jersey shirt and stretch pants she wore. Chapman came up behind her, as she had to him, hands cupping the bowl of her belly, pressing against her. She didn't move; she didn't respond; she stood fast, a bent-over L of acquiescent resistance, and grunted, "With you, Nathaniel, it's always the same. Hurt and bruise, then fuck to make it up. You must have Teutonic blood in your veins."

His erection shriveled, desire sluiced away. "At least," he replied, his arms falling from her waist, "we have *some* way to make it up. That's more than most people have."

Helga remained leaning on the table as if momentarily expecting him to return, then abruptly straightened up. "All right," she said, throwing the washcloth into the sink, "let's do it on the veranda. At least there you can look at your beloved elms, and I, I can watch the moon rise."

Remote in the heights of the night, the moon made the elms ghostly and ethereal, no infantrymen at all. He loved those trees. The house and farm and elms had been a solace—a joy he had never anticipated, nor probably deserved. It had helped begin the long, slow recovery from Moscow, the touching earth that restored him and made him stronger.

"It's never going to get better for us, is it?" Helga entreated, pale as porcelain, her flesh glinting on the porch glider as she held her arms up like the throats of swans (like the ballet dancers of *Swan Lake* that he had seen two dozen times in Moscow in order to meet Valya). "There's no asking for love, Helga," he said as kindly as he could, trying to comfort and be candid too, Valya's ikon glitter shimmering before him. "If you have to ask for love, then it's just no good, *kaputt* from the beginning. No justice in love, either. The loving are not necessarily loved, the giving are not necessarily given. People don't have reciprocal trade relations. One can strike the stone of indifference, or even affection, with Moses' rod and simply hurt one's fist. Nothing happens. And then another simply touches the rock with a fingertip and the secret springs of love will make an oasis of shade, pleasure, and cool waters in the very desert. Why? Who knows?"

Helga responded as if she'd understood nothing he'd

said. "I'm disaster prone," she mused. "If I believed in this astrology—*Virgo, Venus, Cancer*—I'd say the fault was in my stars, but even if we are star-crossed lovers, I don't believe that. My whole history proves I'm disaster prone. I was born the year Hitler took power. What more unfortunate introduction to the world did I need? No one has to cast my horoscope or read my tea leaves."

The combination of self-pity and determination that betokened Helga's past never failed to surprise him. Though she'd told him the story of her life too many times, and in so doing had forfeited his compassion, he always listened to each repetition of the tale as if mesmerized, pouncing alike on new detail or old repetition, to see if beneath the repetition he could search out the truth of what had happened to Helga, what she had become.

Helga von Waldecke was a member of an old Prussian family which prided itself on being able to trace its ancestors back to some of the Teutonic Knights who, in the early thirteenth century, had exterminated the Baltic inhabitants of Brandenburg and settled in their place. For generations the family were landowners and soldiers, whose holdings slowly branched into Pomerania and Silesia until after the First World War, when most of their lands were ceded to the new Polish state created by the Treaty of Versailles, an event the von Waldeckes never forgot. For them the name Woodrow Wilson was a malediction and the word Poland a profane oath.

Helga's great-grandfather, Friedrich, had been a maverick. As stiff of spine and martial of temper as the other Junkers of his clan, but shrewder, he had taken advantage of the new conditions in Prussia. After fighting in the Austro-Prussian War he moved his family to Ratibor, in Upper Silesia, where he owned a schloss and some ancestral acres. Clever enough to recognize that he didn't have the capital to compete with the *nouveaux-riches* coal-mine owners and steel magnates from Westphalia and the Rhineland, whom he despised, he planted his lands to tobacco and was soon drying and curing it as well as growing it. His son, Kurt, Helga's grandfather, was born while his father was at the front. He expanded the family landholdings, began to sell snuff and tobacco, and, in time, also manufactured cigars —and later cigarettes. He had energies to spare, enough to exercise his traditional Junker passion for arms in the Franco-Prussian War.

Helga's own father, Werner, born at the turn of the century, was just old enough to volunteer and fight against the French on the Western Front during the last year and a half of the Great War before he left the army—full of spleen— convinced that the Reichswehr had been stabbed in the back by treacherous politicians at home. He returned to Ratibor to join his father in supervising the family estates and tobacco business. The revolutionary upheavals and ruinous inflation of the 1920s almost bankrupted them, but reinforced father and son's contempt for Weimar, and hatred of the hoi polloi of social democracy and communism. They read Junger's *Feuer und Blut* approvingly and threw their support—behind the scenes, of course—in with their own kind, von Papen and von Schleicher. When von Papen became Chancellor they rejoiced at seeing Otto Braun, the Social Democrat Premier of Prussia, booted out after a dozen years in office. Their reward came in the form of Hermann Goering, put in Braun's job by Hitler, who set out to prepare the Third Reich for war. Werner von Waldecke was impelled thereby to rejoin the officer corps of the revamped *Wehrmacht* almost immediately, leaving the tobacco business to his father.

A few years earlier Helga was born, a disappointment to her father because he wanted another son and an event made even more grievous because her mother—who had endured a number of stillbirths and miscarriages—died not long after. Werner von Waldecke tried to take heart from the fact that his beloved Margret had already given him one son, Wolfgang, with all the proverbial virtues: physically brave, devoted to duty, with a military bearing, blue-eyed, blond, handsome, and already a champion horseman at fourteen. But at nineteen Wolfgang was to die, in the winter of 1944, fighting a desperate rearguard action against the Red Army in Prussia. When the Russians overran Ratibor on their way to Berlin, Helga's grandfather, old Kurt himself, invalided out minus one leg after the 1942 battle for Moscow, had taken Helga and his second wife, Lotte, in the vast flood of refugees to the West, to the Americans. En route, stopped by a Nazi deserter from an SS battalion who at Luger point commandeered their car and began to search Lotte's person for what family jewels she might be carrying, old Kurt had bravely grappled with the SS man, furiously roaring, *"Canaille!"*—Helga always joked that even at such moments one had to find a foreign imprecation for one's own countrymen—and had his head blown off for his pains. Her grandmother, all iron will and hauteur, had managed to get to family friends in Cologne, to whom she entrusted Helga and the few jewels she'd been able to save, and then died—of hunger, shock, love for her departed husband—depending on how Helga felt when she was recounting the tale.

Postwar Germany was a place where friendship died swiftly, and soon Helga knew that only one course was open to her; she had to leave the Vaterland. Only fifteen then, she was wise beyond her years, a fully developed woman, beautiful, speaking flawless English, French, Italian, and Polish—her home town Ratibor was now Raciborz, part of the new Communist Poland—and she found an American soldier in the Occupation forces, one who had not fought against her countrymen, and "persuaded" him to marry her.

Three years after they returned to the States, she divorced him and married a prosperous middle-aged dentist from Memphis, who not only supported her through university, but who then had a convenient coronary—sometimes Helga would wink, implying it was the result of the lewd exertions with which she tried him—and left her all his considerable life insurance. With that money she was able to continue her education unhindered. By twenty-five she had a doctorate in European history and by twenty-eight had written half a dozen scholarly monographs and one short book of the Polish Corridor question, all characterized by a loathing of things German, that earned her an associate professorship at Vanderbilt. Not too long after that she moved further north and east to Princeton, where Chapman had met her at a faculty cocktail party. Each time he heard her tell the story, or parts of it, Chapman was again persuaded that life was cruel, politics crueler, and history the record of the latter's monstrosities, as biography was the record of the former's.

"I hated that town," Helga was saying. "Wolfgang and I both detested it, small, stinking, and provincial. Always cold and damp. Cross the street and you were black and needed a bath. Blow your nose and the handkerchief was sooty. And did it stink! From the boats on the Oder, from the steel mills, from the tobacco-curing flues. My parents wouldn't let us play with the town kids either, because, after all, *we* were the von Waldeckes. And the other children weren't too eager to play with the scions of the schloss. So Wolfgang and I were thrown together, despite our differences in age, more than a brother and sister should be. He taught me to swim and to ride horseback, and whenever we could escape from the servants, we rode or went down to the Oder, filthy though it was, and swam. He even taught me to read, and when my parents were entertaining we sat up together at night and he'd tell me stories about Attila the Hun, who had left his footprints at the bottom of the brown Oder at Ratibor, or read me tales about Attila's alter ego, the Etzel of the *Nibelungenlied.*"

Helga shuddered, and slipped into her jersey and stretch pants while the glider swung and squeaked. She balled up her underwear, held it up as if for bidding, and asked, "Premature?" She found her pocketbook, stuffed the underwear into it, and explained apologetically into the face of his silence, "I was cold." Biting her nails, she asked for a cigarette, and when she'd exhaled her first deep drag, said, "I smell smoke."

"The cigarette?"

"No. Smells like fire."

Their eyes caught, and Chapman ran through the rooms, pausing in the kitchen only long enough to make sure nothing was scorching in the stove or smoldering on the burners, then pounded down the corridor to Fedorov's room. Halfway there he saw the serpents of smoke slithering under the door. He slammed the door open, dragged Fedorov from the burning bedclothes, and rolled him into the carpet on the floor, the smell of singeing hair rank in his nostrils. He seized the pillow, saw the Luger under it, and left it there to beat the flames down, making them flare at first, then snuffing them out with flat blows of the pillow. The smoldering mattress he turned off onto the floor at the far side of the bed, heard the Luger slam, but stamped on the mattress to keep it from bursting into flames.

Coughing in the smoke, he staggered to the windows, opened one, and its screen, a second, but the third—nearest the bed—was wide open already, its screen completely raised. Had he left it open before? He was sure he hadn't. A window perhaps, but not a screen. Choking, his lungs feeling seared, he put his head out of the window and breathed the cool night air. When the smoke had cleared, he soaked the mattress with pails of water, then examined everything—bedclothes, mattress, springs, the floor—but except for the Luger, he found nothing. The window had been open and had marks on the sill that could have been made by a knife used to lift the screen, but he could have made those marks himself when he'd put up the screens earlier in spring. As he began to unwind Fedorov from the rug, Helga asked from the doorway, "Is he all right?"

"Sleeping like a baby," Chapman answered. He felt Fedorov's pulse, listened to the slow, even breathing. Drunk, passed out, asleep and unhurt. Having freed Fedo-

rov altogether from the carpet, he saw the burnt-out cigarette stub scissored between the blistered second and third
fingers and held the hand up for Helga to see, but she was
staring at the Luger in his back pocket.

"Fell asleep while he was smoking?" she asked.

"Must have. Absolutely bombed. Fatigue, empty stomach, and vodka are a knockout mix," Chapman told her, but
he didn't believe it.

Together they managed to carry him into the next bedroom, where they dropped him on to the bed. Helga
stripped him down to his underwear, then covered him
with a quilt Chapman brought from the linen closet, where
he left the Luger. "He's a lot heavier and stronger than he
looks," Helga muttered.

"Fedorov's a tough old bird. Hard to kill."

"To kill?" she repeated.

"Only a manner of speaking."

Back on the porch she asked if he wanted her to stay and
help him clean up, but he said no.

"Let me stay the night," she pleaded.

He considered it for only a moment before he said, "I'll
call you."

"Don't call us, we'll call you," Helga observed bitterly.

When she had driven off—the tail lights of her Porsche
animal eyes in the darkness—Chapman went back to the
rear bedroom to make sure that all the fires were quenched,
then looked in on Fedorov. He was still peacefully asleep,
the hair of his head and beard slightly scorched, and two
fingers blistered, but otherwise unscathed. But when Chapman looked into the linen closet for the Luger, it was gone.

# 7

# *Birdwatching*

The early mysterious mist had lifted only enough for them to see their legs in the dawn darkness. On Chapman's back the knapsack was light, but the binoculars hung heavy around his neck and the Walther automatic in his waistband was sticking in his side. The enveloping obscurity unnerved him, although usually such a spring morning with its sweet smell of wet grass filled him with anticipation because he knew the mist would shortly lift, the sun rise, and the rolling green meadows, the brown rutted marshes, the blunt mottled hills would be revealed. Far and wide there would be only earth and sky and slanting sunlight on water, birds, and animals, and not a sign of man. Behind him Fedorov complained, inquiring if birdwatching was always so uncomfortable, the mist muting his voice so that it seemed to come from a great distance. Because Chapman couldn't see him, Fedorov seemed disembodied. He wondered if the Russian had an equivalent for the American slang, "It's for the birds," but instead explained that birds were early risers or stayed awake all night. Fedorov groaned something about energetic and puritanical Americans who rose before dawn, ate enormous breakfasts of orange juice, hotcakes, bacon and eggs, drank gallons of coffee, then went out into the fog to—of all things!—watch birds. What had possessed him, he wondered aloud, to indulge himself and Chapman in such masochistic idiocy. The complaint was good-humored and a dry chuckle accompanying it was a reminder that they had had only coffee and vodka for breakfast.

American birds, Chapman knew, were often able to fly to Europe because the prevailing winds were in their favor, but European birds who came the other way had to be especially powerful because they flew against the wind. He had heard of several sightings of European birds in that very area, so he was always on the lookout for a Ruddy Shield Duck or a Curlew Sandpiper or a European Woodcock, but so far he had not been lucky enough to spot one. Speaking softly and moving carefully so they wouldn't alarm any nearby birds, Chapman told Fedorov about how birds flew both ways, observing that the best he'd been able to do in the way of Russian birds was a Russian peacock: Fedorov himself. Fedorov's laughter was followed by the remark that at his dacha only other kinds of birds, "swallows," awoke him early in the morning, or kept him awake all night. Yet he had to admit that on occasion he had risen just to see the sun come up, to watch the brightness fall from air, but chiefly to persuade himself that the Lord did not deny some light even to the black Russian earth; but even seeing was not believing: even the Lord's sun did not persuade him.

"If not the Son, then perhaps the Father?" Chapman asked.

The mist had lifted enough for him to see the pained look on Fedorov's face. "Do you still believe, Alek?" Chapman wanted to know.

"Believe, Nathaniel?" His eyes were hard, his mouth set. "I believe in nothing. Neither man nor God, neither rulers nor ruled, neither East nor West."

They walked, their shoes and trousers soaked with dew, until the sun had swept the mist away, now and then catching sight of a low-flying goshawk, its quick gray wings beating a convulsion in the air, its long predatory glide over the treetops a quest, a search. For what? They saw a fine flight of formally clad barn swallows, blue-backed, swallow-tailed, their cinnamon-buff breasts like cummerbunds. Rusty-bosomed bluebirds and yellow-beaked robins hopped and whirred upward, flights of swifts, purple grackles, and red-winged blackbirds were blown like sheets of driven hail into shrubbery or trees, then soared out of them like locusts. The best was a single hermit thrush imperially perched on an oak, slowly cocking its tail and letting it fall back to the branch, its flutelike song timed to each cocking, each keynoted phrase lyrically separate.

"There is something to your birdwatching after all," Fedorov acknowledged when at last they sat under the oaks at noon, their shoes and socks laid out to dry in the sun, eating slices of Danish salami and Swiss cheese on *Roggenbrot,* washing it down with a bottle of Montrachet Chapman had lugged along in the knapsack.

"Life can be beautiful," Chapman observed.

Fedorov, stretched full-length, hands behind his head, fixed his eyes on the canopy of leaves above, as if they had suddenly intruded between him and the sun. "You're sarcastic, Nathaniel," he mused, "but in my whole life I have had perhaps half a dozen mornings like this, when my spirit could run calm and clear as the brook near my father's house. A day when there was no anxiety that I might say or do the wrong thing, no fear that I might be under surveillance, no terror that if I did not remain always alert, the sun above might be blotted out and before nightfall I might find myself in the cellars of the Lubianka or in a cattle car on my way to the Sea of Okhotsk."

In spite of all the buffetings he'd endured and would still have to endure because he was a Soviet defector, a middle-aged KGB officer, Fedorov would make it. He was a sturdy bird, one of those who had made the transatlantic crossing against the wind, from Europe to America, and survived. In only a few weeks he already seemed much like his old self, his body filled out, his hair with a new luster, his skin shining from their daily walks, the prison pallor gone. He looked thirty-five, not fifty. A remarkable resilience—and willpower?

"You know," Fedorov went on, "that was what separated us from the beginning, back in Vienna, although I didn't realize it then. Or even later, in Moscow. Only when I finally made the decision to come over did I understand what it was. You believe that something can still be done for my countrymen and I don't. You were a specialist on our affairs, a volunteer who came to my country not because you were assigned but because you wanted to. No matter what the Abrasovs and Saribekyans thought, you came to help. You were sure that the differences between us could be settled, because otherwise the world had no future. All this"—he waved his hand at the trees, the meadow sloping greenly away, the white sky vaulting overhead—"was finished, and earth—and man on it—cinders, unless all could be persuaded that 'peaceful coexistence' was not a slogan but a necessity. Without accommodation between us, between the United States of America and the Union of Soviet Socialist Republics, you were sure that history was at an end.

"You really did come to help, you know, don't deny it now," Fedorov insisted, cutting off Chapman's protest with a peremptory gesture. "It's nothing to be ashamed of. Naïve? Yes. But you meant it sincerely. You were really— how do you call it in American argot?—a 'do-gooder,' but in the right way. Not that you didn't see the mote in our eye and the hump on our back—God knows that you saw us plainer than we saw ourselves—but you were imbued with that awesome and terrifying American optimism. *Something could be done! Progress could be made! We could be saved!*"

"Something *can* be done," Chapman reiterated.

"You lived among us and saw how we behave. You went to Moscow University and studied our history. You talked to Party and government leaders, workers, teachers, intelligentsia, even peasants—when you had the chance, which wasn't very often—but you're still mistaken: Underneath all the terror and tyranny in Russia there is *no humane face of socialism*, no warm heart of concern to be unearthed and washed clean, no political and moral archaeology which can reconstruct the Russian halt and lame, and make us walk upright and behave decently, which can wash us clean of the detritus of centuries, of our bloodthirsty and murderous deeds. We Russians crave tyranny and terror. We can't live without them. We wouldn't know how to live unless some boyar, count, *vozhd*, Tsar, or First Party Secretary was ordering us what to do and what not to do."

"No people is irremediably damned," Chapman insisted.

"Nonsense. Many are damned. Maybe all. By history, by geography, by their institutions, by their very nature. Maybe the whole stinking human species is beyond salvation. Stalinism with us is the end product of a thousand years of Russian history, not just a Marxist-Leninist aberration. It's the apex of the pyramid that began who knows where—with the Varangians, the Tartars, Goths, Huns, Avars—who knows with what insane mixture of genes and tribal customs? Stalin is truly the heir of Ivan the Terrible, of Catherine the Great, and Nicholas I."

"And the heir of Stenka Razin or Pugachev? The Decembrists? The Herzens and Kropotkins? Or the Solzhenitsyns, Yakirs, Grigorenkos, and Bukovskys of today? Don't they count? Aren't they part of the Russian heritage too?" Chapman said stubbornly.

"Splinters under the blind Cyclops' fingernails. Where did Stenka Razin and Pugachev end up? Beheaded in Moscow. The Decembrists? Shot down by cannon and hanged. Herzen? Permanently exiled. Kropotkin? Imprisoned and exiled for most of his life, and disregarded when he returned to Russia. The others? Who can tell what will happen to them? They've all seen the insides of our prisons, our Russian universities, Lubianka, Butyrka, Vladimir, and the great waste sections of our earth where the camps are, the archipelago of Gulag."

"Yet they continue their struggle."

"Futile, Nathaniel. Absolutely hopeless. Stalinism persists even without Stalin. One man's tyranny may for the moment be in abeyance, but the tyranny of his heirs remains."

"The terror too is ended. Mass murders and deportations are over."

Fedorov's face was grim. "For how long? They are shrewder in one sense than before. Psychiatric wards for some instead of prison, stelazine instead of the 'conveyer.' But the camps are still there, full of inmates. The whole *apparat* of terror remains intact—KGB and Komsomol, Gulag and Glavlit, *kolkhoz* and *sovkhoz*, Gosplan and the trade-union councils. None has been dismantled, so that whenever they wish, the terror can be resumed . . . tomorrow . . . or the day after. Who's to say?"

"Is that why you left, because you'd lost hope?"

"I had no hope, period. For my country, for my people, for myself."

"Then nothing will change."

"Nothing. Oppression, exploitation, terror, all will remain the same. Only overwhelming catastrophe can change things—nuclear war, floods and famine, which might bring widespread suffering. Then the people might rebel. Brutally. With unbelievable violence and bloodshed—and with incalculable results. The 'final conflict' the Internationale sings about, the apocalypse the Bible tells about."

"The apocalypse?"

"Those in power will defend their power and privilege to the last. Marx was right that ruling classes did not willingly surrender such things—power and privilege must be wrested from them. But today those in power have nuclear weapons, nerve gases, germs, and if necessary, they will use them all."

"Against their own people?"

"The masses are *not* their own people."

Fedorov drank some more vodka and Chapman considered how, under the canopy of sunny sky and glittering oak leaves, such talk was truly sacrilegious. "By your accepting defeat before it occurs, you hasten defeat. I don't think the struggle is hopeless. Even in our time there was East Germany in 1953, and the rising in Vorkuta after Stalin's death, Hungary and Poland in '56, and Czechoslovakia in '68. And in the last fifty years Western society has been transformed—"

"Whatever its contradictions and injustices," Fedorov interrupted, "capitalism was never the equivalent of a police state, never what Russia is or was. Perhaps the West is doomed, precisely because its freedoms have turned to license and its prosperity to contentious wastefulness and show. Perhaps we *will* bury you, perhaps the 'new societies' will drag you down. But what good were all those risings and rebellions against them? The risings were crushed. And remember, except for Vorkuta none took place in Russia, and even Vorkuta was among prisoners. I know that living in 1984 is more than I can bear. I've had more than enough. Up to here." He held his finger across his mustache.

"What do you want?"

"To be left alone. To till my own garden. To speak or be silent as I choose. To work at something with my hands— once I was a good carpenter, maybe I can be again—to loaf in the sun, to whittle, to play chess, to read what books I please, to make love, to take long walks—even to watch birds—if I can winnow the corruption out of my soul and the fear out of my bones, maybe before I die I can write one book, just one, that would tell what I have been and what I have seen, what my people and my country have lived through in my lifetime."

Fedorov's rumbling bass was abruptly echoed by the flapping wings of a covey of killdeer rising steeply on whitestriped wings from nearby underbrush. Chapman caught two of the birds in his glasses, their longish tails flicking over golden-red rumps, the feathers of their white throats ruffled with double black necklaces. Their noisy complaint

—kill-deah! kill-deah!—was shrill, as they wheeled and scattered. *Kill dear,* to kill expensively? Or *kill dear,* to kill that which you cherished? Again he was anguished by the thought of Valya nearby. He had waited for Fedorov to speak of her again, soberly, on his own initiative, but Alek had not said a word.

"Did you see those killdeer?" Chapman asked, lowering his binoculars.

"No. I was having a vodka." Fedorov wiped his mouth with his hand and offered the flask.

Chapman drank, warming the sudden chill in his vitals.

The sun was beginning to sink when they awoke from their nap. They lay in the shade under the oak until Fedorov exulted, "A peaceful day, one whole peaceful day." He stretched, sat up, and put his shoes and socks back on. He pointed to the butt of the Walther sticking out of Chapman's waistband. "Always carry a pistol to watch birds?"

"Never before this, but now I'm protecting an important bird—you."

"Has Wheelwright appointed you my guardian, Nathaniel, or my jailer?"

"Your host."

"I need a friend, not a guardian."

"Friends are hard to find."

"Once we *were* friends. *True* friends. Are we still?" Fedorov looked into his eyes and Chapman felt as if he were being searched. He looked away and Fedorov sighed. Chapman began to gather their things into his knapsack. "Why don't you go to see her?" Fedorov asked. "I told you, Valentina Andreyevna is in New York."

"You didn't tell me enough."

"Because you didn't seem eager to talk about her."

"I can't." He shouldered the pack, adjusted the Walther, then set out briskly down the knoll toward the house.

Fedorov opened the conversation again. "They sent Martynov to the UNO last year. Part of the Russian quota.

Deputy Director of their public information service—a perfect cover—he's *rezident* for the 'illegals' here."

"Still KGB?"

"Once KGB, always KGB."

"Even you, Alek?"

"There are some exceptions. For almost thirty years, since before the war, Fyodor Martynov has belonged to Them heart and soul."

"Didn't you belong to them too?"

"Never heart and soul. Or mind." Fedorov's face was downcast, and his eyes watched his feet as they trod down the grass. "Yours is always a vote of no confidence," he said at last, a note of entreaty in his voice, a difficult note even for a consummate actor to strike, but that was what they had been trained to be: diplomacy or intelligence, both of them knew the masks and motions, the guile and the guilt. "Valentina Andreyevna was permitted to go along with him to the UNO," Fedorov added, "though just why, I don't understand."

"Not punished for me, for the films?" Chapman pressed him. "Didn't Martynov divorce her?"

"After you left she didn't appear on the stage for more than a year, and I didn't see her in Moscow. I was having my own troubles then, too. Possibly she *sat,* possibly they sent her to the camps, and possibly Martynov divorced her. She could be here on an assignment, working out her 'salvation' as part of her sentence, and no longer his wife. But I would doubt that. It is not Their way, nor Martynov's."

They sat on the veranda as the sun dipped below the horizon, meditatively drinking vodka and tonic. Fedorov resumed the conversation as if it had never stopped, and what he spoke was a eulogy and epitaph for the day. "I have longed for a day like this as an afflicted sleepless man longs for dawn. We have done nothing today, you will say. Nothing has happened. You are quite right. And that's the point. *No disaster has befallen. No humiliation been imposed.* A day in which two *almost* friends talked *almost* honestly with *almost* no fear of informing or reprisal. A simple day. A good day. Almost a holy day."

"Except for all those *almosts.*"

"Yes, except for those, and that." Fedorov pointed to the Walther.

"Maybe the most you can ask of men and societies is *almost,* even good men, and tolerable societies."

"Would you use it—the gun—Nathaniel, if I put my glass down, said good evening," he set his drink on the arm of his chair and stood, "walked down the road under those elms and simply disappeared?" He strode slowly to the veranda steps and balanced on the upper step, his back turned and his head lifted at an angle as if waiting to hear something. Fedorov spoke into the dusk so softly that Chapman had to strain to hear him. "No slavery is worse than the slavery which you persuade yourself is freedom. I persuaded myself that way for the best half of my life. More. Like a horse I kept myself putting one hoof in front of another by wearing blinders so I could stick to the strait and narrow. Yet in spite of the blinders, my eyes saw, my ears heard, my flesh felt, and my heart hoped and feared and was moved by the agony of others. My conscience could not be put to sleep. They could ring their bells to make me salivate like one of Pavlov's dogs—university, good job, flat in Moscow, dacha in the country, vacations in Sochi or Yalta, shopping in the special stores. But they couldn't satisfy my hunger. The more I salivated, the hungrier I grew. The more they fed me, the more starved I was. The freer I told myself I was living, the more enslaved I felt. They could not make me belong to them—and neither could I.

"I tried. Make no mistake about that, Nathaniel. I was as eager to belong to them, heart and soul, as any little 'swallow' who comes to Moscow from the provinces, so eager to stay in the big city that she will bed down with the devil himself for them. But I couldn't. I couldn't. A stifled cry kept sticking in my throat like a dagger—*Justice! Justice! Justice!* My eye had a tic, my hand a tremor, I couldn't sleep, and after a while I couldn't always make love, and when I did I couldn't enjoy it much."

Moved in spite of himself, Chapman asked, "Did you tell Wheelwright all that?"

Fedorov spun around on his heel. Angrily, he spat out, "That's not his language. His language is Theirs. For him there are only interests and power, nothing else, no ethics, no feelings, no loyalties, no guilt or remorse."

"What does he want from you, Alek?"

"Hasn't he told you?"

"No."

Fedorov's eyes and mouth went slitted and vicious. "Did he inform you that he was the man who counseled your ambassador to break his word to you, to send that dissenters' film out of Moscow and not to intervene on Valentina Andreyevna's behalf."

"I'm not surprised," Chapman said slowly, though he was disappointed. "Probably wasn't in the 'national interest,' as Andrew saw it." Somewhere at the back of his mind he'd always suspected that they had all betrayed him—Alek with Kornilov's flat, Wheelwright with the Ambassador, Valya with Fyodor Vyacheslovich—because they were part of that juggernaut, the machine of state, which took no account of individual human beings, only of interests and powers. Until now he'd refused to acknowledge such suspicions in the light of day. What was it old Charlie Simmons had said to him and Andrew at college? *Paranoia is the mother of invention.* Since the war he had worried that he might be inventing enemies, only imagining the causes of the disasters that befell him. He had fought a long lonely uphill struggle against his despair that nothing could be done, that the world was inevitably sliding over the precipice into the pit, and his victory—such as it was—over that despair had been his decision to go from AMG into the Foreign Service, agreeing to cooperate with the Agency. Otherwise, after the war, it might have been either suicide or paranoia.

He had fought—others, himself, the Department, the Agency—to remain true to his conviction that something *must* be done, *could* be done, and even as he did he was never quite free of remembering Charlie Simmons's look of loathing in the grand old man's class in diplomatic history when he quoted *Feste, Farina, Forche*—festivals, pasta, and the gallows—as instruments of state policy, from the Bourbon kings of Naples to Il Duce. Nor had Chapman forgotten the too admiring nod of Andrew's head when he heard it, as if something he'd accepted and known all his life under its Roman version of bread, circuses, and coliseums had thus been given intellectual and historical respectability.

"Here," Chapman said, as Fedorov continued to teeter on the top step. He tossed the Walther automatic to Fedorov, who only just managed to catch it awkwardly by the barrel. "Take your walk, Alek. I quit hunting and killing a long time ago. As you saw this afternoon, I don't even hunt birds, I just watch them."

## 8

# *UNO*

On the drive up, Fedorov seemed lighter-hearted and gayer than at anytime since his arrival, delighted to be visiting the great metropolis, to see and mix with crowds, to eat some Russian foods, to go to the theater. Most of all he wanted to see the United Nations, he said, because some Russians still hoped that it might become a true "parliament of man," although he knew, sadly —though he said it quite cheerfully—that such an idea was a chimera. Yet, as they sped up the turnpike, Fedorov threw his head back and in his booming bass recited: *"We are determined to save succeeding generations from the scourge of war, which twice in our lifetime has brought untold sorrow to mankind, and to reaffirm faith in fundamental human rights, in the dignity and worth of the human person, in the equal rights of men and women and of nations large and small, and to establish conditions under which justice and respect for the obligations arising from treaties and other sources of international law can be maintained, and to promote social progress and better standards of life in larger freedom . . ."*

"Sounds like the rhetoric of the Stalin Constitution," Chapman commented sarcastically.

"You really don't know it, Nathaniel? It's the preamble to the UNO charter."

"Scout's honor. I never heard it. When I was growing up, they only taught us to pledge allegiance to the American flag, and the League of Nations was called Wilson's folly." It was hard to believe that Alek's desire to see the United Nations was anything more than Fedorov's folly. Why come up to one of the two places in the United States where large number of Russians were likely to be, where someone might recognize him? Unless Alek had something else in mind.

The city skyline came into view bathed in lemony sunshine and Fedorov exclaimed, "A magic city!"

"Didn't you come in this way?"

"No. They flew me in at night, Russian-style, to a military airbase near Washington. I've never seen New York, though I know it from photographs." He was lost in admiration, for the towers, the cars which trapped them in a traffic jam, the scores of gas stations, the tunnel which took them under the Hudson. When they were in the city, Fedorov teased him, saying, "Even in the greatest city in the Western world you carry a pistol in your belt?"

"This is one of the few places in America where you really need it," Chapman remarked, and then told him about urban crime, and how in that one respect Soviet cities seemed superior to American ones—the control of crime—although that, too, was part of a police state. Nonetheless, he admitted it might be wiser not to carry a gun in New York, so he stowed and locked the Walther in the glove compartment.

The permanent headquarters of the United Nations is situated on the brink of the East River, housed in four buildings, the two most prominent, the General Assembly, with its cantilevered lines and hump on its back, squat and immovable, and the curiously frail-looking Secretariat, thirty-nine stories of blue-green glass and gray-white marble. As they stood and looked, Fedorov was dissatisfied, saying that the building was not as beautiful as the Palais de Chaillot. They walked along the street looking up at the Secretariat, while above them the fresh spring breezes blew the more than a hundred flags of the nations stiffly away from the flagpoles, halyards metallically clashing against poles. "Flags!" Fedorov snarled. "I hate them. All. Hammers and Sickles. Stars and Stripes. Crosses and crescents. They all make me sick! For those colored rags millions have murdered each other."

His outburst set Chapman on guard. Fedorov seemed anxious, irritable, looking over his shoulder time and again. They watched the flow of automobiles—many long luxurious Cadillacs and Lincolns with diplomatic license plates—as they pulled up to the guarded gates, then past them along the ramp to the delegates' entrance of the Assembly, to disgorge passengers. Abruptly, Fedorov turned his face away and seemed to shrink in size. "What is it?" Chapman asked, alarmed. "Are you sick?"

"Speak English!" Fedorov commanded in a hoarse whisper, not turning his face. "See the car just passing the guard? The chauffeur in it is KGB. A member of the 'special bureau.' I think he recognized me."

Chapman positioned his body to mask Fedorov, calmly pointing over the fence at the huge, one-eyed stone sculpture and fountain in the plaza, pretending to discuss it. The chauffeur in the car had turned and was craning his neck to see where they were. He suggested that they walk off, but Fedorov stood frozen. "No," he said, "a man's walk is more revealing than his face. Stand still, do nothing, blend with the landscape."

The perpetual good advice to combat-infantrymen, prisoners, intelligence agents, to anyone who wanted to survive in a hostile environment: don't move; movement more than anything else attracts the eye. The hunted had long known that almost by instinct.

"If he recognized me," Fedorov muttered, "he will drive around a second time to make sure."

"Or drive like hell to the nearest telephone, if he doesn't have a phone in the car."

Fedorov's eyes were swiveled so far into the corners of his sockets, trying to peer sideways at the autos on the ramp, that he seemed to have gone white-eyed and blind. With an explosion of breath, he whispered, "He's waiting there. Maybe he didn't see me." Quickly, he hurried them past the delegates' entrance and only when they had turned the corner and gone through the visitors' entrance into the main lobby of the Assembly building did Fedorov seem to breathe easier.

"You sure you knew him? Or that he saw you?"

"Count on my eyesight and memory, Nathaniel. Neither is impaired and both are trained. His name is Khlakov. Lev Mitrofanovich Khlakov. He is a *spetsi*, a KGB assassination goon."

Chapman knew that They usually had a couple of strong-arm types in every mission or embassy, and plenty of KGB officers served as chauffeurs. Some were even *rezidents*, with more power than the ambassador or head of mission, but why a *spetsi* at the UN Mission? Like the Boy Scouts, Chapman thought, they're always prepared.

Looking lonely and small in that immense, four-story-high lobby, Fedorov sat on a bench, exhaling cigarette smoke with a sound as if he were in pain. Clearly he wanted to be left to himself, so Chapman wandered about the lobby, picked up some pamphlets from the information desk, reserved a table for lunch at the delegates' dining room, found where the official tours began, then found himself staring up at the first Soviet sputnik, hanging fixed and certain above them, its antennae a Buck Rogers menace of the future. On a heavy pedestal solid on the floor, a statue of Poseidon with arms outstretched pointed—but to what? Symbols, both of them, for space above and the sea below? At the other end of the lobby, the Foucault pendulum was also suspended from the ceiling, its swaying gold ball dizzying contrast to the fixed silvery ball of the sputnik. Its deliberate pace was like the clock that had kept time in his grandfather's house, and its graceful undulation, precise and certain, solaced him. If above the earth hung the menace of sputnik and below the sea Poseidon had been enthroned by Polaris submarines, the pendulum was an assurance that the earth still turned. A small plaque announced that it had been donated by the Dutch government and engraved on it was a single sentence: *It is a privilege to live this day and tomorrow.* Fedorov's voice at his ear startled him. "You see, Nathaniel, someone agrees with you." Fedorov read the inscription aloud, mocking it derisively, "It is a torment to live this day and tomorrow. For most people in the world that is truer."

They'd been over that so many times in the past week that Chapman saw no point in renewing the argument. He had tried to explain that life was privilege *and* opportunity, that neither should be sacrificed one to the other, but Alek remained unconvinced. He saw how upset Fedorov was, took his arm and led him to where the tour guide was to meet them. At his side, Fedorov nudged him, whispering, "Remember, speak only English, please," though he himself was speaking Russian. The whisper distracted Chapman so that he missed the announcement of their tour guide's name. The guide, a young, dark, ugly girl in a sleeveless orange dress that might have been a modified sari, was either Indian or Persian. She wore bright orange plastic sandals, her feet bare in them, and her lacquered toenails jutting orange from the front of them. She was an altogether modern-looking and polyglot young woman, but her magnificent nose and sculpted nostrils were pure and classical, a profile that might well have been cut from a Persepolis frieze. Her fluting, high-pitched British English was clearly a foreign language to her and spoken so shrilly that she was sometimes incomprehensible.

The first exhibit was a wall montage of enlarged photographs showing the Arab refugee camps in Israel, intended to demonstrate the UNRRA's role in maintaining them. A tall, lean man in his sixties, with a distinguished face, horn-rimmed glasses, and thick gray muttonchop sidewhiskers, burst out, "Why is this the first thing to be shown? There are more than thirty million refugees all over the world, yet you choose these four hundred thousand. Why?" The guide, flustered, shrilled something about the UN High Commissioner's Office being responsible for other refugees, but it was lost on the members of the tour. One of them, a shirt-sleeved man in a Hawaiian shirt, a Yashica camera hung around his neck, said in a Midwestern *sotto voce* to his wife, "Must be a Jew." Everyone heard and ignored the remark except the man who had asked the question and Fedorov, both of whom turned to glare. The incident spoiled the holiday atmosphere of the tour for Chapman.

They made their way slowly through the buildings, dutifully admiring tapestries, murals, stained-glass windows— Candido Portinari, Marc Chagall, Fernand Leger—and all the visitors took snapshots, jiggling their light meters and lenses, bobbing up and down for effective angles. They were ushered through the empty Security Council chamber, silent and portentous. They sat in on a session of the Economic and Social Council, while a member of the Commission on the Status of Women gave a long, dull report in French on the flourishing slave trade in young girls in the Middle East. Because the Trusteeship Council was in closed session, they were barred from entering the room, and their guide led them on to the General Assembly. The "parliament of man" was truly impressive: more than a hundred nations embodied not by their flags but by their human representatives identified by small signs, from Afghanistan to Zambia, all gathered before the UN emblem on the wall, a polar view of the planet embraced—as though two arms—with the olive branches of peace.

"The view from the Arctic ice cap," Fedorov snorted. "Appropriate indeed. Mankind's prospects are truly glacial."

"The emblem probably means that the 'cold war' must be contained by the olive branches of peace," Chapman countered, only half in jest.

The great hall, its dome and overhead lights like the dome of heaven, was immense, but the huge, groping Leger murals, the green, red, and yellow voting lights, the galleries for newsmen, translators, and visitors seemed gimmicks—and the debate was appalling, frightening. Unbelievably self-interested and self-righteous, irrational and bellicose, long-winded and pompous, it was a blight on the hope for man's future, an anguish to hear. Here, where only the striving for peace and harmony should be manifest, where truths delicately stated should be made to work for man's survival on the planet, there was the maelstrom of fierce rivalries, greeds, and lies.

"Nothing can be expected from this!" Fedorov said. "A bullring full of matadors and the stink of death on every one of them. Each of those fools thinks himself a Manolete in the suit of lights, trying to get as close to the horns of catastrophe as possible while showing off his *cojones* and his graceful veronica. And if it lands mankind on the horns and disembowels him, okay, it won't be the torero's fault, but the bull's—and mankind's."

Fedorov stiffened, again turned his back. "In the news gallery," he remarked quietly, "the Tass man. I knew him when I worked on Radio Moscow. What is he doing?"

Chapman couldn't see and Fedorov growled impatiently, "Fifth window on the right."

This time Chapman saw a burly blond Russian nudging a colleague and pointing toward them. The colleague snatched up a pair of binoculars and began to focus it on them. "He's got a pair of spyglasses," Chapman warned, but Fedorov had already dropped to all fours, and, hidden by the benches, began to creep toward the end of the aisle as their tour group filed out. Fortunately they were the last, so no one noticed, but Fedorov asked, "Is he still watching?" Chapman looked back, glancing casually around the rest of the hall as if appraising it, before noting that the Tass man was still sweeping the visitors' gallery with his binoculars. He handed the glasses to his colleague, who repeated the sweep, then they began to argue, gesticulating angrily. As they were distracted, Chapman held the door open and said, "Now, go!" Fedorov, still on all fours, like an animal, scooted out of the Assembly chamber into the corridor, then swiftly stood, acting as if he had only bent down to tie his shoe.

"A mistake to come here," Fedorov murmured. "Too risky. That's the second time today someone here has recognized me."

"I didn't know you were so well-known to your countrymen." Chapman made light of it, wondering if this was defector's paranoia—*The guilty fleeth when no man pursueth*—yet he himself had seen that chauffeur looking back to see him, and the two Russian newspapermen raking the gallery with their binoculars, and, although he hadn't mentioned it to Fedorov, the burly blond one had reached for the telephone just as they were leaving. Coincidence? Perhaps, but it didn't pay to risk it, so he suggested that they leave. Fedorov did agree not to go to the delegates' dining room for lunch as they had planned, but he wanted to finish the tour: he'd come to see the UN and he'd be damned if he'd let Them frighten him off.

The tour ended on the public concourse with souvenir shops—where handicrafts from many countries were for sale—jammed with buyers. Chapman asked if he'd like to buy anything, but instead Fedorov led him upstairs to the Meditation Room their guide had pointed out in passing. He left Chapman at the door, and in the almost bare room, stained by the blue and gold light, facing the suns, moons, and double helix of the stained-glass window, Fedorov knelt on the floor, his eyes shut tight, his palms together, and his face in the crook made by his thumbs. His lips began to move and only after a time was Chapman able to make out some parts of the Old Slavonic Biblical cadences:

Thou, O Lord, knowest;
Remember me, and think of me, and
> avenge me of my persecutors. . . .

I sat not in the assembly of them that make merry,
      nor rejoiced;
I sat alone because of Thy hand;
For Thou hast filled me with indignation.
Why is my pain perpetual,
And my wound incurable, so that it refuseth
      to be healed?
Wilt Thou indeed be unto me as a deceitful brook,
As waters that fail?

Fedorov continued to kneel there until the mutton-chop-whiskered man who had been on their tour and protested about the refugees entered the room and coughed uncomfortably. Fedorov looked up, the two recognized each other and nodded. Fedorov rose, unself-consciously brushing off his trousers, and as he began to leave the room the two men passed close to each other, a thick brown envelope moved from the man to Fedorov, then Fedorov was out of the room. So swift and deft was the transfer that no sooner was it over than Chapman was not even sure he had seen anything occur. Fedorov's prayers had been answered. And, at last, Chapman thought he knew why Alek had taken the risk of visiting the UN.

Outside, the sun glinted off the blue-green windows of the Secretariat building. High up, carefully swabbing it down and wiping it dry, a washer clung precariously to one of the thousand windows, held there only by two leather straps. "I'm just like that," Fedorov remarked, "barely holding on and trying desperately to clean off my little square of fogged glass so I can see through the window." Prompted by blind impulse, his hand sought and caressed the coat pocket where he'd secreted the envelope he'd been given.

The gardens were in bloom, daffodils stiffly yellow, flowering cherry trees—soft masses of pink blossom—hawthorn, oak, and locust greening along the walks. Like the

Foucault pendulum, the gardens were evidence for him that earth could be fair, that life renewed itself, that spring did come; but Chapman knew that he was making an effort to convince himself. Near the river they passed an enormous bronze nude man, all ridged, straining muscle and titanic energy, a sledgehammer clutched in his powerful raised right arm, his left holding and bending back a gigantic broadsword already broken and being shaped to a plow. Carved into the plinth was the legend: *We Shall Beat Our Swords Into Plowshares*. Beyond, the blue and white UN emblem blew, stiff in the wind, from an aluminum flagpole. "Stalin Gothic," Fedorov declared.

"Yet," Chapman countered, "there is something of the passionate strength and energy in it necessary to make swords into plowshares."

"How shrewd they are," Fedorov remarked, "to seem to have preempted the cause of peace. Even the Isaiah quotation itself isn't good enough for them. Not *They* shall beat *their* swords into plowshares, as the Bible has it written, but *We*. Not they, not you, only we. The earth shall rise on new foundations, *we* have been nought, *we* shall be all." He wagged his head disconsolately.

In silence they strolled along the river looking at the tugboats and barges, the factories on the far side, the tracery of the bridge ahead. At the end of the walk, Fedorov said he was hungry, and as they turned to retrace their steps they found the two men waiting for them, blocking their path. One, blond and slender, wore an old-fashioned chauffeur's uniform buttoned up to a stiff collar. He had uncommonly small hands, which he kept flexing, like a pianist warming up for a concert, looking down at his fingers as if to convince himself that they were still in good working order. His face, beardless as a boy's, seemed almost bland, except that his eyes were banks of gray fog, impenetrable. A step behind him and to the right loomed a squat hairy man with thick black mustache over thick lips, arms too long for his body, his enormous hands balled into fists. He wore an awkwardly cut double-breasted blue suit, beneath which Chapman saw the outlines of a shoulder holster. "Good afternoon, Aleksei Mikhailovich," the chauffeur said in Russian.

"Sorry," Chapman responded in English, "I don't understand what you're saying."

"I speak to your friend," the chauffeur said in English.

"I think you've made a mistake," Chapman insisted. "We're only visitors here." He took Fedorov's arm and tried to walk by them, but the men wouldn't let them by. "I don't know what you want, but would you please get out of the way."

"I want your friend say something," the chauffeur declared.

"Ma buddy and ah are in this heah city to see the sights," Fedorov spoke up, his voice higher pitched than its usual bass, his words slurred in a Southern drawl. "If you fellas is aftah ouah wallets, you mighty much mistaken."

The chauffeur, puzzled, hesitated, then flicked his hand out, his tiny fingers tugged hard at Fedorov's beard. "Son-of-a-bitch!" Fedorov bellowed. The American imprecation startled the chauffeur, and Fedorov followed up his advantage by shoving him hard, pushing him back on his heels, then himself falling into a boxer's stance, left out, jabbing, "Ah tell you, boy, y'all lookin' fo' a fight, y'all found you'sef one. You gon' get youah ass kicked."

The chauffeur gave ground, but a revolver appeared in his companion's fist. "Stand!" the companion ordered.

"You were clean-shaven when I knew you," the chauffeur said thoughtfully to Fedorov in Russian, "and your hair was different." He switched to English, saying to Chapman, "My friend in my time did not have beard."

"I don't give a damn about that," Chapman exploded. "Get your friend to put his popgun away before I call that policeman." A UN security guard had just emerged from the conference building on to the esplanade.

Not taking his eyes off Fedorov, the chauffeur asked his

companion in Russian if there was truly a policeman behind them. The mustached man covered them with the gun, but turned enough to see the security guard. Chapman began to wave his arms, yelling, "Help! We're being robbed!"

"Silence!" the chauffeur commanded, in a voice used to being obeyed.

Chapman continued to wave frantically and pushed forward, but the squat man shoved the gun into his belly. "You no quiet, I kill," he threatened.

"Y'all ain' gon' kill nobody, mistuh," Fedorov said. He shoved the gun-toting man so hard that the man fell back half a dozen paces before he brought the gun up and trained it on Fedorov's chest.

The security guard began to walk toward them and Chapman continued to wave his arms and shout. "No shooting!" the chauffeur commanded in Russian. "Put the gun away." They turned to go and the chauffeur called over his shoulder, "I think you are Aleksei Mikhailovich Fedorov, only with beard and mustache. Perhaps you have dyed them or age has changed your hair color. But we shall soon find out." He repeated the words in English, for good measure, before they broke into a trot across the garden, heading for the street.

When the security guard came up and asked what was wrong, Chapman told him that the two men had been asking directions and then turned quarrelsome. "Directions!" the guard expostulated. "Crazy Russians! Those two work for the Mission here. They know their way around better than I do." He saluted them and strolled off.

"You'd have made a great actor, even if that Texas stuff was a bit overdone," Chapman complimented him.

"We KGB are well-taught. Perhaps only well-selected in the first place. Chameleons who can swiftly change their color or their coats to suit the circumstances," Fedorov said somberly. "Acting or not, he recognized me."

"He's KGB too, with good eyes and a trained memory."

"Khlakov. The Spetsburo. Now They'll be certain that

I'm alive and with the Americans—and they'll have to kill me."

"I thought they'd tried twice."

"Not them. They weren't even sure whether I had defected or 'had an accident,' and disappeared." Absentmindedly stroking his beard, Fedorov stood glaring after Khlakov and his henchman until they disappeared, then murmured, "The only way is to disappear again."

# 9

# *Reunion*

The irony of being in a Chinese restaurant was borne in on them when Chapman ordered Polish vodka and Fedorov, laughing harshly, suggested that at the very least he might have called for Stolichnaya or even Smirnoff, because, otherwise, as a Russian, he found himself once more surrounded, Poland on one side, China on the other. Chapman laughed with him. "The Communist encirclement now that the capitalist encirclement is over, eh, Alek? But always an encirclement. Be glad I didn't order German schnapps."

"I am, I am," Fedorov responded, throwing his hands up in mock horror, but still tense.

Both of them drank the first vodkas in one gulp, then Chapman ordered doubles for seconds. They sipped those slowly, waiting for the food which the waiter said would take some time to prepare because the regular lunch hour was over—it was almost four in the afternoon and the restaurant was virtually deserted—and also because they hadn't ordered from the regular menu. Chapman said they weren't in a hurry, and because Fedorov had rejected his advice to get out of the city as swiftly as possible they weren't. Fedorov insisted that since Khlakov was sure he was alive it no longer made sense to run, at least not right then; yet, Fedorov seemed to have something else in mind.

"They're going to try to kill you," Chapman told him. "You know too much and they'll want to make an example of you. You know how the Spetsburo people work. They'll keep after you for years until they murder you, the way they did Krivitsky and Ignace Reiss and Dmitry Navachin. and Juliet Poyntz, who probably ended up in the East River, not far from where we're sitting."

"I can't cut and run every time they threaten to kill me. Or your people do."

"My people? You mean Wheelwright?"

"Your Wheelwrights and my Abrasovs are the same. They want things, and unless you're prepared to give them what they want . . ." Fedorov drew a finger across his throat. "A defector is a peculiar creature, Nathaniel. His freedom is especially precious to him because, to acquire it, he's given up most of the other things that men think worthwhile—their native land and native tongue, their families and friends, their work and properties. He is also in a no-man's land, because those he left consider him a traitor—and so do those to whom he has come."

Those transatlantic birds flying full against the wind, wing bars straining, tail coverts swept back, breasts and throats bruised, Chapman thought. Never piss against the wind, Wheelwright was fond of saying. You only got wet that way, but flying in the face of the wind was liable to kill you. "To risk your hard-earned freedom unnecessarily," Chapman said, "is criminal. If those Spetsi hoods murder you, you have death, not freedom."

"Death itself is freedom, release from the enslavements of life."

"You could have bought that freedom cheaply enough in Russia," Chapman replied impatiently.

"So I could have, Nathaniel. Maybe freedom is only a snare, and I'll have to sprint like a hare until the hounds run me to earth."

"The time to go to ground is when the hounds are out."

Unreasonably irritated by the Slavic passivity and melancholy, Chapman stood up. "I'd better call Wheelwright to
tell him what happened."

"I wish you wouldn't."

"I have to."

"Then you *are* my keeper."

"I *am* my brother's keeper," Chapman said, solemnly.
"But not his jailer. We may need help. Wheelwright can
supply it."

"What help?"

"I don't know. An escort? A helicopter? Anything that
will prevent Khlakov and his friends from converting you
into a corpse."

The waiter told him there were banks of phones at the
rear and downstairs near the washroom. The downstairs
phones were more private, and he preferred that Fedorov
not hear what he had to say to Wheelwright. It took a while
to put the call through to Virginia and then Wheelwright
wasn't "available." His secretary wouldn't say where he was
or when he'd return. For an instant of pique, Chapman
considered switching the call to Logan Pearsall, but he
knew that would infuriate Wheelwright, and besides it
wouldn't make sense. Exasperated, he left his name and a
message that some Spetsburo hoods had recognized Fedorov and that he, Chapman, thought it dangerous. If Wheelwright were to return within the hour, they'd be at the
restaurant—and he left the telephone number.

When Chapman came back upstairs, Fedorov was hanging up a phone at the back of the restaurant. He offered no
explanation and Chapman refused to ask any. He was willing to go some distance to protect Alek's life, but in spite
of Wheelwright and Khlakov, not willing to be his turnkey.

The food arrived, succulent shrimp fried in batter and
wrapped in thick slices of bacon, crisp segments of roast
duckling, the color and texture of tree bark, a mound of
pork cubes, snow pods, vegetables, and almonds. Looking
happily at the steaming food, Fedorov said, "If all the Chi-

nese ate like this, my countrymen could eat their borscht and kasha with quiet hearts." Eating restored some of their good spirits, as did the double vodkas which Fedorov poured into his tea. "A fine international combination, vodka and Chinese tea," Fedorov grinned.

"Better than bourbon and tea, or vodka and coffee," Chapman granted.

"At least you admit Russia does have some virtues."

It was almost dusk before Chapman broke open his fortune cookie and extracted the tiny strip of paper from it. Aloud, he read the legend: *"Trust your friends today, not your enemies."*

"How simple," a woman's voice behind him said in Russian. "I thought the Chinese were more subtle than that. The real difficulty is to tell your friends from your enemies."

Hemmed in by the table, Fedorov still half-rose and bowed from the waist. "Valentina Andreyevna," he greeted her, kissing her gloved hand. Unable to speak or move, Chapman sat, the fortune cookie strip of paper taut in his fingers. The sun setting behind her blinded him and he saw the Madonna of Tenderness with a nimbus of gold around her head, as she'd appeared on the wall of the dacha. Fedorov mumbled something about going to the washroom, and left them. Valya sat in his place, the light radiant on her face and iridescent in her eyes. Her hands were folded on the table, encased in brown kid gloves that made them seem cast in bronze, the outlines of her nails beneath the skin-tight leather etched into the metal.

The fortune cookie strip of paper snapped apart in his fingers, and he dropped the pieces and watched them flutter on to the table in front of those metallic hands. In utter disbelief, his fingers touched the vein beating in her temple, caressed the outline of bone in her cheek, and settled lightly on her trembling lips. "Valya," he spoke at last, "my beloved Valya." Her gloved hand drew his fingers along her throat, caught them between her cheek and raised shoulder. "Why didn't you write?" she asked.

"I did. Many times."

"I never received your letters. Did you get mine?"

Chapman shook his head. "I sent them to," he hesitated, then skipped Wheelwright's name, "a friend at the embassy. He was to put them into Russian envelopes and post them to you in Moscow. You *must* have gotten them. Some? One?"

"Nothing. Ever."

For more than a year, he had written letters and sent them to Wheelwright via diplomatic pouch to be remailed to Valya. When Wheelwright had returned home, he'd given him the name of his replacement in the Moscow Embassy who promised to continue doing the same service, but by then there seemed no point because Valya had not written a single word in reply. Had Andrew duped him? Had Fyodor Vyacheslovich intercepted the letters? Or had the KGB simply examined all Valya's mail, letting through only what They wished.

"I didn't know what to do," he explained. "I was afraid to ask our embassy people to inquire, because that might do you harm. And after the way they'd betrayed us with the dissidents' film, I didn't trust them."

Valya looked puzzled. "Then you didn't break your word?"

"Did you think I had?" Reluctantly relinquishing the warmth of her flesh, he took his hand from the crook of her neck and shoulder. "I made a bargain with Abrasov."

"A bargain is only a word."

"Not mine. My word is my word." He saw they were about to quarrel and, to avoid it, asked, "How did you find us here?"

"Aleksei Mikhailovich telephoned me."

So that was the call Alek had been making. Or one of them. He had known that Valya was in New York, had even known her phone number.

"Didn't he tell you that I was here, that"—she hesitated
—"we were at the UNO?"

"I couldn't believe him."

"Why didn't you put him to the test?"

Why hadn't he asked Alek for the phone number or the
address, or simply for more information? A part of him
wanted so desperately to believe that she was in the States,
that another part even more adamantly refused to acknowledge the possibility, stringently preventing him
from putting the truth to the test, from putting his faith in
Fedorov to the test, lest both fail him. He had given himself good enough reasons: if Valya were in New York,
she'd be under surveillance, her mail opened, her phone
tapped, but that wasn't what had held him back. "I
couldn't take the chance," he began, then switched to,
"Why didn't you . . . ?" and finally lapsed into uncomfortable silence.

Valya answered his question nonetheless. "I didn't know
where to find you. I wrote to the only address I had, your
flat in Washington. The letter was returned—*Moved, No
Forwarding Address.* After we got to New York I tried all the
Nathaniel Chapmans in the city, then in the Washington
and Philadelphia directories, but the men I reached were
never the right Nathaniel Chapman. So I wrote another
letter, but Fyodor saw it, and warned me."

"Warned you?"

"I was not to get in touch with you. He said you were an
American intelligence agent. *They* would find out and it
would be the end. They'd send us both home." Valya
frowned. The fine lines etched around mouth and eyes had
not been there before, and they stung him. She caught his
look. "I sat," she confided, "for almost a year, in Vladimir
Prison and in camp in Mordvinia. Article 58. Fyodor persuaded them to release me, finally, but I knew it wouldn't
take much to make them send me back."

"Why did they let you leave Russia, come to New York?"

Her bosom rose and fell, as if she couldn't quite catch her
breath. "They co-opted me," she said. "I agreed to work

for them, so they let Fyodor take me out of the camp—and out of the country."

Chapman put his head into his hands. She had let them co-opt her too. Yet he knew what the camps were, what her fate would be if she remained there. Her hand caressed his hair, but he couldn't look up at her face. "There's no way for you to understand, Nathaniel, is there? Especially when what they asked me to do, what I did, is so much more than that. For you know, they co-opt you to do a job for them, not for nothing. My assignment was to be a 'swallow.' " Her hand stopped stroking his hair. "Do you know what a 'swallow' does?" she asked.

Chapman nodded, felt her fingers fall away from his head.

"They used me in their 'games' against foreign diplomats. Some American, some English, one French," she said, bitterly, "because, you see, they said I now had prior experience."

"With me?" he whispered.

"With you," she replied.

"And Fyodor Vyacheslovich consented?"

Her laughter was a discordant choking that sounded as if she were being gagged. "Consented? He was delighted. He's one of theirs in his heart, and has been for a long time. I think he's a Colonel by now, a Colonel in the KGB! What a very long way for a man to come who was born in a one-room hut, a miserable peasant *izba* near Omsk. Even further than the Stalin Prize."

Chapman looked into her face, saw her eyes bright with tears, the tense gloved hands, animal-smelling of leather, on the table between them. Words were stirred in the depths of him, but though he tried to speak, his voice was buried in his throat, the sound lost.

Valya waited a long time for him to speak before she continued. "Truly, you live on the other side of the earth. It's easier here to indulge yourselves in such courtly abstractions as love, honor, fidelity. On my side of the world, we can't afford such luxuries. Everything there is the struggle simply to survive, to keep one's head above the waters. Do you understand that, Nathaniel?"

He shook his head.

"You can't. Even if you study us until you're a graybeard, even if you live among us for the rest of your life, you won't understand because you'll only be among us, not of us. You'll never know what it is to lie there at night waiting for the knock on the door, keeping that little bag always ready in the hall, waiting for the Lubianka, for Vladimir, for the Butyrki, for the transports to the camps. You've read about such things, talked to people who have lived through them, but you can't imagine its happening to you. Here, you live your well-ordered lives. As far as you're concerned, all that is the other side of the moon, not simply the other side of the earth. But in our part of the world, terror is as intimate as a toothache, as debilitating as diarrhea, with us all the time, and for which there's no doctor, no dentist, no pain-killer, no cure. We have to live with it. To *survive*! Before all, *that*'s necessary. Surviving one more day, and then another day, hoping to live out our lives. Dishonored, perhaps. In shame, surely. But alive and breathing.

"If you want to stay in Moscow to study, to act, you marry a man who has a flat in the city, who has connections in the theater, who is, you learn later, one of Them. And if you make a mistake, a human mistake, and fall in love—and falling in love is the most grievous of mistakes, because it means caring for someone else more than you do for yourself, and when that happens you can't look out for yourself —then you try to make up for it."

"And I," Chapman asked, "was that mistake?"

Valya peered narrowly at her bronze fingers, stretching them to their utmost in their kid confines, her nails projecting. "We are primitive still, we women. We want our men to protect us, to cherish us, to keep us unsoiled by the world. Maybe keep us from soiling ourselves. But the world soils everyone, all of us, men and women alike. Do you hear, Nathaniel? Even you. Are your hands so clean that you can say my body is dirty? Is your honor so unsullied that you can say my soul is besmirched? Weren't you a spy in my country?"

"I was a foreign-service officer, a diplomat," Chapman declared, "not a spy."

"You cooperated with your own spies, then, didn't you?" She was angry. "They co-opted you just as They did me. And didn't you leave me to Abrasov and Saribekyan, to their tender mercies and those of my husband? For what? For a strip of celluloid film, for half a dozen heroic martyrs and a half-hour's conversation for the world to see and hear, that will do no one any good—neither them, nor my people, nor yours." Her hands, clenching and unclenching, were like the claws of a bird of prey about to pounce.

"I had no alternative," he began to explain.

"Neither did I," she snapped.

"What is it you want, Valya, my forgiveness?"

"Your forgiveness!" Her voice, darkened by fury, was altogether a stranger's. "I committed no crime and I ask no forgiveness. Not from you. Not from Fyodor. Not from anyone. For me to ask your forgiveness I would have to believe that I had wronged you—and I don't."

Precipitously his anger rose to meet hers. "Then what *do* you want?"

Her eyes appraised him as if he were an object, foreign and distasteful. His rage vanished and spontaneously he reached out to smooth away the hard, unforgiving lines her face had set in, but she averted her cheek. Hopelessly, he let his hand fall and accidentally it grazed the tip of her breast. Her gloved hand exploded against his cheekbone, deafening him. He thought she was going to slap him again, but by some gigantic visible effort of will that shook her, she restrained herself. "That's always men's idea of love . . . touching," she said. Only then did he realize that what she wanted was forgiveness from herself, a way of surrendering the notion that she had wronged herself.

From a respectful distance, he heard his own voice, detached and dead-sounding, "Touch is what we're left with when words fail."

"Or when feelings fail."

Dizzy and nauseated, Chapman leaned his elbows on the table and held his head. Eyes closed, he watched the spiraling nebulae and comets exploding in the darkness behind his lids, heard the ringing in his ears like a tocsin, felt himself swept away by an unfeeling tumbril to where the guillotine of love had made him lose his head.

When he opened his eyes, she was gone. He leaped to his feet, looked around, then raced outside, but she was nowhere to be seen.

In the restaurant, he met Fedorov coming up from the washrooms. "Sorry," he apologized, "I'd have given you longer, but the washroom attendant was beginning to stare at me as if I were a homosexual waiting for trade at the urinals." Only then did he see the look on Chapman's face. His eyes flicked to their booth. "Where's Valentina Andreyevna?" he asked.

"Gone."

"Where?" Fedorov persisted. "Why?"

Throwing his hands up, Chapman said, "*It would be very wrong to think you were a vestal; you came in with a chair, took my life as from a shelf and blew away the dust*—and now she's put my life back up on the shelf to gather dust once more."

"You're drunk," Fedorov accused.

"No, neither on Pasternak nor on vodka."

"What in God's name happened?"

Chapman tried to describe what they had said, but none of it made any sense to him.

"Women!" Fedorov exclaimed. "Vestal indeed! Neither virginal nor guardians of the sacred fires of hearth and home, but wanting always to be thought both."

"I don't know what she wanted," Chapman said plaintively.

"To be fucked," Fedorov retorted harshly, "to be relieved of her guilt."

# 10

# Chase

Walking toward the garage they crossed an oil-slicked gutter and stopped on the far curb to stamp the sticky black muck from their shoes. "Fuel-oil delivery truck leaking," Chapman explained. Behind they heard the tap-tapping of the blind man's stick on the curb they had just left, his long aluminum cane describing a small impatient arc in front of his shoes. Dark, in a well-cut black suit, dark glasses, with a head full of dark curly hair, he stood muttering mournfully, waiting for someone to help him across the street. No one was in sight so Fedorov started back. Chapman tried to stop him, but Alek was too quick. As he trotted across the street, the aluminum cane came up and Chapman yelled, "Down, Alek!" The cane hiccupped, a soft popping sound like an umbrella opening, and Fedorov fell on one knee. Chapman ran across the street. "You hurt?" he asked.

"Slipped on the oil. Lucky. Otherwise . . ." His voice was shaking. "Never mind me," he ordered, "get that bastard!" But it was too late. The man had already raced two blocks down the avenue and was turning onto the side street. Chapman jumped into the middle of the avenue to flag down a car, his only chance of overtaking the "blind" man, but no one would stop for him, and two cars barely missed running him down.

"You'll only get yourself killed," Fedorov finally shouted.

"Save the Spetsi the trouble."

Ruefully trying to brush the oil stains from his trouser knee, Fedorov grumbled, "I don't think they're after you."

They were well out of the city before Chapman brought up the question he knew Fedorov must be asking himself. "How did they find you? Valya?"

Fedorov winced. "You think that was why she provoked the quarrel, stormed out?"

"I don't think Valentina Andreyevna is one of Theirs. More likely my stupidity, and They followed her to the restaurant."

"The blind man?"

"Him and others, probably waiting in a car on that street."

"I've watched the rear mirror since we left the city. No one's following."

"They may be working two and three cars, switching. They often do."

"Three cars? We're not worth it, are we?"

"Speak for yourself, Nathaniel," Fedorov tried to make a joke of it. "I'm worth a convoy."

They had driven another five miles when Chapman suggested some coffee. At the next service area he pulled into the restaurant parking lot and waited. The cars immediately after them went right through to the service station to gas up. In the restaurant they got a hard-eyed stare from the thick-legged, bleached-blond waitress when they ordered only coffee, but she grew friendlier when he switched his to Irish coffee and Fedorov added a double vodka. "If I'm going to get killed for this, Alek, I'd like to know what it's all about."

Fedorov's eyebrows arched. "You called Wheelwright. Did you give him the address?"

"You think the blind man was one of *our* people?"

"Did you give him the address of the Chinese restaurant?"

"No, Andrew wasn't there. I left the phone number with his secretary."

"Wouldn't be too hard to get the address, would it?"

"Simple, but I don't think *we* keep any Spetsburo types on tap at the American Mission, so that Andrew could get back to his office, run down the phone number, call New York, and have some hoods sent to the restaurant in—what —half an hour. We're not that efficient."

"Not impossible though?"

"No," Chapman admitted reluctantly, Fedorov was driving at something else. "Besides, why would Wheelwright want you bumped off?"

Fedorov took another tack. "You and he are school-friends, aren't you?"

"Andrew, Charlie Simmons, and I roomed together in New Haven. But friends? I don't know."

"How can you *not* know?" Fedorov's glance was skeptical.

"I'm not sure I *know* anyone, in the way you use the word."

"If you know a man for a long time, you can usually gauge what he will *not* do," Fedorov asserted, "as I knew you would *not* kill me when Wheelwright brought me to your house."

Chapman let that pass.

"How long has he been an intelligence officer?"

"Since the war. Andrew was one of the 'Oh So Socials.' "

"The what?"

"The O.S.S. That was the American wartime intelligence service. An amateur group at first, recruited mostly from upper-class families and good schools. Other people—outsiders like me—called them 'Oh So Social.' "

"He must be quite high up by now, a colonel at least," Fedorov hazarded.

Chapman was increasingly uneasy at the direction Fedorov's questions were taking.

"Were you in the O.S.S. too?"

"No, in the infantry. Then, after the war, as you know, in Military Government. But Andrew was in intelligence from the beginning. He came back home right after the war, so he was on the ground floor when the Central Intelligence Agency was organized."

"You remained friends?"

"We were posted in different parts of Europe. When I was on home leave, he was off somewhere else. When I was in Berlin and Vienna, he was mostly in Washington. But I was one of his ushers when he married."

"Doesn't that mean you were intimates?"

"In a way."

"Did you know," Fedorov asked, "that They compromised his wife in Moscow?"

"Phyliss?"

"They had pictures of her."

"The same techniques over and over again."

"Because they work. They never tire of such means because people are subject to the same urges, pressures, compulsions—sex, money, power. They had photographs and also tapes."

"Does Andrew know?"

"He knew," Fedorov said, staring into his coffee.

In the parking lot, they stood for a while looking up at the new, polished stars and the ruddy profile of the half-moon. "Alek," Chapman asked, "are you saying that they doubled Andrew in Moscow with those pictures of Phyliss?"

"Friends cannot be traitors, school chums cannot be doubled. 'Gentlemen' from 'good schools' don't do that sort of thing, eh, Nathaniel? I thought you Americans were a little smarter than the English."

"I remember Philby, and Burgess and MacLean."

When they settled into the car, Chapman unlocked the

glove compartment and took out the Walther. He checked the safety and the clip before handing it to Fedorov. "Until you get your Luger back."

"You know about the Luger?"

"I saw it the night of the fire."

Chapman was less concerned about the gun's disappearance than upset by what Fedorov implied had happened to Wheelwright in Moscow. Had the KGB's compromising Phyliss been what led to their divorce? If Andrew had divorced her, then could they continue to hold the pictures over him? Even as he asked himself the question, he knew they could. One of Andrew's jobs in Moscow had been to seem to be a double agent passing carefully prepared information to Soviet agents, to persuade the KGB that he was indeed a traitor. Had Phyliss been part of that scheme so it would appear that Andrew could be blackmailed? He found it hard to believe that the Agency would permit such a thing, much less Andrew. They used "swallows," but did we?

Assignments like Andrew's exposed a man to the greatest peril. First he dangled reliable information as bait, then gradually misleading information would replace it which was intended to confuse and misinform Them, but in such an operation a man might be killed by either side, mistaken for a traitor by his own people—such assignments were very secret, had to be in the nature of the job, and Andrew had told him only, he said, because he wasn't sure that his case officer would stand by him if he were caught by their own security—or murdered as a double by enemy counterespionage. Yet, once a man took such an assignment, there was always the danger that he would move to the point where he no longer knew where his allegiance really belonged. Once he'd made contact with enemy agents, fed them information, taken their money, enjoyed their plaudits, how could one be sure that he had not passed over the line irretrievably? Was that what happened to Andrew, or had he used the KGB's clumsy efforts to blackmail him with evidence of Phyliss's playing Lady Roundheels, to fool everyone, including Fedorov and Them?

In the rear mirror he saw the automobile come smoothly off the shoulder. A big gray Mercedes, it fell in behind him, about five cars back and in the right-hand lane while he stayed in the center lane, but no matter how he varied his speed, it stayed there. "They picked us up," Fedorov remarked, without turning his head. "Waiting on the grass outside of that rest area, the only way we could drive out. Well-trained." A note of professional pride crept into his voice which amused and appalled Chapman. "I don't think they'll try anything on this highway. Too many cars, too many witnesses. Unless they can manage an accident."

At first Chapman tried to outrun them, eighty-five, ninety miles an hour, his hand bearing down heavily on the horn, narrowly missing collision after collision, praying that a state police car would hear his horn, see them, pick them up, but no police appeared. Their Mercedes was faster than his Pontiac and they clung to him without apparent effort, their headlights dead in his rearview mirror. Chapman tried slowing down then, to thirty-five, to see if they would pass him, but the Mercedes dropped back and waited. Waited? For what? "Look out ahead!" Fedorov warned, just in time for him to see and avoid hitting the second Mercedes, dark-green, which had come up from behind on the other lane and slid in front of him. The drivers, interchangeable in tan raincoats and turned-down hats, had obviously handled such assignments before. Now that they had him boxed in they began to increase their speed, the rear one forcing him on, to keep from being rammed, the one in front keeping just enough ahead of him to keep from being rammed, but not far enough for Chapman to swerve out of the lane. They had him in a trap in which he had to go slow or fast as they wished, and stay in the lane they wished. Seventy. Seventy-five. Eighty-five. Cars swerved out of their lane, bug-eyed drivers cursing, but the gray Mercedes kept pushing him faster and faster until he was going over a hundred miles an hour.

The arrow on the speedometer was, at the last reading, a hundred and twenty miles an hour, the Pontiac, chassis shaking, yawing in the wind, and Chapman fought the wheel to keep the car running straight, the sweat pouring off him. The green Mercedes dropped back now, pulling to the right, into the lane beside them, but never giving him enough space to get out of lane. They roared along like that until they seemed certain that the Pontiac could go no faster, and then the green Mercedes edged in, forcing him toward the road divider. He held the car straight, heard the Mercedes' wheelring tear against his, once, twice, then the Mercedes veered off. Then returned again. And again. Each time forcing him farther toward the divider until the side of the Pontiac scraped along the concrete. At that speed, if he swerved just a little more, the car would jump the divider into the oncoming traffic and they were dead. And so would be some innocent people in cars going in the other direction. Grimly fighting his own fear, sweat almost blinding him as it poured down into his eyes, Chapman fought to hold the car on course with all his strength.

Once more the green Mercedes swung closer, bounced his front fender slightly so he was driven half up on the divider before it edged away. He saw the driver's grin, gleaming like chrome in a headlight. "Alek," he roared. "The Walther. Kill those bastards, before they kill us!"

Fedorov took a long time before he got his window rolled down, and just as he braced the Walther, Chapman put the accelerator pedal down flat on the floor, standing down on it. The Pontiac leaped ahead and Fedorov fired twice. The green Mercedes suddenly careened crazily, the driver fighting the wheel, and then it skidded into their lane and hit the gray Mercedes full tilt. The explosion shoved the Pontiac ahead with a hot giant hand as the flames roared behind them.

It was almost a mile before he could bring the Pontiac down to thirty-five miles an hour, but even then his heart continued to pound. Behind him in the rearview mirror he had watched the two cars burning fiercely—relieved, angry, sorrowful—had seen the belated flashing yellow light and heard the yowling siren of a state police patrol car.

He got off at the very next exit of the turnpike and took the local roads. After they had driven a few miles, Fedorov asked, "And now?"

No lights were on in the house as they drove up the *allée* under the elms, but when they got out of the car a porch rocker squeaked, light glinted on something, and they fell flat on the ground. Walther in hand, Fedorov motioned for him to go around the other side of the porch, and began to creep forward when Helga's voice asked, "You two boys gone up to the city for some debauchery and got it? So drunk and worn out by the pretty girls you can't even stand on your feet." She was sitting on the porch rocker, her feet on the rail, a glass in her lap. "I waited dinner for you two bastards!" She threw her drink at them, the ice cubes in the dark like shiny starlings.

Although Helga was swaying next to the rocker now, Chapman didn't believe she was drunk. He also remembered that he had *not* invited her for that night, but for the next night. Had Helga simply confused the dates or had she known they wouldn't be there? Was Helga the one who'd taken the Luger? And was he himself beginning to be a paranoiac?

Fedorov was brushing the dirt from his coat and trousers, the Walther out of sight, and they went up the porch steps together. Helga weaved forward to meet them. "You invite me to cook dinner and stand me up!" she raged. "You don't call, you don't leave a note, you don't say a goddamn word. And I work and waste good time, energy, and sauerbraten, dumplings, and red cabbage." Her arm came up to slap him and Chapman twisted it down, then let her free. No woman had slapped him or tried to since his college days, and now twice in one day. "You're drunk," he remarked not unkindly. "What are you sitting here in the dark for?"

Helga beat his chest with her fists. "I didn't want to see myself. I didn't want to do anything except get drunk and forget that you treat me like . . . an object, a thing. Something to be taken off the shelf when you need me, and put back and forgotten when you don't." He grabbed her wrists and held them, but she twisted away from him. *It would be very wrong to think you were a vestal; you came in with a chair, took my life as from a shelf and blew away the dust.* Pasternak's poetic insight was unerring. Helga *was* right. He had treated her that way, because always there was the ambivalence, almost a physical distaste to be overcome before passion could flow. And Helga had known. All along he had withheld himself because of Valya. There'd been no room for anyone else.

When she pulled free of him, Helga turned and threw her arms around Fedorov, kissing him full on the mouth. Even as she continued to kiss him, chin, throat, mouth, hands running up and down his back, Fedorov's eyes, open and questioning, stared at him over her shoulder. A question, urgent and silent, passed between them, and Chapman nodded. Then, slowly, even unwillingly, his arms came up from his sides. In his right hand, outstretched, was the Walther, and Chapman took it from him without Helga noticing. Not until he had tucked the gun away under his coat did Fedorov close his eyes and sink hungrily into Helga's embrace.

# 11

# Old Friends

They met at the Knightsbridge Arms, a pseudo-English pub with a highly polished knotty-pine bar lit by stained-glass ships' lanterns and furnished with beamed ceilings and knotty-pine wainscoted walls. Leaded windows permitted only the very minimum of late afternoon light to enter the premises. Chapman had been introduced to the pub by Helga, who took him there because, she maintained, it was one of the few places they wouldn't run into either students or faculty from the university. Wheelwright was immediately uneasy because the barman greeted Chapman by name and remembered that he drank vodka neat. "The phonier they are, the more popular, and the more expensive," he commented acidly. "Taste in America is on a toboggan slide."

"They bring you real Stilton cheese, the drinks are strong, and they have good brown ale," Chapman apologized.

"Still looking for the bright side." Wheelwright snapped his fingers and said nastily, "Always fastidious qualifications, refusing to come down clearly on one side or another."

"My mind doesn't run that way," Chapman remarked.

"Such people always get caught in between," Wheelright noted.

Chapman shrugged.

"Not tough enough, Chappie. Not enough *cojones*. Too much sentimentality."

"Good that I'm out of situations where *cojones* are an essential qualification."

"I wasn't one of those who saw your leaving the service as an irreparable loss. This is where you belong, Chappie, the pub, the university, the adolescent world of ideas and talk without real consequences."

"But you belong in the serious world of action where adults spend all their time betraying or murdering one another? Come off it, Andrew, stop talking like your hypocritical Calvinist ancestors. It makes me sick. If anything is more adolescent than your cloak-and-dagger games, I don't know what it is. And if I'm so useless, why did you need me and my house to stash Fedorov in?"

"A fluke. In the shipwreck of Aleksei Mikhailovich's life, you were the only flotsam he thought he could hang onto, so we played along. Now the coddling is over. We've had nothing from him, or you, except that maybe someone tried to burn him up in bed, which sounds like that idiot fell asleep smoking, and that he lost the Luger we gave him to protect himself, and now this cockamamie story about being accosted, followed, shot at by a blind man with a fun gun hidden in an aluminum cane. Talk about cloak-and-dagger fantasies!"

Chapman was furious. "What point would there be in my lying to you?"

"You're imagining things, full of defector's paranoia."

"That blind man did shoot at Alek," Chapman said quietly, "and those two Spetsburo hoods did try what I think was a kidnap attempt in the UN gardens. And those two Mercedes did try to kill us on the turnpike. Why don't you check with the state police and see who those cars were registered to, and who was driving them?"

Wheelwright took another tack. "For all the good Fedorov's done us, it wouldn't make much difference if They'd gotten him."

"And me too?"

"You're expendable." Wheelwright tempered the remark with a grin and a flourish of the cigarette lighter. "What the hell made you take him up to the city anyway?"

"He wanted to go to the theater, eat some Russian food, visit the United Nations."

"Why the UN especially?"

"He thinks it's the hope of the world, he even knew the preamble to the Charter by heart and recited it for me." Chapman was unable to keep the sardonic note out of his voice and disliked himself for it. He disliked himself even more for not mentioning the mutton-chop whiskered man at the UN who had given Fedorov that envelope.

"The Russians have more agents in their UN Mission than in the embassy in Washington. Their *rezidentura* for all North and South America. They run agents from there, pay them off, and even have a section to keep their people from defecting. The boys in the Bureau keep an eye on the mission but we can't put a finger on Them because they all have diplomatic immunity, or most of them anyway."

"Spetsburo types there too?"

"Ninth Section of the Special Division of the Second Directorate, Section for Terror and Diversion, if you please, Chappie. Unless you know them so well you can tell them by their aluminum-cane shooting irons."

"Wise guy."

"I prefer to think of myself as a wise man." Wheelwright jabbed the cigarette holder between his teeth. "We need that information Fedorov brought out."

"That's your problem. I let you foist Alek off on me."

"I thought you were going to kill him," Wheelwright interrupted.

"So did I, but . . ." He wondered if Wheelwright had hoped that he *would* kill Alek. Had that been one of the reasons for farming Fedorov out to him? But why should Wheelwright want him dead? Was Fedorov telling the truth that Wheelwright was a double? If that was so, then all

Wheelwright's talk of getting information was a cover for finding out if Fedorov actually knew that he, Wheelwright, was being played back by the Russians. If Fedorov knew, then Wheelwright would have to see that he met with an "accident." Only if Fedorov was dead could Wheelwright be certain.

"You didn't even have the *cojones* to kill him. And you had the Walther."

"He had a Luger."

"Yes, he did, didn't he?"

Was that the scenario Wheelwright had planned? A romantic duel between him and Alek, one or the other, or both of them, being killed. With weapons that Wheelwright had considerately supplied. Over a woman. An old score settled. Revenge for betrayal in Moscow. *Former State Department officer and former KGB agent and defector kill each other in an impromptu duel.* He could see the tabloid lead lines now. Did Wheelwright think both of them so simple? Or was Alek's defector paranoia really infecting him so that he suspected everyone?

"We haven't got much more time."

"You want Fedorov back, take him."

"You've been endorsing all those checks to your account every week, a goodly sum by now. What are we paying you for?"

"You think you're threatening some cheap thug? I didn't ask you for money. You insisted I take those checks for my 'time and trouble.' And I didn't want Alek either. But he's as 'back to himself' as he's going to be. You want to interrogate him again, come on back to my house. He's all yours." Chapman began to get up, but Wheelwright pushed him lightly back into his seat.

"Calm down, Chappie." Wheelwright sat still, eyes closed, the frail blue network of capillaries in his pale eyelids disturbing. "All right," he said, teeth clenched on the cigarette holder distorting his words, "I guess the time for talking turkey is here."

"Long overdue."

"Even if it means no Thanksgiving."

"You want thanks from me!"

"No, from Aleksei Mikhailovich Fedorov, whose life we saved, to whom we promised a new identity, papers, money, whatever he needs to start a new life."

"For a price?"

"We're not a charity organization. We pay off only quid pro quo. We wanted the information Fedorov brought with him."

"You debriefed him for months. What could I find out that you didn't already know?"

"Aleksei Mikhailovich didn't work hard enough at remembering. Maybe we didn't work hard enough at jogging his memory. I thought he might let something drop, or take you into his confidence. . . . We think he has a list of all the KGB agents in this country."

"That wasn't Alek's side. He worked Western Europe, and against Russian intellectuals and foreign diplomats at home. He wasn't really inside, or high up enough to know about their American networks. He was co-opted and on the fringe."

"Co-opted, yes, but on the fringe, no. He had the rank of major, but the rank wasn't it. He was bunghole buddies with the general who ran their American section, Major General Igor Semyonovich Galtsev. They drank together, chased ass together, even went hunting other game together. Galtsev's wife died a few years ago. His children hated him, his subordinates were afraid of him, most of his friends and colleagues had perished in the purges, so he was a pretty lonely man. For some reason, he seems to have liked and trusted Fedorov. We think that's how Fedorov got the information."

"Galtsev just took it out of the safe and gave it to Alek?"

"Some of the heavy drinking was in Galtsev's office."

"You'd have to write that kind of information down, or photograph it, even if you had a superb memory. Then

you'd have to get it past their people and yours. I'm sure
you searched him and everything he brought out."

Wheelwright sighed. "We did everything, including
sticking a finger up his ass, X-rays, all of it, and didn't find
a thing. But he's no fool. If you defect, you take insurance
with you, for bona fides, for trading, maybe even for blackmail. He gave us his 'entrance papers' "—Wheelwright's
admission was grudging—"but nothing more than that."

"What were they?"

"A two-hundred-page report of the operations he was in,
or knew about personally. Names. Places. Dates."

"That's a hell of a lot of bona fides."

"He's got to have more," Wheelwright declared, punch-
ing out his cigarette. There was urgency in his voice.

"How did he get a two-hundred-page report out?"

"Microfilmed it. With his own camera. A very ingenious
man, your friend Fedorov. Persuaded one of his KGB colleagues, a cameraman, to lend him special lenses because
he said he had some dirty pictures he wanted to work up.
Attached the lenses to his own camera, photographed the
report page by page, then destroyed the original. He returned the lenses with some pornographic pictures he'd
prepared for the contingency—KGB files have plenty of
those which They use to entice foreigners and Fedorov had
access to those files as part of his operations—so the cameraman wasn't suspicious."

Was the cameraman Kornilov, Chapman wondered, the
man who had lent Alek the flat for his rendezvous with
Valya? "So you think he microfilmed this other information
the same way?"

"Exactly."

"Why didn't he give it to you with his two-hundred-page
report? Why one and not the other?"

"He's such a complicated, mixed-up Slavic son-of-a-
bitch, I can't tell why. The operations he gave us are old
hat, people we can't get our hands on, because all of them
are over there. But the other stuff is here. Maybe he just

wants an ace up his sleeve to bargain with us, or with Them if They run him down."

"That's no sale. The moment Fedorov let onto them he had such a list—had even seen it—he's dead. They'd never deal on that. Too risky."

"Fedorov isn't stupid. He even used one of their devices to smuggle his microfilm out. A hollow-handled hairbrush from his Berlin days. They didn't remember he still had it . . . poor inventorying. He gave me the brush as a souvenir when he gave us the report. Even so, he was crapping in his pants at the airport because he was sure they'd search him and find it."

"Wouldn't you be too?"

Wheelwright regarded him quizzically. "No, Chappie. All part of the job. I enjoy the tension, the excitement. You see, I like the work." He leaned confidentially across the table. "Do you know what it would mean to us to get such a list? Names of agents, networks, methods of communication and codes, payment arrangements, safe houses? What a coup! We could switch some off, sweep up a few others, carefully, and play some back to Moscow."

"They're not stupid. They'd figure it out sooner rather than later. They know Fedorov's here and they'll remember that he was friendly with Galtsev. They'll draw the right conclusions."

Wheelwright snapped erect, abruptly formal. "State got a note from the Soviet Embassy this morning. They say they've got letters from Fedorov's wife and son, and they want to see him."

"If their note arrived this morning, that corroborates my story about what happened at the UN, doesn't it?"

"Blind man's buff again?"

"You've had Fedorov for months and suddenly they send you a formal inquiry? Too coincidental."

"I didn't say Fedorov wasn't recognized up at the UN. I doubt the kidnapping, the shooting, the auto accident stuff."

"Are you going to let them see him?"

"Depends on how cooperative he is."

"Bastard!"

"Such language, Chappie. Don't get carried away. Only we upper-class types are allowed the luxury of vulgar language. You middle-class fellows are the ones who must be prim and proper." His voice switched to the organ tones of diplomacy. "The Soviet Ambassador formally requests that two representatives of his embassy be permitted to confer with Aleksei Mikhailovich Fedorov who, we are advised, is presently in the custody of United States officials."

"Inform the Ambassador of the Union of Soviet Socialist Republics that Mr. Fedorov does not wish to speak to him or to any members of the embassy staff," Chapman growled, "nor does he care to communicate further with the official organs of the Soviet government."

"They'll charge us with kidnapping."

"Let them. It's been months since they reported him missing, so why the delay in asking to see him?"

"The notes from his family?"

"Andrew, their embassy representatives will be KGB officers who'll have family letters all right, forged or coerced for such an occasion and kept in the files. They'll try to use them to get him to redefect or threaten him to keep his mouth shut. You have nothing to gain from it, so why let them see him?"

"If we could gain anything in return, I'd turn him over to Them in a minute."

"What a nice fellow you are, Andrew."

"It's not my job to be nice, Chappie, just effective."

"Can't you see the stink in the newspapers? You'll have all the press and half Congress down your throat."

"I'd see that it didn't get into the papers. I'd drop him in their laps and Their Transport Department would take care of him—fast."

"You do that, and if Alek can't get to the newspapers, I can."

"You're threatening *me?*"

"Just forewarning."

"Why the hell should you be concerned about that crud anyway? I thought you'd want us to give him a cement footbath and drop him into the river. He set you and your girl up in Moscow. He's done that to a shithouse full of other people too. Goddamn it, you should see that two-hundred-page report, the thing makes your stomach turn."

"I'd like to see it."

"It's classified."

"I thought I was cleared."

"Your clearance lapsed when you left the Department." Wheelwright lowered his voice. "That microfilm has, among other things, a contingency plan for sabotaging American missile sites, tracking stations, railroads, air-fields, electric-grid systems, and natural gas pipelines."

"If you've never seen it, and no one else here has, and Fedorov denies that he has such a thing, how did you get such a clear idea of what's in it?"

"I don't like the implications of that remark, Chappie. You've got to trust me."

"Trust you!" Chapman began to laugh, his jaws so tight with anger that the laughter hurt his throat.

"You trust Fedorov? How do you know he's not a sleeper, a double, a plant?"

"Hell, no, Andrew, I don't trust either of you. I remember what your assignment was in Moscow. You wanted a witness, someone to protect you in case you got too far out on a limb and they cut you off. I was your friend, you told me, someone you could trust. Or I was then. Clearly, I'm not any longer. How do I know the Russians didn't cut you off that limb and double you?" The moment the words were out of his mouth he knew he'd made a mistake, had gone too far. The familiar face of the man he had known as a colleague, the face of the boy in it he remembered from school, was submerged by the thin-lipped, cold-eyed features of the intelligence officer. For no reason he remembered how, when they were first introduced at Yale, Wheelwright had explained very carefully that he wanted never to be called Andy, only Andrew.

"You're walking in a minefield," Wheelwright said, "and one wrong step is going to blow you ass over teakettle."

Their eyes engaged and Chapman found himself in a staring contest. Unwilling to drop his eyes first, yet feeling childish in continuing such a contest, he finally turned away, searching out the barman to signal for another round of drinks. A half-assed way to save face, he thought, amused to be reminded that he'd already lost one buttock in that minefield. "Not much of this makes sense, Andrew. I'm confused, so try to see it my way for a minute."

Wheelwright's throw-away gesture of the hand was noblesse oblige, I'm listening, but what you say won't really matter. Chapman hid his displeasure and continued. "An old friend of yours comes to ask your help in hiding a Soviet defector you once knew and who you thought had betrayed you. You finally agree, because both your friend and the defector seem to be in danger. But you also agree because you want to know the truth of what happened to you in Moscow. You do so, reluctantly, because you've given up such things since you left the foreign service, and you never did like it much. Now you're a teacher, and a political scientist—however much the last is a metaphor—and maybe your friend is right that you lack the *cojones* for real politics, that a library, a university, is where you belong. You're also writing a book on Russian dissidents and you think, maybe, the defector can help you, because you've been back from the Soviet Union for a couple of years and things have changed. You know that part of his job was work against the dissidents, among them, and he knows their lives and ideas intimately. So your reasons are mixed, selfish and unselfish, but you take the whole business on against your better judgment.

"From the moment you do, your life becomes a maelstrom. Fire, an attempted kidnapping, a shooting, an attempt to kill you on the highway. Your old friend doesn't believe a word of what you tell him about these things. His attitude is that of a complete stranger with whom you're doing business. It's true you have not seen him for some years, but can such a thoroughgoing change take place, a virtual metamorphosis? You wonder if you ever knew him at all. You try to review all the things you knew, thought, felt about him, and you're not sure about anything in the relationship except that you know you're being used. The more you wonder about not understanding anything about him, the more you worry about not understanding anything about yourself, because if you have misconstrued such a long-term relationship, then something must be seriously wrong. With him, with the relationship, with you.

"Your old friend tells you about a microfilm the defector brought out with him, but did not turn over. He doesn't say how the defector got it, smuggled it out, or where it is now. He also admits that the defector did give him a two-hundred-page report on his KGB activities, plus whatever other information months of careful debriefing could supply. But the old friend insists that is not enough by half. He wants more, wants it badly enough to threaten to turn the defector back to the Russians. More what? And how does he know any more exists? And if he doesn't know, why all the pressure and urgency?

"The defector, who was also once a friend, though not for so long or so intimately, insists that he never betrayed you in Moscow, that he was himself a dupe in the operation. What he says seems to be the truth, although you have no way of verifying it. There is in him the candor of the man who has nothing more to lose, so it's hard *not* to believe him. He doesn't ask for trust. He just gives it, and speaks his piece. He expects not to be trusted. Yet you know too that he is a well-trained intelligence agent, a skillful dissembler, so all of it may be another Potemkin façade.

"With it is the painful circumstance of meeting once more the woman you loved in Moscow because the defector knows and tells you that she is in New York with her husband, which the old friend has never bothered to tell you, although the friend must know, for the husband is, after all, a senior KGB intelligence officer, and it is the friend's business to know such things. When you meet the woman—which the defector arranges for you—she tells you that things between you are over, partly because she never heard from you after you were flown out of Moscow, though you wrote perhaps a hundred letters over the period of a year and sent them to your old friend in Moscow, who assured you that he had forwarded those letters as they arrived.

"The friend, however, doesn't speak his piece, doesn't give his confidence, only demands cooperation and trust. He is evasive, tough, threatening, caustic, contemptuous. His is the kingdom and the power—and no one better get in his way."

Wheelwright expelled his breath audibly as if he'd been swimming underwater for a long time and had been holding it with difficulty. "Is that the way you see it?"

"That's the way."

"That's not the way it is."

"Tell me how it is then."

"I can't—altogether."

"Then how do you hope to convince me?"

"I don't—altogether."

"Try your best."

Wheelwright pursed his lips, rearranging the disarming pince-nez on his long aristocratic thin-nostriled nose, masking those unyielding blue eyes. He still looked like Roosevelt, but like Roosevelt at Yalta, grim, sick, wrapped in a cape to keep off the chill of death. "Do you know who Aleksei Mikhailovich Fedorov really is?" he began. "A major in the Russian political police, first and foremost—an intelligence officer for whom his job, his assignment, is more important than anything else. You may think he is—

was—your friend, but for intelligence agents friendships are a luxury, and precarious."

"For Americans as well as Soviet ones?"

Wheelwright nodded his unwilling agreement. "The good ones can't afford profound personal relationships because they drain off too much caution, involve too much confidence. Good intelligence men can't even afford wives and children and family lives. Mistresses, casual women, if they can find them, are okay, but familiar ties are too binding, debilitating, and an ever-present source of compromise. Poor security. We're loners. Or should be. We may tell you that we regret it, that we're lonely—and we are—but the sense of being a power behind the scenes, the sense that *one man*–not a division, a computer, a Gyros satellite, not They—can change history, is what drives us. We are the last individualists in an increasingly collectivist world."

Chapman noted the change from *they* to *we* without comment. He had heard such a Wheelwright talk the same way in all-night bull sessions, but that had been a long time ago, at school; he had never heard him talk that way as a grown man. "Paranoia," he said, "delusions of grandeur."

"Every good agent is a bit of a paranoiac, Chappie, more, if he wants to survive and be effective."

They sat looking at each other, uncomfortable, until Wheelwright resumed, in another voice, "Fedorov was recruited right after the war, in 1945, after he'd been demobilized. Like a lot of other young Russian officers, he didn't know what he wanted to do, and there was enough disarray in the society so that making a decision was difficult. The GRU tried to recruit him too, but he chose the KGB instead. Why? He knew that military intelligence was not where the real power would be—that belonged to the security police. But he claims that the KGB persuaded him that the disasters of the early war years were due not to Stalin but to the domestic and foreign enemies of the USSR. Spies and saboteurs. Fedorov remembered those early days with bitterness, the Panzers tearing divisions to

shreds, capturing whole Red Armies, while Russian troops
didn't have enough guns, tanks, planes, ammunition. He
himself was wounded twice in those early engagements
because he ran out of ammunition. Those defeats, those
deaths and maimings, the sense of being demeaned and
impotent, were events he couldn't forget."

"A patriot."

"Semi-patriotic, maybe, yet not very discerning," Wheelwright conceded grudgingly. "But Fedorov was young. He
had a gift for languages and was already a skillful and colorful journalist. He'd written some good frontline reports
and his KGB mentors thought they might have another Ilya
Ehrenburg or Simonov in him, a man they could use
against their own intelligentsia as well as abroad. Hadn't
Stalin himself said that Ehrenburg was worth two divisions
all by himself? So they set about training him, in languages
and as an intelligence officer, and he was an apt pupil.

"Journalism provided a natural cover. They got him jobs
with Novosti, with Tass, with Radio Moscow, wherever for
the moment it seemed best to use him. They had him sent
to 'interview' leading scientists, writers, artists, because
that was his forte—and because they wanted to keep a
finger on the pulse of their intelligentsia. Fedorov fingered
the 'unreliable' ones for them, those who were to disappear
in the Zhdanovschina after the war, and the Doctors' Plot
after that. Fedorov was especially effective with Jews, almost as if he had some special insight into them, some
peculiar charm that won them over. His case officers joked
that he must have some Jewish blood, and they even
checked him carefully, but he was Russian for generations
back. After each interview, he wrote reports for his case
officers, shrewd, detailed, intuitive, as if he was able to
penetrate into the very marrow of his victims' thoughts and
feelings. His superiors had great confidence in his work.

"And the writers and artists, physicists and geneticists,
students and teachers, all trusted him too. Good old Fedorov. Sensitive, charming Alek. How could he be one of

Them? There was the occasional rumor, but no one believed it, or at least only a few people repeated it aloud." Wheelwright paused. "Never trust charming men, Chappie, they lack character and they're hiding something."

"Not even you, Andrew?"

In a measured voice Wheelwright replied, "Not even me." He took the pince-nez off to massage the bridge of his nose where they made indentations in the flesh, but he did not close his eyes. He stared, the intent, focused stare of the nearsighted. "Do you want to hear more?"

"You've only just begun."

"All right, then. In 1949, They fixed him with a foreign correspondent's credentials and sent him to Berlin and Vienna. That was about the time you met him."

Chapman nodded. "I was in AMG working as a press officer, occasionally cooperating with your people, as Fedorov was cooperating with his."

"No, Chappie, you were cooperating, but you were in AMG and then in State. Fedorov was KGB from the beginning, co-opted, but an intelligence officer. Then, after Stalin's death, and after Beria's, his career went into a decline. Lean times. He was considered a 'Beria man,' though he maintains he had no special ties to Beria and, in fact, detested him. That was when he returned to working as a writer, wrote a couple of plays, a handful of moving-picture scenarios, some literary essays. They still had the string on him and it was only a matter of time before they'd yank him back."

"Or purge him."

Wheelwright ignored that. "And yank him back they did . . . after he'd written a movie script about an American falling in love with a Russian girl and wanting to marry her. . . . You'll recognize the theme. Bucking the bureaucracy. But the girl couldn't get official permission to marry him or to leave the country with him, so the lovers loved—and like some other people we know—were separated when the American had to leave Moscow."

"Lieutenant Pinkerton and Cio-Cio San."

"In Fedorov's play the American truly loved the Russian girl, but the Soviet censors wouldn't hear of filming it that way. *Glavlit* recommended a few minor changes." He smiled, cynical and weary. "They turned things about a bit. The girl became an American code clerk at the embassy and the man a Russian worker, an electrician, who comes to the embassy to repair some wiring. The girl gives up her citizenship to marry the Russian and remain in the USSR because love flourishes in a 'true democracy.' Ukrainian folk songs, the sun setting over the onion domes of the Kremlin, the two of them riding away in a sled, heads together, the troikas pulling away in front of them. . . . Overnight Fedorov was famous. This new literary reputation not only gave him further entrée into the circles of the old intelligentsia, but *cachet* with the foreigners.

"That was just when They reactivated him, only now against the foreign diplomatic community in Moscow. And in a quite new way. Fedorov became a Russian Don Juan, his 'game'—against the wives of diplomats, in order through them to compromise their husbands. It was an assignment for which he was perfectly suited. He was good-looking, suave, sophisticated. He spoke several languages and, unlike most Russians, had traveled abroad. And he was a writer, a decorated war veteran, and, to all appearances, an available bachelor, although by then he was in fact married and father of two children.

"From then on, his work was mostly with those foreigners, although he kept his hand in with the intelligentsia, or the KGB kept his hand in with them. Fedorov's job was to get what They wanted not with a gun, or with money, but by suborning with friendship, by blackmail through love. Because his manners were attractive, and his charm contagious, he made friends in the foreign colony easily, especially with diplomats' wives. He would insinuate himself into their lives because they were so isolated, so eager for relations with Russians, almost any Russians. He gained their confidence by indicating that he was out of sympathy with the Soviet regime, subtly of course, with an ironic smile or gesture, an offhand comment, nothing crude or provocative, so that what the foreigners believed of him seemed justified because they sensed in him a real under-current of fear. And he was afraid—of Them, and of what he might say.

"Fedorov made himself useful. That was very important. He always knew the best restaurants, how to get tickets to the theater and the ballet—even at the last minute—how to make travel arrangements, where to shop—all of which his KGB mentors took care of for him—and he could always manage to bring the prettiest and most willing party girls, all KGB 'swallows,' if you needed lovely young things to decorate your reception, or, for that matter, handsome young men, KGB officers co-opted for the occasion, if that was what was required. A veritable factotum, Fedorov, Figaro's frigging brother. He could even serve as an inter-preter if need be. Altogether a useful man to Them.

"He blackmailed a French Embassy code clerk who, with Fedorov's help, had managed a few blackmarket currency exchanges. For three years afterward, the KGB had their hand in the till of top-secret French confidences via that code clerk, until the French security finally nailed him and sent him home.

"Fedorov befriended an English radio engineer who had a taste for young men, pretty young men, having been well brought up in British boarding schools and a Guards regi-ment. One night Fedorov got him looped, took some photos of the poor Limey being buggered and enjoying a taste of the whip. For better than four years, then, They got most of the secret traffic into and out of the British Embassy until the man was finally rotated home to England where SIS security finally got on to him, a bit belatedly, because the KGB *rezident* there made a muck of contacting him in London.

"But friend Fedorov's forte was fucking. To the diplo-

matic colony's women he was the perfect escort, a shoulder
to cry on, a willing ear to listen, never"—Wheelwright's
face twisted into a leer—"pressing his point home, and
doubly successful because of that. He screwed the attractive if foolish young wife of the Australian military attaché,
taking all the appropriate down-under photographs, and
taping the grunting and groaning. He presented the colonel with samples of both to remind him that if he didn't
produce what they wanted—information on Aussie military
strength and plans, the Woomera range, participation in
Viet Nam, American space-tracking stations in Australia,
security measures at the embassy—the tapes and photos
would find their way to his ambassador and to the diplomatic colony at large. That time, Fedorov and his masters
misjudged their man. The Aussie colonel was a tough old
bastard and when he discovered what They wanted, saw the
photos and heard the tapes of his beloved—and much
younger—second wife in action, he blew his brains out with
his service revolver."

As Wheelwright detailed "game" after "game" that
Fedorov had worked against foreign diplomats, their wives
—in one case a daughter—Chapman's nausea grew, but
also he heard the undercurrent and knew that Wheelwright
hated Fedorov with more than the professional animus of
an agent. This was not an intelligence officer coolly appraising and disliking the "opposition"; it was the throb-
bing personal loathing of a man talking about another who
had done him injury, a man he feared and envied.

"Was Alek the one who seduced Phyliss?" Chapman
asked without warning.

Wheelwright blanched. "Phyliss was just an easy lay.
Lady Roundheels playing Lady Bountiful."

"Did Alek 'do' her, Andrew? Is that why you hate him
so?"

Again, Chapman knew he had gone too far. Wheelwright's head lolled as if severed at the nape, before—like
a Punch and Judy marionette—it snapped erect. "Yes,

Fedorov did my wife," he conceded, his voice a whisper, the shaded emphasis on the words *my wife,* "did her up brown." His laugh was rich, vulgar. "Unfortunate choice of phrase, Chappie, but then I don't know what appeals to Comrade Fedorov, though I do know—" and then he caught himself.

Chapman was tempted to take the risk a third time, to ask if that was how, why, the KGB had doubled him, but Wheelwright's face seemed to have been laid bare to the bleeding flesh and pale bone, and he desisted. In a spontaneous turmoil of compassion and distaste, he put his hand over Wheelwright's and Wheelwright tore it away as if his fingers had been scorched.

"Tell Fedorov he's got a week, one week, or ten days at the outside to spill his guts."

"And then?"

Wheelwright catapulted himself from the chair. "You'll see," he said. Then, head rigid, arms swinging, not turning back even to remark on Chapman's feeble farewell, "Don't call us, we'll call you," he marched out of the pub.

# 12

# Counterpoint

It was not yet dark when he drove slowly up under the elms, the car headlights on high so that in his darkened house Alek and Helga would know that he was returning. About three-quarters of the way up the *allée* he parked, left the engine running and the lights on, and went out to lean against one of the elms and watch the slow moon rise. Wheelwright had unnerved him. There was no mistaking the menace he intended, nor his power to make that menace effective, so his ultimatum to Alek would have to be delivered, even if the substance of what he intended to do was not clear. Chapman squinted into the darkness, imagining cardinals and chickadees, jays and juncos, grosbeaks and goldfinches, hearing their songs and seeing them leap before his eyes like the scintillas of light struck off the thin curved blade of the new moon, yet what he really heard was only an invisible hoot owl. His spirits were leaden, the fantasy of birds and birdsongs did not cheer him, and he felt manacled to the trees, though their trunks were far too thick for his arms to encompass.

The lights went on in the house, and Chapman stood looking at it, an old-fashioned, comfortable, ramshackle house he loved and that had stood him in good stead. How his parents would have been pleased to know that he hadn't sold it, was living in it and finding the pleasure in it that they would have had—if they had lived.

He shuffled back to the car, wondering if Wheelwright was right about Alek. Even if Alek had been a KGB stud, did that make him altogether a whited sepulcher? It seemed the kind of sexual hypocrisy they were all guilty of, not the least himself. If I do it, it's eccentric; if you do it, it's a mortal sin. Could he justify what seemed to be giving Helga to Alek? Yet he knew that no one "gave" Helga; she conferred or withdrew herself at her own prompting and pleasure, for reasons beyond his control and probably beyond his ken. The electricity between them, jolting and shocking as it had been, was now shunted to Alek, for many reasons, the least obscure of which was Valya's return. *Valya.* The name was a spasm of love interrupted midway and painfully unrequited. And then he remembered that Andrew had not explained why he had not told him that Valentina Andreyevna was in New York at the UN with her husband.

In the living room in front of a fire that had been burning for a long time, Alek and Helga were playing chess. Alek lay on the floor on his side facing Helga, who sat with her legs tucked under her smooth strong haunches, voluptuously outlined in wine-colored stretch pants. Redolent of burning wood and pine cones, mixed with the subtler odors of cooking from the kitchen, the lamplight soft beneath the shades, the logs hissing on the grate, the room was the picture of domestic tranquillity, except that Helga, biting her nails, was concentrating on her next move. Chapman saw from the board that her position was hopeless. Without being able to say how he knew, Chapman was sure that they had only recently made love in front of the fire. A pang of jealousy wracked him, but because it had not been he and Valya instead. To forestall that line of thought he called a greeting from the entrance to the room. Both looked up together, a shade too casually and simultaneously. Helga reported that dinner was almost ready while Alek pointed to the vodka bottle, suggested that he pour himself a drink and pull up to the fire they had laid to take the evening chill off. Chapman took a stiff vodka and sat staring into the flames. It was not long before Alek had Helga checkmated and sent her off to the kitchen with a friendly pat on the buttock to prepare the rest of the dinner. He took great pains with mixing himself a drink before asking, "Things went badly?"

"Very."

"How long have I got?"

"A week, maybe ten days."

"And then?"

"He didn't specify." Chapman began to outline what he and Wheelwright had talked about. Fedorov didn't seem in the least surprised by the embassy move. He'd expected that Khlakov would report, that They would try to threaten or cajole him into redefecting. No, he didn't want that. But, his face was very grave—if there were really letters from Genia and the children—though he knew there couldn't be —it might almost be worth seeing them. "You think Wheel-wright was serious about turning me back?" Fedorov inquired.

"I don't see how he could."

"Privately, I imagine. A deal. Once arranged, the KGB Transport Department will organize my journey. They'll have me on a fishing trawler off the coast or drugged in an airplane packing case on my way back to the Lubianka. That is, if they don't decide to kill me and save themselves the trouble."

Chapman reported his gaffe about Wheelwright's being doubled and Fedorov winced. "You've tipped our hand."

"*Our* hand?"

"You're still not convinced he was doubled?"

"I have only your word for it."

"And my word's not good enough?" Fedorov challenged.

"Trust comes harder to me these days. I'm older."

"And wiser?" Fedorov jiggled the ice cubes in his glass. "You want bona fides too, Nathaniel." It was not a question.

"Just the truth, Alek."

"Just the truth." Fedorov's laughter was harsh. "How absolutely American. Which truth? Whose truth? There are so many truths." Awkwardly he spun around, raising his glass, and flung it into the fire, a smashing of glass and a flare of burning vodka. For a long while he stood warming his hands over the fire, as if he'd forgotten what it was like to be warm, before he turned back and apologized. "I'm sorry," he said. "Slavic temperament and Russian melodrama. I'll try to be as truthful as I can, with my life at stake."

His pacing was an irregular lope, full of pauses and twists and turns, like an animal at bay not yet ready to surrender to his pursuers. "Human life is all duplicity and guile." He grinned lopsidedly, nervously tweaked his beard. "The grand Russian generalization to overpower the mean, small, ugly facts of truth. Duplicity and guile, those are what I have practiced most of my life, acting one way while feeling another, subtly deceiving others, and on occasions more frequent than I am yet able to admit or recognize, myself.

"Wheelwright probably gave you a more or less accurate picture of my work for Them, Nathaniel. My version of truth departs from his only in what may seem to you slight matters, small particulars, matters of shading, explanations —or rationalizations?—of motive. Yet a life—my life—is made up of just such particulars, nuances, complex and conflicting motives, all odd-shaped little tiles that make up the mosaic of my duplicities.

"They did come to recruit me after the war. In Moscow. I was still gray with war, gray skin on the outside, gray ice on the inside. I'd come back to Moscow because my mother was there. Somehow she'd managed to hang on until I was demobilized. When she saw me, her face lit up like one of those haloed ikons. 'Now I can die in peace,' she told me, 'now I can go to my rest.' That glow from her face was the first warmth that began to thaw the ice in me. Officially, the doctors told me she died of pulmonary tuberculosis and hardening of the arteries, but one of them, an elderly physician of the old school, explained that it was really the result of wartime privation. She stayed in Moscow all during the war years, even when the Nazis were at the doorstep of the city—unlike the brave Generalissimo.

"That room in Moscow was my inheritance. My mother left it to me. Four meters by three meters, sharing a kitchen and a toilet with twenty-three neighbors. It was the only thing she had to leave me aside from a few personal mementoes, *and it was a great deal.* A room in Moscow. People married and divorced for such a room, bribed and blackmailed, even killed, all for a room in Moscow so they could live and work in the city. Twelve square meters. *Lebensraum.*

"My father had been swept away in '37 with Yakir. A major in the Red Army and one of Yakir's adjutants, a good, bluff, and naïve man, an old Bolshevik and a fanatic patriot. Two days after They arrested Yakir, they took my father. He refused to testify against Yakir, he refused to incriminate anyone, he would not confess nor bear false witness, so he was murdered at 11 Dzerzhinsky Street on a sunny afternoon in April 1937 when one of the NKVD officers interrogating him was a little impatient and over-zealous.

"Many of the wives and children of the military who died in that purge were sent to camps, Potma, Vorkuta, Magadan. Some were executed. My mother managed to weather the storm without being sent away from Moscow and she saved me from them. 'By making myself small,' she explained to me. She was far shrewder than my father—he came from a worker's family, but she from an old gentry family—and she had no politics. She knew which way the wind blew and that standing against it would break the strongest oak, so, to protect me, she decided to be a willow. I don't think she cared about her own life after my father was killed, but she cared passionately about mine. Otherwise, she probably wouldn't have gone on.

"I was only a boy, but even then, without knowing Livshits' dying cry, I asked myself, 'Why? What for?' and could get no answer. Years later, in Khrushchev's time, when he told about Yakir's last words, 'Long live the Party! Long live Stalin!' I cried bitterly, because I was sure my father had died with such words on his lips, in blind anguish that enemies of socialism had somehow penetrated the NKVD, certain that Stalin and the Party really couldn't know that such things were being done to good Party comrades and soldiers. That poor, stupid bastard!"

From the kitchen, as from a great distance, Helga's off-key contralto sang "Lili Marlene" in German. Their eyes caught and both of them grimaced. As Helga's singing died away to a distant humming, Fedorov declared, "Woe not to the vanquished, but to the victors." In front of the fire, again he rubbed his hands as if he were washing them. Softly, he continued, "I made up my mind then that I wouldn't be like my father, an oak, but a willow like my mother. When the wind blew, I would bend, to the very ground if necessary, but I would *not* break.

"So, when they came to me, I said yes. I was trying to write plays then, and writing a little journalism to stay alive. I kept myself away from everyone except a girl I had fallen in love with, Evgenia Borisova Pozerna. I had the insane but pure notion that I could penetrate the NKVD myself, an 'enemy of socialism' who would be a true Chekist, who would save the real socialists and the real lovers of Russia. And I would tell no one. I would do my small part to save those I could—what I could—without pride, without boasting, without recognition."

"Paranoia *à rebours*," Chapman commented.

"Worse. A foolish Dostoyevskian idiot, an Alyosha *manqué*, a self-deluded nincompoop," Fedorov conceded.

"Yet I was able, admittedly only a few times, to save a man's reputation, or his life, have a sentence reduced, an 'interrogation' made more lenient, though not very often."

"Few of us do even that much," Chapman solaced him.

"I know, I know. But I was a fool. And Stalin was no fool. And They were no fools, his henchmen, the rubber truncheons of the Revolution. They were so skillful, as if they knew more of men's souls than any priest or psychoanalyst. They knew just where to 'touch' me, where to burrow into my spirit. My ambition, my desire to be known, my lust for power-behind-the-scenes, my false humility. Worst of all my passion to do good, *to do good.* How they understood that best of all, and manipulated it. 'Aleksei Mikhailovich,' they said to me when they sent me to spy on the intelligentsia, 'you understand these people. You're one of them after all, so you will not permit violations of socialist legality, miscarriages of justice.' Ha! Permit! I was myself a violation of socialist legality, myself a miscarriage of justice, a miscarriage altogether, because my plans and purposes completely and utterly miscarried. They were shrewder by far, more purposive than I, they 'played' me as they wished. I was their puppet, they pulled my strings and I danced to their tunes whether I willed it or not. Oh, they gave me an illusion of freedom. 'Of course, Aleksei Mikhailovich, we understand that you do not wish to be a regular employee. You will only be co-opted.' But, of course, they paid me— well, gave me rank. Perhaps on occasion I outwitted them with a spontaneous jig, or they let me believe that I was calling the tune and dancing my own *gopak* to it, so I'd imagine I was doing some good by continuing to work for them. Who knows?

"They did get me jobs as a journalist, good assignments. They encouraged my writing and helped to have some of it published and produced—what was useful to them, of course. Getting me published and produced was a useful cover. They saw to it that I had access to the 'special stores' so I could wear English tweed jackets and smoke Irish briar

pipes and buy Genia French perfume for her birthday. I
thought I was penetrating them, but they were penetrating
me. Buggering me. Corrupting me. Nothing corrupts like
privilege.

"Genia, of course, was opposed to my working for them.
She had her own reasons, her own scores to settle with
them, but I found that out only later. She knew they'd come
to see me, she suspected that they'd made me an offer, so
I lied to her, told her that I'd refused. In theory refusing
them was possible, but as a practical matter, impossible. If
I'd said no, one way or another, sooner or later, it would
have meant prison or camp for me. And maybe for Genia
too.

"At least I thought so. Sometimes I believe it was only an
excuse for my cowardice, because there were people who
managed to refuse and 'get lost,' slip away to the provinces
or to Siberia, where they 'buried themselves.' But to be a
journalist or a writer meant remaining in Moscow and I was
not yet prepared to be humble. My mother had taught me
to be flexible, but I had not yet learned to be nondescript.
The idea of being a nonentity offended my pride and ambition, and I suffered for it.

"As far as Genia was concerned, I was a writer by preference, a journalist by necessity. She wanted me to stick to
writing plays, or screenplays, because she was convinced
that that was what I really wanted to do."

"Was it what you wanted to do?"

"Then, Nathaniel, I would have said yes. I liked journalism because it allowed me to travel, it gave me all sorts of
privileges, even a kind of power. It catered to my vices, my
pride about being in the know, my ambition to be close to
the sources of power, to be one of the elite, without being
responsible for their actions.

"Yet once you eat the heel of the bread you're in for the
whole loaf. They moved me around a good deal, Berlin,
Vienna, as you know, but also Warsaw, Prague, Budapest,
even Paris and London a few times. Each time I was 'out,'

it took all my what—courage? determination? stupidity? fear?—to make me return home. But Genia and the children were there. They had hostages. And each time I returned, of course, They trusted me a little more. I was being reliable, loyal.

"At first Genia didn't mind my foreign assignments. She liked to see my work in the newspapers, or hear it over the radio. Most of all, she enjoyed the occasional magazine article with my byline, though those were fewer and further between. The children were little and needed her, she was studying for her own degree at the university, and she was so busy that my absence was perhaps more help than hindrance. Still, as time passed, we began to become estranged—the children were altogether strangers to me—and both of us became aware of it.

"I'd be back in Moscow for a few days and Genia might have an exam or a field trip or a report, or the children would be sick, or some other urgent matter would come up. If I could be home for a couple of weeks, or months, as sometimes I was, it was better. Good—in fact, often marvelous. Simple things we did together, a picnic in the country with the children or taking them to the zoo, going to the ballet, an ice-skating outing in Sokolniki Park, and I felt cleansed, renewed, and human.

"Yet one strong part of me did *not* want to come back. Outside of Russia I was happier, precisely in those assignments They gave me, more than in the real journalism. True, every now and then I was able to write a good piece of reporting without its being shredded at the editor's or censor's desk. But They'd been very knowing when they assigned me to pretend I was disaffected, ready to sell myself as a foreign agent. It gave me my chance to speak almost freely, because that was the bait. Some American official, or British, or French, might get wind of my discontent and make me an offer.

Once they did, once any foreign intelligence service had approached me, I would 'sell' myself to them and then They could 'play me back.' You know the game."

Chapman remembered Berlin and Vienna. "I was right then, wasn't I? In Berlin?"

"Completely. It became too dangerous for me."

"So They called you home?"

"Maybe. I'd asked to be recalled because of Genia. I loved her and didn't want our marriage to dissolve. And I didn't want to be a stranger to my children. They didn't recall me then—when I asked—and when they finally did, it was because they were disappointed in me. I hadn't been able to sell myself to anyone. I'd brought back some information, but that wasn't what they were really interested in. They began to worry too, I think, about my conversations and my reports, about my *really* selling myself and being played back on them. They also considered that I might defect to the West. I had spent too much time with foreigners—although on their orders—and some of the things I said publicly, though they knew it was part of the 'cover,' disturbed them. They didn't like my free and easy relations with Americans either, especially with you."

"They knew about me that early?"

"At first I reported my contacts with you. Later, when we became friends, I began to stint on such reports."

"Thanks. Yet They remembered to send you to see me again when I was assigned to Moscow."

"They have long dossiers, if not long memories, and computers with memory banks now, to help out."

"You think anyone will ever be smart enough and brave enough to throw the dossiers away altogether, burn the tapes?"

Fedorov shook his head. "The Hungarians tried in '56. They tried to burn the AVO headquarters and files, but even the Nagy government wanted to keep the dossiers. Whoever is in power wants the dossiers for their own uses."

"Freedom," Chapman lamented.

"Even a touch of freedom is infectious, a kind of sickness, They would have said. I enjoyed that. As part of playing the role of being disaffected, I could really speak my mind for the first time, I could be myself publicly. It was exhilarating, it made me lightheaded. I was frightened that I might act that way when I went home, burst out with such comments unaware. It reminded me that there was much of my father in my spirit still, bluff, open, even naïve. I had to watch myself every moment."

"Must have been impossible. I warned you," Chapman reminded him, "because you were talking more freely than the situation warranted. You weren't selling yourself, only giving yourself away by being so unguarded."

"A fine way to get killed. I might have, you know, if you hadn't called matters to my attention, Nathaniel. It took courage and I have been grateful ever since."

"Wheelwright would have said I'd betrayed my trust."

"I never seem to understand such words. *Trust. Loyalty. Betrayal. Treachery.* Even when I felt my trust had been betrayed."

"By Genia?"

"By Genia. After I was recalled to Moscow, she discovered that They had co-opted me."

"How?"

"*How* doesn't matter, only that she did. Maybe They told her. Or had one of their cats-paws take her the news. Perhaps she figured it out herself. It wasn't that hard, what with my trips, our privileges, the extra rubles we were getting. She confronted me and I lied. But she wasn't taken in. She wouldn't speak to me or let me touch her." Fedorov closed his eyes. "It went on for weeks like that. Genia getting up in the morning—having slept on the couch—sending the children off to school, not giving me meals or making me a cup of tea or ironing my shirts. She'd do all the chores scrupulously, and look after the children, but she did nothing for me.

"They'd left me in Moscow without a new assignment,

putting me off. I was nervous and uneasy about that. I was
hoping for a miracle, but nothing produces catastrophe as
swiftly and inevitably as waiting helplessly for miracles. I
was trying to write a new play, because a friend of mine, a
KGB colonel then, later a general—Galtsev—warned me
that I was under suspicion, that I'd better write something
appropriately anti-Western and orthodox to restore myself
to Their good graces. My failure to 'sell' myself to Western
intelligence services was looked on not as a sign of inepti-
tude, but as a sign of treason. I couldn't fathom that logic,
but I didn't even try. I couldn't concentrate, I couldn't write
a word. A sword of Damocles from Them hung over my
head, a spear from Genia was stuck in my side.

"I knew I had to do something, anything, that I couldn't
let my life drift like that. I decided finally to tell Genia the
truth. I broke down and confessed. I tried to explain to her
what it had been like. I cried, I groveled at her feet, but
Genia was unmoved, unforgiving. This was a Genia I hadn't
known before, not the loving, easygoing, warm Genia.
She'd heard of some of the 'games' I'd been in, heard
rumors—and some of the facts too—of my operations
among the intelligentsia, which outraged her most of all.
She wouldn't listen to what I said, and everything I did tell
her only confirmed her notions of my depravity. I grew
angry and beat her. What did she know of life, there in her
cloistered university, I raged, what did she know of the
sacrifices I had had to make so she might finish her studies
and the children live in peace and security? She stood
there, head bent, letting me rain blows on her, telling me
that I had done it *not* for her, or for the children, but for
myself. For privilege, for preference, for Scotch whisky and
Irish briars and English tweeds. Besides, she didn't care
why, only that I had gone over to Them. That was unforgiv-
able. She looked at me as if I were a cockroach she wished
to grind under her heel, saying, 'Your hands are covered
with blood and your tongue with the blisters of lies.' It went
on like that for hours, blows and screams I tried to stifle so

that those twenty-three neighbors would not hear and report what we were saying. And Genia repeating over and over, 'Your hands are covered with blood.'

"I went out and got drunk, and stayed drunk. I was in a stupor all the time. Day after day I drank a liter, two liters of vodka, until I fell unconscious in the streets, to be picked up by the militia and taken to the drying-out stations. When I found my way home again I promised Genia I'd do anything she asked—I'd tell Them I was quitting—but we both knew that short of death there was no quitting. Once you were their creature, you were theirs forever, like a serf on one of the gentry's estates under the Tsar. Another dead soul.

"I begged her to tell me what to do, but Genia said it was too late. We were finished. She wanted a divorce. I told her I'd never give her one. I threatened to get Them to help me take the children from her and she shrieked that if I did, she swore—yes, swore before God, her hand on her heart —she'd kill me. Even through that alcoholic haze I recognized the face of Medea, and knew that it was no idle threat.

"I did not know until then how implacable my wife was. And now, too, she told me her father had been a Chekist from the very beginning, for Dzerzhinsky, for Yagoda, for Yezhov, had done all their biddings in everything, against everyone, against the peasants in the Ukraine, against those accused of murdering Kirov, against the Bukharinites and the Trotskyites. In 1938, some neighbor denounced Genia's mother as a German spy. It didn't matter that the charge was a vicious fantasy built around the single fact that her mother's sister was married to an Austrian comrade with whom she lived in Vienna, and that the sisters wrote to each other from time to time. That was enough—writing to and receiving letters from 'foreigners'—Austrians were by then Germans because of the *Anschluss*. Her mother was taken to Lefortovo, tortured, and sent to a plank bed in Magadan. Within six months They had worked her to death.

"Genia continued to live in the same house with her father for three years after that, never speaking a word to him. No matter what he did to her, she wouldn't talk to him. She kept house for him, cooked, cleaned, but would not utter a syllable. Finally, when Beria and his Georgians purged Yezhov and the NKVD, it was his turn. Her father was accused of being an agent of Hitler and, ironically, part of the 'proof' was that his wife had been convicted of being a German spy. When they took him away to the Lubianka, Genia's farewell was a single sentence, 'You had my mother's blood on your hands, now let her blood be on your head.' Eight months later, in Vorkuta, he cut his throat with a piece of glass."

"Had you never asked about her family before?"

"Many times, but she was always evasive. She told me about her life as a child, about her schoolmates, and gave me the impression that her father was a minor bureaucrat in the government. After she described what she had done to her father because he had not stood up for her mother against Them, I knew it was hopeless trying to continue, so I agreed to a divorce."

"She wanted to persuade you that she was irreconcilable."

"She succeeded. And she *was* irreconcilable."

"You let her have the children?"

"I knew they were better off with her. Yet, if I'd kept the children, I wouldn't be here, I'd never have left Russia."

The fire dwindled. Fedorov took more logs, put them on the grate and blew the embers up with the bellows until the fire was roaring once more, first carefully poking the shards of the vodka glass to one side. Helga bustled in from the kitchen, face gleaming. There was enough hausfrau in her to enjoy cooking for "her men." She stretched out her hand and Chapman put a drink in it. "How grave you both look," she remarked.

"A fine and quiet place where none, I think, do there embrace," was Chapman's rejoinder.

"Add your New England sobriety to Alek's Slavic melancholy, and what have you got?" Helga inquired.

"Prussian bleakness," Fedorov replied.

"Wise guy!" Helga examined their faces, then called over her shoulder as she departed, "Get rid of all that gloom before my dinner. I want my meal eaten in a light and frivolous atmosphere."

When she was gone, Fedorov said, "A few more vodkas and we may achieve that blessed state."

"Haven't you heard, Alek, alcohol's a depressant."

"Who knows better?" He watched the fire, then held his empty glass up to the light.

"Don't throw another glass. I haven't got enough to go round."

"No one ever has enough to go round," Fedorov observed, and he didn't mean glasses. "The divorce notice appeared in *Evening Moscow,* and it was over. What was in some ways the happiest time of my life was finished. Genia had gone and the children with her. She'd managed to get another room in Moscow from one of her fellow students who'd gone back to Yaroslav, a room only a little larger than mine. I visited a few times after the divorce, presumably to see the children. Sometimes Genia was there, more often she was out and had left the children with an old grandma who lived next door with her son and daughter-in-law."

"When was the last time you saw her?" Chapman asked, thinking of Valya.

"A few days before Stalin died, in the winter of 1953. She was taking the children ice skating in Gorki Park and asked me to meet her there. They'd flooded the paths in the park so there were long trails for the children to skate on. The day was cold, the air crisp and clean, with a taste like light smoky wine distilled from leaves and bark and snow, a taste that always comes back to me like the taste of bitterness in my soul. I came up the path and saw the children skating. Dmitry was showing his little sister how to do turns, and she, trying to imitate, was falling on her rump. Both were laughing, their teeth snowy, cheeks red, their faces much like mine and not at all like Genia's so that it all seemed even more unjust. And then, incredibly, I could barely breathe. It was as if the air in my lungs had frozen into ice. Because I really knew for the first time that they were lost to me forever.

"I was so childish then. I'd been working hard writing *Damn the Dnepr*. I knew it was going to be a success, be produced in Moscow, make me money and reputation, and restore me to Their good graces, enough—I hoped—so they'd leave me alone. I thought that would change everything, that there'd be some road back for Genia and the children and me. You know the psychology. See, I've been a good boy, I haven't been drinking vodka or sleeping with young girls or working for Them, and I've written a new play. Now you must forgive me, take me back. . . . What an idiot I was!"

"Not idiotic, Alek, only human."

Fedorov waved his compassion off impatiently. "When I came up to Genia, she was standing next to one of those wooden shacks they use, for changing, you know. She told me she was leaving Moscow and taking the children with her. She had a new job in Novosibirsk, half a continent away, a good job as an architect, helping to build the Akademgorodok. She was excited, happy, and expected I'd be happy for her too. This was what she'd worked for, what she wanted to do. She told me the details, mentioning that she'd be leaving in a few days—*in a few days!*—and I tried with everything I could muster to wish her well, to congratulate her on her good fortune. But I didn't have enough . . . courage, or tact, or character, or just plain goodness. Instead, sobs came roaring out of me like ice floes cracking, and I turned and ran, slipping and sliding on the ice, falling and picking myself up. Literally ran away. Without saying good-bye. Without saying anything, just barely avoiding Genia's hand reaching out to comfort me, but not to take me back, not to take me with her. Then, like some Fury never sated, she yelled after me, 'You'll end up like my father, Aleksei, without a wife, without children, without a home, without faith.' She might have added, without a country."

"You never saw her again?"

"I couldn't go to the station to see them off. I couldn't. I heard from her once more, three years later, in 1956, just after the Hungarian Revolt. From Novosibirsk. She was married again and wanted my permission for her new husband to give the children his name."

"You gave it?"

"By then they were mine in name only, so why not? Genia was right, Nathaniel. Her prophecy is fulfilled. I have ended up exactly as she predicted."

"The game's not half over yet. You're not dead yet."

"A cheerful thought."

"Not uncheerful. The beginning of something else," Chapman insisted.

And then Helga called them to come in to dinner.

# 13

# Who Does What—
# To Whom?

It was late afternoon when Chapman returned from the library. Helga was on the porch rocker, drink in hand. "Where's Alek?" she called before he was out of the car.

"I left him here after breakfast."

"I had two early classes this morning, a nine and ten o'clock, so I thought I'd visit and have lunch with him," Helga explained, "but he was gone when I arrived."

"Was he expecting you?" Chapman walked up on the porch.

"Sort of, I think." Chapman suspected that probably they'd arranged an assignation and Helga was feeling stood up. "Maybe he just walked into town for a change of scene."

"A good long walk."

"What's four or five miles to a Russian, Nathaniel? Remember Alek's not a car-spoiled American."

"I remember."

Helga laughed. "Don't look so alarmed. You look like someone pressed your panic button."

"Nobody's even pressed my belly button," Chapman replied.

"Ah-ha! I told you you'd miss me, Nathaniel."

"I knew I would."

"You should have told me."

"And if I had?"

"I might not have let you 'give' me to Alek."

"No one ever gave you to anyone, Helga."

Helga tossed her head as he went past her and indoors. Chapman looked at the roll-top desk, the typewriter, the message pads next to the two telephone extensions downstairs, all the places Alek had left notes before, but there was nothing. He got himself a vodka and went back out on the porch.

"Convinced?" Helga asked, but Chapman didn't answer. He watched the sun plummet toward the horizon, then a jet plane cut a straight red line of vapor trail across the sky's throat. "Only men draw straight lines," Helga observed, almost to herself. "In nature, nothing is straight."

"Man is a crooked creation, which is why he learns to draw straight lines."

"Is Alek really in danger?"

"Of falling in love with you?"

"Don't joke."

"Why not?"

"Because you and Alek are hiding in your house as if both of you were running for your lives."

"Everyone's running for his life. You know . . . the appointment in Samarra."

Helga slammed her glass down sharply on the rocking-chair arm, splashing vodka on her wrist and forearm where the droplets clung to the dark hairs like diamonds. "Why must you treat me like a moron. I'm not, you know."

"I know, Frau Doktor Professor."

"You make fun even of that."

"I'm sorry, Helga, really," and he was truly contrite.

"Don't apologize. Just tell me why Alek's so afraid, always looking over his shoulder as if someone were chasing him."

"Even in bed, Helga?"

"There, too."

"Is he better than I?" Chapman asked, aware that he asked not only to divert her.

"Always the same stupid question. Why do men ask it? Why do they want to know, have to know?"

"We're a competitive gender."

"It's not a question women ask, or even can answer truthfully."

"Why? Because they don't really know? The latest being always the best?"

"Did your wife issue Nielsen ratings, Nathaniel?"

"My ex-wife. Betsy may have—and I undoubtedly ranked low. Is Alek better than I was?" he repeated.

"No," she answered, discouraged, "just different."

"They're all different, or all the same."

"'*La nuit, tous les chats sont gris*' is a man's motto not a woman's. With Alek, I have the feeling that he needs me— or someone—and I'm there. With you, I felt you needed no one. Or if you did, it wasn't me."

"Sometimes I wished it had been you."

"When you talk like that, Nathaniel, you're another man, gentle, shy, considerate. You were that man to me occasionally, and then I thought I loved you."

"You mustn't exaggerate," Chapman cautioned, touched in spite of himself.

"Then there was the high prickly hedge you usually hid behind. Hidden but not protected. *Noli mi tangere*."

"A hedge against inflation, of feelings, of ideas, of expectations. I didn't want to be touched for loans I couldn't afford."

"That defensive humor."

"Offensive, isn't it?"

"So much part of the prickliness. Yes, even the prickiness. You're so smart about some things, so very stupid about others." She was on the verge of tears. "Alek's not afraid to be touched, or to touch," she said. "So, yes, he's better than you are."

"I'm glad for you," Chapman replied, and he half was. "You and Alek have a lot in common."

"Strangers in a strange land." She laughed bitterly. "But only geographically."

"The geography of love?"

"No, only the topography of passion, the configuration of affection and loneliness, a surface, but a better surface for me than our depths."

Chapman hated her then, with a rush of hot feeling, hated her refusal to cater to him. He wanted to shove her off the rocking chair on the porch planks, throw himself on her, enter her, plumb her painfully.

"How I recognize that look. Do you know what it says, how loudly it speaks? I want to screw you, it shouts, screw you in both ways, as much screw you out of, as much cheat you as fulfill you. How many times when you were with me have I seen that look leap crazily across your face, like scarlet rain, your whole body beginning to quake like a volcano about to erupt lava all over me. That look roars, I want to hurt you, overwhelm you, fuck you, fuck you, fuck you!"

"You know me too well, Helga," Chapman said, trying to make it sardonic and a denial, knowing that he was unconvincing, to her or to himself. Yet he was too petty to leave her with her petty insight and victory. "If it's true, it was what you wanted, wasn't it?"

"I suppose so." Sadly, she shrugged. "The miserable masochist meets the superlative sadist."

"Oversimplified," he declared.

"Sure, but not untrue. In the sadist's view there's no place for love. Love is an exchange of affection between equals, a surrender of one individual to another, or of each to the other. But the sadist never surrenders himself. Surrender is only on his terms, slave to master, object to subject, never person to person. He must do anything, everything, to maintain his superiority, so he keeps his distance from what he desires because it might find him flawed, might make him human. Instead, he invents fantasies on a grander scale where he is the absolute dictator, lord of all he surveys. Everything is his to command, everyone slave to his desires.

"The sadist is a child, Nathaniel, what the psychoanalysts call an infantile omnivorous. And, therefore, polymorphous perverse. He wants everything and nothing. He cannot fulfill himself, content himself anywhere, either in fantasy or reality. Because he cannot give himself to anyone, cannot lose himself, he cannot find himself. He trusts no one, not even himself. And no woman can give herself to him, because he will not allow it, cannot accept it."

What she said was true enough to shake him, enough of it repetition of what Betsy had said before the divorce, so that he couldn't simply dismiss it. Yet he knew it to be only a very partial truth, not the essential of what he was. If there was validity in Helga's views, it was and had for a long while been a diminishing factor in his life, and never a controlling one. Helga, like Betsy, brought all that out in him. Valya never had, not even in that scarifying encounter in the Chinese restaurant. Helga and Betsy would both say, he was certain, that he hadn't known Valya long enough, well enough, that at the beginning things had been good between them too, but Chapman knew that was false. There was a chemistry of human combinations where in some the center held, while in others it dissolved. He didn't pretend to understand what it was, but it was there. The vodka glacial and smooth in his throat, he rocked himself in the chair as if he were his own child to be soothed. "Not only left-wing Communism is an infantile disorder, Helga," he remarked, but the joke fell flat. At best, it was a half-hearted evasion.

"How you became anti-totalitarian, anti-Communist, baffles me," Helga observed. "You'd have been a perfect candidate for the Party, either CPSU or NSDAP."

"The tyrant in the privacy of his boudoir can be the democrat in the public forum," he retorted, but he knew that there was the lucky accident of birth. He had been born in the States, not in Germany or Russia.

"Only if the democrat is a respecter of persons."

"Yes, but only of *some* persons. The democrat discriminates."

"You haven't answered the question."

"How I became a libertarian in three easy lessons, rather than a Communist or Nazi in one? Jekyll and Hyde? Alienated from my best self? Perhaps you just bring out the beast in me, Helga."

"My first husband always said that to me. *You bring out the beast in me.*" She mimicked a small-town Southern accent. "When he said that he was always undoing his fly, or making me undo it for him."

Chapman grinned. "You bring out the beast in me, so I can put it back into you, and together we can make the beast with two backs."

She laughed. "That was the usual case with me and my men."

"Blame your bloody Prussian ancestors for making you so good-looking."

Their silence was sexual, heavy, like musk in the air, and she deliberately broke it. "I doubt that Alek came to his anti-totalitarianism so relatively painlessly."

"Painlessly! I can see you've never had a bad conscience."

"The two of you are so similar, both disenchanted idealists, intellectuals who wanted to put their hands on the levers of power to guide the locomotive of History—"

"Whoa! Your Germanic slip is showing."

". . . without getting grease and blood on your hands. But Alek wanted to be a gentleman, always worried about what was cultured and uncultured, what one should and should not do."

"*Nekulturny* is one of the dirtiest words in the Russian lexicon."

"Once such gentlemen's standards break down—and in societies like Russia they break down very easily—a man like Alek has very little left to go on. He has to cut and run. But you, Nathaniel, were different. You set up an ideal America that never was and never could be. When it didn't measure up to your expectations, you cut and ran too. Alek, from Russia to the States, you, from State to the academy.

"You've answered your own question about why we're hiding here in my house."

"But why that sense of running for your lives?"

"You know, sometimes when you're sick, you become your own worst enemy. The most intimate and familiar man you know, your own body, is suddenly strange, hostile. The enemy within wracking you with pain is all the more cruel and pitiless because he is you. You're alienated from your own self. You seem to have deserted to the enemy, and you're filled with guilt and self-loathing, as if you'd just turned your best friend in to the political police for torture."

"Which, of course, you have."

"Being alienated from your country is like that, Helga. You're filled with self-loathing and guilt. You're the cause of your own pain. Your body—and sometimes your mind—are both traitors. You're a traitor to yourself."

"The moment you stop being a slave to a cause, you become a traitor to it."

"Don't you ever feel that way about Germany, Helga, about the Nazis and the Thousand Year Reich?"

"I never was a believer, Nathaniel. My brother was. My

father and grandfather surely, but not I. Maybe because I was a girl."

"Kitchen, kirk, and kids only?"

"That's not such an unholy trinity as you would make out, but it's not what I meant. No, the only lever of power most women want their hands on is that one." She pointed to his crotch.

"Power or pleasure?"

"Both. Certainty that comes of sexual security, social security—and not the old-age variety either. My brother was sure of what he wanted, what everyone wanted, what the Third Reich wanted. Even what I wanted. He was always sure, brought up to be sure. After all he was a von Waldecke, the boy from the *Schloss*, the descendant of Teutonic Knights, and he'd heard a thousand times from my father and grandfather that Hegel nostrum—*Life has value only when it has something as its object.*"

Astonished, Chapman remarked, "You hated him."

"Nonsense. I loved him. Passionately. Wolfgang was everything I myself wanted to be, everything I believed in until I left Germany. Then, as I saw more of the world, I learned how wrong he was.

"By then I thought he was dead."

Helga's face worked, as if she would have preferred to keep something secret, but she said, "*I* was alive. Only half-alive, maybe, because Memphis, Tennessee, was a tomb and I was a mummy in it. Even when I didn't want to remember Wolfgang, I couldn't seem to help myself. It was as if we were twins, formed of the same flesh and blood, so that I had to carry forward his life with mine, so that I kept imagining he was inside me—"

"Had he been?" Chapman interrupted.

Again Helga gnawed the bitten fingernails with her even white teeth. Imperiously then, eyes shining with tears, she confessed, "It didn't seem wrong. We'd been so close all along, alone so much together, we had so much opportunity and so few others to play with. We had played with

each other when we were young, at first only the usual
childishly curious, 'You show me yours and I'll show you
mine.' Later curiosity grew—and capacity. When it happened, it was the right consummation after a long wait—
and an anticlimax."

"Incest."

"A name . . . like love."

"Names describe acts."

"They only try to. The original Latin *incestrus* meant to
be unchaste. Even now the word means sexual relations
between individuals who are closely related."

"Ah, the virtues of a classical education! One even has
the Latin roots to justify one."

"The way to do is to be," she concluded.

"I thought it was the other way round, the way to be is
to do."

"Always the puritan, Nathaniel."

"That kind, sure."

"Is there another kind?"

"Of the flesh," but even as he said it, he wasn't sure that
the two could be separated. Responsibilities underlay them
both.

"You should have seen your face when you said the
dread word *incest.*"

"I was an only child, Helga, without such opportunities.
It's harder for me to understand."

"But you had a mother, Nathaniel?"

"Touché! I do understand."

"It happened only three times, at home, in Ratibor, just
before Wolfgang went back to the Russian Front. He was
home on leave and haunted by a premonition that this time
he would die. He had never done it with another girl, nor
I with another boy."

There was something naked and hurt in her face that hurt
him, something poetic in that love and commitment of
brother and sister that he didn't want to contemplate, so he
asked how old they were then.

"Wolfgang was just under twenty. I, a bit more than fifteen."

"So young?"

"In a war one ages overnight."

"At the front."

"At the rear too."

Only after the words were spoken did they hear the *double entendre* and feel their mutual embarrassment.

Their rockers complained like old bones as they rocked, and Helga nipped at her nails until she drew blood, a sudden scarlet crescent on her ring fingernail.

"Do you still think of him?" Chapman asked.

"Every day."

"With love? With hatred?"

"With longing. For a simpler time when what Wolfgang said was law, justice, truth. He was going to restore Germany to greatness. The Wehrmacht would bring unity and order to all Europe, and the Third Reich—like a new Holy Roman Empire or the old Roman Empire—would stretch from the Atlantic to the Urals. A new Europe, reborn under German hegemony, strong, peaceful, and prosperous."

"And Hitler?"

"The Führer and his thugs would be disposed of as soon as victory was achieved, before, if necessary. Then the 'right people'—like the von Waldeckes, of course—would once more direct Germany's destiny and decide Europe's fate." She sucked the blood from her fingernail with distaste. *"Und zo weiter."*

Darkness hid them from each other and Chapman could no longer see Helga's face or fingers, but heard her breathing. Small evening sounds carried to them, a dog baying the rising moon, the faraway throb of an automobile engine racing. Helga stood up, the rocker rocked back and forth until it squeaked still. She stood with her arms across her breasts, stepped toward him and leaned her head into his shoulder, murmuring, "I'm scared."

Chapman put his arm around her, held her tighter to

stop her trembling. When he lifted her face, her eyes were shut and tears ran down her cheeks. "Alek will be all right," Chapman told her, more confidently than he felt.

"What do you mean, will be?" It was Alek at the foot of the porch steps. "*Is* all right."

They broke apart, almost guiltily Chapman realized, and Helga ran down the steps into Fedorov's arms, sobbing, "You idiot, why didn't you telephone?"

"What, and miss surprising you in Nathaniel's arms!" He was joking to calm her and Chapman took up the joke.

"Like the cavalry, you arrived in the nick of time. If only you'd waited a little longer, Alek, you might have found us in flagrante delicious instead of saving Helga from a fate worse than."

"Indian giver," Helga said, laughing in spite of herself.

"I trust you, Nathaniel," Fedorov declared, "because you're my friend."

"Friends are precisely the ones you can't trust! They're the only men who have opportunities with your women."

"Don't you trust *me*?" Helga asked, drawing back, mock-horrified.

"Are there trustworthy women?" Alek wondered.

"*Go and catch a falling star,*" Chapman said as he went to switch on the porch light. Helga's gasp was alarmed and he whirled to see Fedorov covered with mud and bits of grass. "What happened?" he asked.

"Someone tried to run me down."

"You sure?"

"Do I look like I made a mistake?"

"In one way, yes," Helga answered.

"I decided to try the great American pastime, hitchhiking," Fedorov explained. "Cars were few and far between. I tried to flag three or four down. The fourth slowed and looked like it was going to stop for me, so I waited on the side of the road and it tried to run me down."

"You sure it wasn't an accident, the driver stepping on the accelerator when he meant to hit the brake?" Helga asked, brushing some matted hair from Alek's forehead.

"I jumped out of the way and rolled down the side of the road. One of the men in the car came after me. Luckily there were trees and underbrush nearby and I was able to hide, but he shot at me twice anyway. Then they heard another car coming and they left." His voice was flat, as if reporting an event that had happened to someone else.

"Are you hurt?" Helga inquired.

"Bruises, scratches, shaken up . . . nothing."

"Come inside and let me clean you up," she offered.

"What I'd really like is a glass of vodka," he said.

Helga went inside to get it and Chapman asked, "Did you recognize him?"

Fedorov nodded.

"Khlakov?"

He nodded again.

"They must know where the house is, Nathaniel."

"I guess it's not a safe house any more, is it?"

"How did they find out?"

"Doesn't matter now, except that it gives you less time. Do you want me to call Wheelwright?"

"Absolutely not. I won't need much more time. I made arrangements in town this afternoon. That's why I went."

"What kind of arrangements?"

"To leave the States."

Chapman was about to speak when Helga's footsteps ended the conversation.

# 14

# Saint Vladimir's
# Trident

Since morning they'd been driving through the ochre and green Jersey countryside, Chapman at the wheel and Fedorov next to him holding a folded map in his scratched hands and giving directions without looking at it. "Beautiful rich country," Fedorov said softly, "like the Ukrainian black earth. What do they grow here?"

"Mostly vegetables. Tomatoes. Asparagus. And they raise poultry."

"Chickens? Ah-ha! To sell in the city. That would be the best thing."

"What, chickens?"

"Idiot! No, to have a small farm in the country where the soil is rich and things grow, but not to have to sweat and slave to make the earth produce."

"A gentleman farmer, you mean."

"Like you, Nathaniel."

"Wheelwright would agree about the farmer, but not about the gentleman."

The mention of Wheelwright seemed to depress Fedorov and he lapsed into silence.

"Why all this secrecy?" Chapman asked after a while. "Why not just tell me where we're going? I'd probably know a quicker way to get there. This *is* my home state even if I haven't spent much time here since I was a boy."

"I want you to forget as much about this trip as possible. That's why."

"Why take me along then?"

"To show I trust you. Also because I needed a car."

Chapman laughed. "In that order? You could always have hired a car."

"No license. And I wouldn't want to have a record of the transaction, or anyone able to figure out where I'd been from the mileage."

"Still thinking like an agent, eh?"

"If I want to survive, I must continue to think like an agent. Besides, I wanted you to come with me because this may be our last chance for a good talk together."

"Now what does that mean? The Slavic melancholy got you by the throat again? Wheelwright hasn't got to you yet, nor Khlakov. Neither has Helga."

"You're wrong, about Helga, at least. Not many women have been truly kind to me, nor I to them. I'll regret leaving her."

"Take her with you."

"Where I'm going, I can't take anyone with me, and I can't tell anyone where I'm going either. For me to survive, Aleksei Mikhailovich Fedorov must disappear from the face of the earth," he said somberly, looking at the scratches on his hands as if they were stigmata.

"What on earth are you talking about?"

"It sounds mysterious, my friend, but it's really very

simple. Tomorrow, if you will be so kind, I shall ask you to take me for a long drive to the Canadian border."

"You're going across into Canada?"

"It isn't safe for you to ask too much, nor for me to tell you. The less you know about my departure, the better for both of us."

"So that's why you wanted to know if I was going to the university or the library today and tomorrow, why you asked me to have the car checked. You plotter, schemer!"

"I didn't want the kingdom to be lost for want of a nail."

"Will you tell Helga?"

"Tonight is our last night together. I shall tell her only that you and I are going up to New York for the day tomorrow to buy me new clothing because the clothes I had were torn in my escape from Comrade Khlakov's automobile. Helga has late classes tomorrow so she won't visit or even call during the day. By the time she does call, the next day, I'll be gone."

"But not I. What do I tell her?"

"That I left without warning and without telling you, you don't know where I've gone because I didn't take you into my confidence."

"That much is certainly true. But what if I call Wheelwright tonight?"

"If you want me murdered, that's exactly what you must do."

"Don't be melodramatic."

"Nathaniel, Wheelwright is Theirs. A double. I don't want to quarrel any more about that with you, but if you will trust me a little longer . . ."

"To the Canadian border?"

"Yes. I shall give you proof."

"Proof?"

"Indisputable proof. Documents. Enough to convince even the most skeptical."

"And then, if I'm not convinced, you'll have slipped over the border. I can see that you really do trust me, Alek."

"I've told you enough about my plans so you can stop me anytime you want. Just telephone Wheelwright."

"You make matters difficult."

Fedorov shook his head. "I can't make them simpler. This is your decision. I've said what I had to say. I can't persuade you any further."

"Have you got papers?"

"After today I will have."

"And money?"

"Some. Not much."

"I'll give you what Wheelwright's been paying me to keep you. You're entitled to that, if only for debriefing."

"I'm entitled to nothing."

"Well, then, for a new start."

"A new start. You think it's possible?"

"Now there's a question I've been asking since I got booted out of Moscow and resigned from the Department. Longer really, ever since Betsy and I called it quits."

"Did you love her, your Betsy?"

"She was easy to be with. Andrew persuaded me that she was an appropriate wife. She had money, she came from what is called a 'good family,' with connections. Andrew said it was what I needed to overcome my petit-bourgeois origins in the Department." Chapman laughed. "You see, we use those stupid terms too, though differently. But the fault was mine, not Wheelwright's. I was ambitious and lonely and stupid, and I took the surface for what was beneath. And there was nothing beneath."

"Your father was a physician, wasn't he?"

"A small-town general practitioner. Not rich. From an old family, brought up on that farm, but declassed because it had no money and didn't care much to make any. You know, the kind of American family full of ministers and teachers, lawyers and doctors. They didn't want to be rich, only to be useful."

"Were they?"

"Most of them seem to have been useful and relatively

content. I guess I didn't take after them. They avoided politics and government like the plague. None of them ever wanted to be elected to anything, and none of them would have thought about becoming a diplomat. Even my father, when he was alive, thought I was wasting my time."

"What was your Betsy really like? I saw her a few times, in Berlin. She was very beautiful and very polite."

"Not beautiful, pretty. There wasn't enough depth of character for beauty. Nor enough experience. Nor even enough desire for experience. And not polite, just detached. I thought she was frivolous, with her horseback and tennis, her shopping and parties and charity balls. She thought I was a bore, even a boor. Too serious, too earnest . . . dull."

"Perhaps you were both wrong."

"No, Alek, we were both right. We married too soon after the war, too impetuously. A mistake. We should have slept together a few weekends and gone our separate ways. But neither of us was that kind then, so we married and wasted years of each other's lives."

"Altogether a waste?"

"Altogether. You and Genia had some good times and the children before it fell apart. Something to show, to remember. Three weeks after the honeymoon I knew it was wrong, only I didn't know how to rectify it. Until Betsy did, by divorcing me. For that, if nothing else, I am grateful to her."

"And Valentina Andreyevna?" Fedorov asked.

Chapman concentrated on the road before them. "With Valya," he replied hesitantly, "I thought I had that second chance, that there would be a way, a marriage, even children."

"Did you think she would leave Fyodor Mikhailovich?"

"Yes."

"How could you have gotten her out of the country?"

"I hadn't thought that far ahead. Stupid, I know. But I

put it out of my mind, as if when the time came, there'd be a key to the door and the door would miraculously swing open."

"It has, you know," Fedorov pointed out. "Valentina Andreyevna is here, in the States. The door *has* swung miraculously open. You still have another chance."

Knowing he'd been properly rebuked, it was some time before Chapman said, "I hadn't thought of it quite that way."

"Then think of it now."

Chapman laughed again. "You sound like a patriarch delivering his deathbed blessing to his progeny."

"If I could deliver her to you, it would be a blessing, and out of friendship, Nathaniel, I would."

"You did try, Alek."

"I'm trying once more, now. A last time. Valentina Andreyevna will be waiting for you at the Russian Tea Room at midnight tomorrow."

Chapman glanced at him. "You've planned a busy day for me tomorrow."

"I want my last day in this country, my last time with you to be—how shall I say?—extraordinary." His face was expressionless so Chapman couldn't tell whether he was serious or not.

"Why do you think They let Valya out, let her come to the UN?" Chapman asked.

Fedorov threw up his hands. "Who knows the mysteries of them and why they do what they do? Maybe Fyodor Vyacheslovich insisted and they wanted him here and indulged him. Maybe they were even more devious than that —and one must never underestimate their deviousness— and they hoped she would help them smoke me out—Valya to you to me."

Tinkers to Evers to Chance. *Chance!* A double, triple, play, but a gamble. Were they that shrewd and farseeing? For an ordinary man it would be hard to believe, but it wasn't for him.

They did not speak again until they came to the center of the town Chapman had known from boyhood. Settled by Russian and Ukrainian immigrants, Russian Mill was the center of a farming community two generations had made rich with hard work, and whose third generation was now leaving to go to the cities, to Trenton, to Elizabeth, and to those Babylons across the rivers, New York and Philadelphia. The town still looked as it had when he was a boy, white clapboard houses with lots of wooden gingerbread on the eaves, giant old maples shading the streets, small vegetable gardens at the backs of the houses, blue spruces screening old pillared open porches, and lilacs, now heavy-laden with purple and white blossoms, framing the doorways. He'd been in dozens of those houses with his father when his father was making house calls. He remembered the heavy, overstuffed furniture, the green plants that climbed up the curtained windows, the crucifixes and ikons on the walls, the smells of sausage, cabbage, vodka, and old peeling wallpaper.

Not until the church loomed up before them, altogether unfamiliar though it obviously had been there long before he was born, did Fedorov motion for him to park nearby. It was that church that made the town different from other similar Jersey towns in the region. A fortresslike plain red-brick building, square, with slitted windows outlined in gray brick, it had the soaring central onion dome and four smaller onion domes, all golden and glittering in the spring sunshine. With a swift look in both directions before they entered, Fedorov led him directly into the church through the main entrance, thick paneled wooden doors carved with scenes from the lives of the saints. Inside, the church was dimly lit by great candelabra whose tall, guttering candles threw wavering shadows of the columns and their intricately carved capitals on the tesselated black- and white-tiled floors. Unaccustomed to the dimness, Chapman followed Fedorov down the nave toward the ikonostasis more by the sound of his heels than by sight. Just before it, Fedorov stopped and motioned for him to remain there. Chapman, reluctant, anxious, gesticulated, but Fedorov shook his head and whispered, "Stay here. I'll be back within a half hour. If not, raise hell and call the police."

"Let me go with you," Chapman whispered back, opening his coat just enough to show the Walther tucked into his waistband.

"That won't help here. Wait for me, please." With three strides, then, he had disappeared beyond the ikon screen into the sanctuary.

Chapman paced before the ikonostasis. On it was painted the usual Easter theme, Jesus demolishing the gates of hell and ascending triumphant from the fires in which he had been confined since the crucifixion. Was that what Alek hoped to accomplish here, behind the ikon screen, smash the gates of his own hell and emerge from those fires in which he had so long been imprisoned? Fedorov *redivivus!* The phoenix risen from the ashes. The second chance. The new life.

The ikon screen rose four tiers high, so high above eye level that no one from the nave could see over it into the sanctuary, the human forever cut off from the divine, the powerful rulers forever screened from the humble ruled. Everywhere there was the smell of incense and burning wax; everything—candles, ikon screen, columns, arches—lifted the eye up, up to the central onion dome where in the cupola, brightly colored mosaics were illuminated by narrow mote-filled shafts of sunlight from the fortresslike windows. Christ the Pantocrator ruled the earth up there, surrounded by an august horde of sacred personages, all stationed in order of their importance, each in his appointed place, fixed, inexorable. It reminded Chapman of the same carefully worked-out groupings of official Soviet paintings. How many of those he had seen in Russia! Serov's *Lenin Proclaiming the Soviets,* or Savitsky's *First Days of October,* or Brodsky's *Second Congress of the Comintern.* Lenin as the main figure, next to him his St. Paul, Stalin, both encompassed by the subordinate but approved Marxist-Leninist saints and apostles, but rigorously excluding the heresiarchs—like Trotsky or Bukharin—who had been excommunicated from the fold. The Soviet figures had the same stylized postures, the same sacerdotal stare, the eyes that peered into the past and into the future but somehow overlooked the present. Pregnant with apocalypse, instinct with eschatology, their bodies were flat and angular and dehumanized, daemons incarnate.

From the crest of the cupola, his haloed head luminous in the sunshine, Christ the Pantocrator looked down. Solemn and great-eyed, his right hand was held up in the traditional two-fingered blessing—for which read the modern clenched fist?—and in his left hand was clutched the book of the apocalypse—*State and Revolution? the Communist Manifesto?*—to be opened only on the Day of Judgment, when all men were equal and the state had withered away?

What mysterious mathematics moved men to invent such rigid hierarchies and ultimate revelations? And the obscure symbols, the cross, the fish, the wheel—the red banner, the hammer and sickle—so heavily freighted with meanings they were too frail to carry, envelopes containing messages of an altogether other reality within, joined only in the Christian dove of the Holy Ghost, and Picasso's earthbound dove of unholy peace. Could Marx be God the Father, as Lenin was the Son, and Stalin the Holy Ghost?

As his eyes dropped from the main cupola—ashamed and aware that he too was playing that melancholy iconographic game he despised, aware that this humble church seemed to have copied so much that was both mundane and soaring in the Orthodox tradition—they fell on the humble images of ordinary men, peasants, tinkers, carpenters, wheelwrights—*Wheelwrights!*—at a feast painted and carved on the beam over the ikon screen. Through that sylvan setting like a serpent, Old Slavonic letters were intricately twisted which spelled out the Biblical: *Come all ye that travail and are heavy-laden.* The lure. Always the lure and the snare.

Chilled by the gray light, Chapman felt dark, as if the hope and exaltation of the slivers of sunshine in the cupola were forever beyond his reach. The devotion of men to their ikons and their hidden significance was doubly intolerable, a snare and a delusion. Was all of it only shifting decorations in an inexorable set of relations, filagreed in gold, silvered in fretwork, glazed in cloisonné? Was the wheel of life fixed and changeless? Who, then, were the faithful and who the infidel? Who the civilized and who the barbarian?

Nervously checking his watch again and again to see how long Fedorov had been gone, Chapman stalked around the church examining and reexamining the ikonostasis, staring up into the sunny domes or peering into the spectral deserted apses. Just as the music began, he saw at the base of one altar the crudely drawn trident, St. Vladimir's pitchfork, with the Russian legend beneath: *Death to the Tyrants!* and recognized that Fedorov had come to an arranged rendezvous. Though he couldn't make out the words, he knew the recorded voices were singing in Russian, earthy plummeting Russian basses and unearthly Russian male sopranos, powerful and plangent—but what they were singing was *Shenandoah!*

> O, Shenandoah, I long to hear you,
> Away, you rolling river,

> O, Shenandoah, I long to hear you,
> Away, we're bound away,
> 'Cross the wide Missouri.

The Missouri. Not the Moskva, not the Volga, not the Yenesei. Try as he would, though he knew the English words by heart, he couldn't figure out what the Russian ones were. Uncontrollably he began to laugh, when he heard Fedorov's footsteps behind him. Even in the dingy light he saw success written on Fedorov's face.

"Why are you laughing?" Fedorov asked. His deep voice boomed loudly off the walls, was absorbed into the resounding chant of *Shenandoah,* then echoed out of it again.

Chapman didn't try to explain. Instead, though Fedorov's face had already provided the answer, Chapman asked if he had found what he came for. Fedorov seized his arm and danced him out of the apse toward the main doors, skipping like a boy, until Chapman pointed to the black-inked Saint Vladimir's trident. Then Fedorov stopped in his tracks and walked back into the apse. As if he could not believe what he saw, he dropped to one knee and with his finger traced the pitchfork's outline, hoarsely read the words *Death to the Tyrants*! aloud. As the music died away, he stood up, his face tragic, and lamented, "O, my country, my country."

As soon as they were back in the car, Fedorov closed his eyes, leaned back, and pretended to be asleep. Chapman knew it was pretense because the currents still twitched in Fedorov's face and shook his frame. He drove slowly, unable to enjoy the high sparse scudding clouds, the greening foliage and shrubbery, the occasional glimpses of white-throated sparrows, titmice, two golden-crowned kinglets wheeling and diving, and a flock of ruddy ducks rising from a marsh like a storm.

A part of his mind and heart insisted on reserving judgment about Wheelwright. How could his schoolmate and long-time friend and colleague be a double agent? All his experience had taught him how precarious such intelligence work as Wheelwright's could be, how easily one crossed or was nudged over the border into enemy territory—as easy as going from the States to Canada—but he still could not believe it.

They had driven halfway back to the farm before Fedorov opened his eyes and spoke as if continuing a conversation.

"You remember the general I told you about, the man who befriended me?"

"Galtsev?"

"Yes, Galtsev. He was my father's friend, which was one reason he trusted me. Because he never had sons, he looked on me as his own son. Sometimes, when we were alone and drunk, he used to recite Scripture, verse after verse, by heart. One line from Isaiah he repeated over and over, told me that my father had recited it to him before his arrest: *'Thy despoilers and thy destroyers shall come from your own midst.'* That is, from your own loins. Both he and my father meant the Cheka."

"What happened to Galtsev?"

"Poor Igor Semyonovich. As They so poetically put it, he outlived his usefulness."

"The KGB scratched him?"

"They were very solicitous of his health. He'd been working too hard, drinking too much, they said, so they sent him on a vacation to the Czech mountains. He loved to ski, had grown up in the north and skiied from boyhood. He used to joke that he skiied like a Finn, but after the Finnish war that was a dangerous joke. They arranged an accident for him in the Tatras, far from home, where no one knew him and no one could help him. Very considerate.

"He went out for a day's skiing with two other Russians, promising to be back before nightfall. A thick mist came down on the mountains in the early afternoon and the two came back later saying they'd lost Igor Semyonovich in the fog. When he didn't return that evening, the Tatra rescue service was alerted. They searched for him all night, until daybreak, when they found his body at last. The Ministry announced that Igor Semyonovich had fallen while skiing and been killed. But some of the searchers who saw his body said his right leg was broken and that he had many bruises. His skis were off and they thought he might have been beaten and left there to die. But the old man was

tougher than They imagined—those two Spetsi hoods they
sent with him—and he tried to get to a rescue hut about a
mile and a half up the mountain from where they left him.
He didn't make it. He died either of cold or exhaustion."

"Is that what finally decided you to leave?"

"Igor Semyonovich was my 'protector,' and my friend.
His murder was the last straw. It was as if They had killed
my father twice over."

"Wasn't it Galtsev who sent them to recruit you in the
first place?"

"You're a shrewd fellow, Nathaniel, shrewder than your
schoolmate Wheelwright. Yes, he sent them to recruit me
because he knew Stalin was planning new purges after the
war, and he'd promised my father to keep an eye on me."

"Is that how your mother escaped the camps and remained in Moscow?"

"You guessed that too. Yes. A strange man, Galtsev, a
man I never fully understood, or even trusted. Yet, in a way,
I loved him. As I owe my first life to my father, I owe my
second to him. And perhaps my third."

"What do you mean?"

"Tomorrow, Nathaniel, you'll know all." Fedorov
grinned crookedly. "At least as much as you want to know."
He fixed his eye on the countryside rolling by, then closed
his eyes and talked on. "The more I got to know my quarry,
the less I felt like a huntsman. At first, after Genia went to
Novosibirsk, what they asked me to do seemed a perfect
revenge, against Genia, against all women. Fuck them,
They said. Fuck them I would. I was sick with a Slavic
melancholy then, an irrational and overwhelming sensation
of death and meaninglessness that I usually suffered, in
smaller doses, every autumn with the dying of the year, and
which my mother told me my father had similarly suffered.
But this melancholy wouldn't pass, it clung to me like black
oil, in my hair, my teeth, my ears, under my fingernails. I
was writing *Damn the Dnepr* then and only the work saved
me."

"A lot of feeling went into that play."

"Probably the best part of it. The rest of me then, and after the play was a success, was devoted to what They asked me to do."

"They started using you as a stud?"

"Vulgar, but accurate, I suppose. Women became the instruments both of my deceit and my revenge. They used me against foreign women especially, because I was supposed to have a special charm for them."

"I can vouch for that."

Fedorov inclined his head, in acknowledgment or defeat. "Thank you, Nathaniel, but that special charm was my downfall. It was based on my 'playing' alienated, but I was no longer playing. I couldn't hold back my genuine feelings, and those communicated themselves to foreigners. I was not feigning anti-regime sentiments, I actually *was* anti-regime . . . and now I knew it. It worked beautifully with foreigners—women, diplomats, newspapermen—the targets They had chosen for me. I made friendships on order, I seduced women on order—"

"What a splendid assignment!" Chapman remarked ironically.

"Shabby, vicious, ugly. Using women who are lonely or unhappy, frustrated, or sometimes just friendly and curious about Russia and Russian life. Using them to compromise them and through them, their bosses or husbands or colleagues."

"Didn't you enjoy it, even a little?"

"At first, of course. It was a way of getting back at Genia. It made me feel attractive and wanted again. Useful. It helped dispel the melancholy, but not for long. In all my friendships with foreigners I could be more myself, and less afraid, less nervous than with my own people, and that I enjoyed."

"Your cover was your protection. You were supposed to shoot off your mouth to foreigners and look alienated."

"The joke was that I *was* alienated."

"The cream of the jest."

"Even with our own intelligentsia I had to be more careful because there were provocateurs among them. Who they were I never knew. They were always checking and double-checking everyone and I knew They would make no exception for me."

"How could you report on your own intellectuals? They were the best in Russia, the ones who should have been your friends. The foreigners were outsiders, maybe even enemies . . . but your own?"

"Slavophiles and Westerners again, still. No, Nathaniel, I tried to help them—especially the good ones—to tone down their disaffection, or to report it in a way that made it seem harmless."

"It couldn't work, you knew that."

"It didn't. When They wanted to nail someone, especially an *intelligent,* they could always find someone to testify against him, to report on him, usually some other *intelligent.* And, of course, they always had the unions to help them, the Union of Writers, the Union of Artists. But at least our intelligentsia knew the score. They knew how it was in Russia and they had the necessary training for protective coloration, for feigning and lying and cheating. I had less sympathy for them. Amalrik is right. They're not the best or most honest or courageous of our people. I prefer an honest worker or peasant any time."

"Still that Soviet sentimentality about the workers and peasants, Alek? You know better than most how much guts it takes for an intellectual to express even the mildest dissent."

"I do, but the intelligentsia just goes along—for the apartments, and the special stores, for their dachas and their Moskvas and Pobiedas, their books published, their paintings exhibited, their plays produced."

"Like you."

"Exactly like me," he admitted. "No better, often worse."

"Tell me, Alek, did you do Andrew's wife?"

"No. Although he doesn't believe that. But I was part of the 'game' against her. It was I who introduced her to Vasily Trofimovich. The son of a peasant, and a marvel with women. A true stud, not a middle-aged fumbler like me. Bogdanov really loved his work."

"And it was Bogdanov who doubled Wheelwright?"

"Through his wife. Photographs, tapes, all of it. You know."

"I know, but I didn't think it was that easy."

"You were lucky. It isn't that easy, but I think Wheelwright likes to blame it on his wife, though in his heart he knows that is not why. He is a very strong man, tough."

"Why, then?"

"Your friend Wheelwright came to the conclusion that dictatorship was the only way out of the dilemmas of modern life," Fedorov said slowly, as if he had thought it over many times. "The kind of dictatorship which might solve all the other questions that beset man that otherwise seem insoluble, especially the question of war. Without a worldwide authoritarianism, a nuclear war seemed inevitable to him, and catastrophic—the end of the species. In a way, his doubling was a form of patriotism, not treason, his way of keeping mankind alive."

"Better Red than dead?"

"The same old choice of evils, yet understandable."

"How understandable?"

"In his own way he loves mankind, and wants most of it to survive. With a single worldwide authoritarianism, man might persist on the planet."

"And you, Alek, don't you care about mankind?"

"I'd rather be dead than Red. I don't give a damn about mankind any more. Just one man, this man. I want to live out my life without deceit and horror."

"You told me that you did only what you could square with your conscience, that you tried to reform the KGB from inside, to brake against the worst excesses, to help the innocent.''

''I tried and failed.''

''And then you decided to come over?''

''I killed a man. A good man. As if I had done it with my own hands.''

''Who?''

''An Australian colonel, military attaché at the embassy in Moscow. I seduced his wife. They had pictures and tapes, and I took some of them to the colonel, so he could see his beloved wife in action. They wanted information from him. He had access to the top military intelligence of most of the Allies, not only Australian. The 'game' was the old gambit. They'd show the film and tapes to his ambassador, leak it to newspapermen, show him up to be an old cuckold.''

''Did he play ball?''

''Even dead he served Their purposes. He frightened others.''

''Maybe he frightened some of those already compromised, but he made those who weren't warier. Did you know him well?''

''Well enough. I liked Brian Sunderland. He was a good man. Brave, tough, and honorable. Straightforward. He fought against the Nazis in Cyrenaica and in Italy, and then later in Korea and Viet Nam. Ordinarily, such a man wasn't the kind They could turn. But they learned that Brian was vulnerable about one thing—his wife—with all the foolish uxoriousness middle-aged men have for their second, very young wives. My God, you should have seen them together! He couldn't keep from touching her, stroking, patting, gentling her all the time as if to reassure himself that she was real and his.

''But his wife was another sort altogether. It was her first time out of Australia. Moscow was the big, wicked, exciting city, you know, like the Casbah. Not that she was a bad woman, only young, naïve, vain, romantic.''

"Did you like her?"

"However odd it sounds, I did. But I liked Brian better. After all, Harriet was young enough to be my daughter and Brian was my contemporary. We had a lot in common. We liked each other as well as men could in such circumstances, when they don't really trust each other, when each is 'playing' the other. In spite of that, we went hunting and fishing together—he was an excellent angler, expert at tying his own flies, which he taught me to do—and we even went on a couple of mountain climbs, really hill climbs, because I'm not much good at it. Brian was an outdoor man, better at sports than I was by far, but he wasn't at home in drawing rooms, or diplomatic receptions."

"Or in bedrooms? Which accounts for your success with his young wife."

"Brian gave me a fishing rod as a gift, a beautiful fiberglass flyrod he had bought in England, perfect for trout or bass. To thank me for all the good Russian fish we'd caught together. He brought it back from London, where he'd gone for a week of Commonwealth briefings. The same week, while he was away, I first slept with his wife, in his own bed. Later, after he returned, They provided me with one of their apartments for our rendezvous, with all the cinema cameras and tape decks."

"Like Kornilov's apartment for me and Valya?"

Fedorov ignored that too. "When Brian gave that flyrod to me, I almost threw up. I never did fish with it. I couldn't. After he killed himself, I gave it to Galtsev, who looked at me out of those piercing little eyes of his and commented, 'English fishing rod. What luxury!' I replied that it was a luxury I couldn't afford, and because Galtsev knew about Sunderland, he understood and took the flyrod and said nothing."

"I'll bet *he* fished with it."

"Said it was the best flyrod he ever had."

Driving past a long stretch of meadow, Fedorov asked him to pull over. Chapman wanted to know what for and

Fedorov, opening his coat so Chapman could see the gun under his belt, explained that he wanted to test a gun. "Have you got ammunition?"

Fedorov tapped his coat pocket. "A whole box full."

"What do you suppose happened to your Luger?"

"Helga took it—and returned it. She was afraid I might do myself in, but later she changed her mind."

"Then what did you need this one for?"

"The Luger's firing pin was filed down so it would misfire."

"Helga?"

"A professional job. Needs expertise with guns."

"So Andrew gave you a Luger knowing it wouldn't work."

"His form of self-protection. If, in a Pushkin-style duel, we'd fought to the death over my supposed betrayal of you and Valya, or if I'd shot it out with Khlakov, or anyone else, I'd have been quite dead. Your faithful friend and my faithful protector was taking no chances."

"You're sure?"

"Look for yourself. The Luger's in the house."

The meadow stretched as far as the eye could see, with patches of marsh and pond mirroring the sun. Chapman parked next to a bordering windbreak of pine and poplar. In August that meadow would probably be full of six-foot-high magenta stalks and hairy sunflower discs but now it was only high grass and weeds. They got out of the car and Fedorov checked the cocking, firing, and ejection mechanisms of the automatic. "This one works," he said. He shoved a clip home, then stood in the shadow of the poplars aiming out at the meadow. He held his gun wrist with his left hand, braced his left elbow against his body, and fired off two shots. The sounds reverberated in the quiet open air. Abruptly, a mallard broke out of the high grass and with a flurry of wings darted straight upward. Instinctively crouching, Fedorov snapped off the shot even as Chapman cried, "No!" The mallard fell like a stone. On the run they reached it together. It lay, chestnut breast still heaving, orange feet scrabbling for a hold on the wet earth, the blue patches of its wings bright as sky, the blood slowly pumping out of its neck where the iridescent green head had been blown off.

They stood over it until it stopped moving, then worked their way back through the high grass toward the road. When they got there Chapman whirled, whipped out the Walther, and furiously fired the whole magazine into the empty meadow.

At the car, they reloaded, then kicked the mud off their shoes, and Chapman said, "You're a dangerous man, Alek."

"All men are dangerous. Some, like me, with proper training—"

"*Im*proper training."

". . . become more dangerous. And not only with a gun. They gave me a few of their choicest photographs, so enlarged and chosen for their pornographic quality that they turned even my stomach. I can imagine what they did to Brian Sunderland when he saw them. I gave them to Harriet and explained what They wanted, but I didn't tell her that I worked for them, only that they had me over a barrel, that they were threatening me too, with prison, with the camps, which was, in a way, true. She believed me, I think, but Brian was wiser and knew better. He understood he'd been twice deceived, betrayed by his friend and cuckolded by his wife." Fedorov covered his eyes. "It was as if I'd shot him down as thoughtlessly as I did that duck back there."

"You didn't kill Sunderland, Alek, he killed himself. He could have gone to his ambassador, told the story, and been sent home," Chapman maintained, but he didn't even sound convincing to himself.

Fedorov didn't seem to hear him. "Harriet telephoned me, hysterical, but wouldn't say what was wrong, only that I must come to their flat immediately. I found a taxi and rushed over. She was stammering, not making a word of sense, only pointing to the kitchen. I went in and Brian was there, folded over the kitchen table, his head on his hands. I lifted his head and his hands, and found his brains and blood spattered all over the table and the gun. He'd put the gun to his right eye and blown half his head off.

"I did what had to be done then, called my control, and They sent the militia and some of their own people too. But I made Harriet call her embassy, and the Australian security officer came right over also, though I left, with the photos, before he arrived."

"Swift and slick."

Fedorov looked unhappy. "They were angry because I'd left without finding out what the Australian security's reaction to Sunderland's suicide was. Later, the Australians let it be known that fighting in the wars had made Colonel Sunderland melancholy and that in a fit of depression he'd killed himself."

"To give the impression that Sunderland had had a nervous breakdown?"

"Exactly. Make it seem he was deranged and really an accident. Hush it up. That suited my control perfectly."

"But you'd failed to recruit Sunderland."

"They didn't want to show that it was a KGB operation. They were sorry that Sunderland hadn't played the game, but the operation was a success for them anyway because Brian was a strong character who resisted them and now he was eliminated and maybe his replacement would be a weaker man whom they could recruit."

"And his wife?"

"They flew her and Brian's body out, back to Australia. He had family there, by his first marriage, two sons and a daughter. They were going to bury him near where he was born, Perth, I think."

Chapman started the car and drove down the road. "So," he said after a while, "that was the beginning of the end."

Fedorov's laugh fell just short of a sob. "The end. They were so satisfied with the operation that they gave me a flat!

My reward for murdering Brian Sunderland. An apartment, mind you, two rooms with private bath and kitchen. Opulence! It took some pulling strings because they didn't want to give me one in a KGB building—that would blow my 'cover,' but within six months I had my own apartment."

"The wages of sin."

"Ironic, because afterward I was no good for them."

"Your conscience?"

"Lower down than that, Nathaniel. I still made friends with women for them, foreign women especially. I was, they told me, as charming as ever, but the instrument wouldn't work. Try as I would, it was dead, dead as Brian Sunderland. I was impotent."

"Then Helga?"

"The second chance. The new life. For the first time since Harriet Sunderland, it performed. It worked fine."

# 15

# To the Border

Long before daybreak Chapman was awake. He'd had trouble falling asleep and half-willing had heard, and listened to, the sounds of revelry and love-making below. Only after midnight, when Helga's car had roared away, had he been able to drop off to sleep. He'd turned and tossed, afflicted with nightmares: brains running over forty-five automatics like ice-floed red rivers over a spillway; headless mallards leaping vertical and glossy into the air from four-poster canopied beds, their yellow-green bills quacking insanely, flying after them; Valya's face, then Helga's, then Phyliss's and Betsy's, and another woman's face he didn't recognize but knew to be Genia's, all exploding from an ikonostasis with hundreds of Virgins of Vladimir, a single face with a thousand expressions: fury, fear, fatigue, lust, love, and longing.

It was dark, the moon still up and a last splash of stars beginning to fade. The house was cold and dark, and he didn't want to put on the lights. He dressed swiftly, packing the gear he'd prepared the night before, filling a thermos with hot coffee, then lugged it all out to the car. He double-checked the Walther and put an extra box of ammunition for it into the glove compartment. Just before dawn he went to wake Fedorov and found him all finished packing, hung over and morose, but moving swiftly and efficiently.

With the first faint light they were driving away down the *allée* of elms. Fedorov, looking back through the rear window, saluted the house. "You have been a happy house for me," he declared, as if appeasing capricious household gods, "the beginning of a new life." Just before they turned on to the road, a pair of cardinals swooped into the elms above them and perched there. The male, brilliantly scarlet as a drop of living blood, his crest cockily erect, looked down at them, then he and his dun-colored mate began their heartening white whistles and Chapman thought that things might work out after all.

By the time the sun began to rise they were on the turnpike speeding north, and Fedorov, with a curt reminder to wake him as soon as they passed Albany, fell asleep. But he awakened long before that, cheerful and restored, the first words out of his mouth: "After a while, you think of almost nothing but getting out. You're obsessed by the desire and beset by doubts. You've done so many evil things. You've compromised yourself so deeply that nothing can ever clear your conscience, so you think God will never allow you to get out. But now I *am* getting out and it seems incredible."

"You're not over the border yet," Chapman cautioned.

"I crossed the really difficult border when I left Russia. Crossing this one should be easy. What happens afterward will be difficult."

"Which reminds me. Money." Chapman brought the envelope out of his breast pocket and passed it to Fedorov. "We got back from your church too late yesterday to get to the bank before it closed. There's seven hundred and thirty-seven dollars in that envelope, all the cash I had in the house plus what I could cash of the traveler's checks in my desk. Not much, but all I could put my hands on, except for about seventy dollars I kept for gasoline and emergencies."

"The Russian Tea Room?"

"That too," Chapman admitted, his cheeks hot.

"Nathaniel," Fedorov's voice was filled with reproof, "with Valentina Andreyevna there is no time to be lost. I learned that once and for all with Genia. At our age it's even more important. There's so little time left. When you love someone, there never is time to be lost because it's all so precarious and so precious, so always poised on the lip of catastrophe. Don't lose this chance because of pride, false pride."

"I'll try my best not to," Chapman promised.

Fedorov took the envelope and, without opening it, put it into his coat pocket. "You know there's no way to thank you."

"And no need. In a way it's good I didn't make the bank. A big withdrawal—especially from that particular account —would have looked bad, shown a connection between my withdrawal and your departure. This way . . ." His voice trailed off.

"Now you're thinking sensibly. Like an agent." He smiled. "When you get back tonight, you can say I was gone when you returned. In fact, call Wheelwright first thing tomorrow to say that I didn't come last night and you're worried. You need say nothing more except that you went up to New York to meet Valentina Andreyevna, which people at the Russian Tea Room will be able to confirm. When Wheelwright asks, when Helga asks, you don't know what happened to me."

"Not quite true though, is it?" Fedorov had thought it all out, carefully, and considerately. He had done his best to make sure that even the rendezvous with Valya was at the right time and place so that he would give him an alibi.

"That's why I haven't told you more about my plans. I want you to have to lie as little as possible."

"No matter how little the lie, Wheelwright won't believe me."

"He won't be important for too long if you use the

documents I give you proving that he's a double. Will you use them, Nathaniel?"

"I haven't let myself think that far ahead because I'm not yet willing to admit that Andrew works for Them."

"You're a loyal friend, and I, for one, should be especially grateful for that."

As they drove along the shore of Lake George into the foothills of the Adirondacks, the tension was like a third presence in the car. Fedorov, husbanding his forces for some imminent and Herculean effort that in prospect fatigued him so profoundly, slept once more. About three-quarters of an hour south of Plattsburg, Chapman pulled the car into a roadside rest and left Fedorov sleeping while he sat outside on the bench and drank some coffee from the thermos, inhaling the healing smell of balsam and fir, looking up at the mountains. *From whence my help cometh?* he thought and laughed at himself. What would he do if Fedorov proved that Wheelwright was a double? Confront Andrew? Stupid. Wheelwright would have to kill him then. The only thing to do was to get the evidence to Pearsall, if evidence there was. In Pearsall's shoes he wouldn't have taken anyone's word about his deputy being doubled without positive evidence, and certainly not from someone who was obviously considered a malcontent officially, one of those who'd fallen by the wayside, so he was going to have to figure a way to get Fedorov's evidence to Pearsall where the evidence could speak for itself.

He finished the coffee, trotted up and back to get the kinks out of his legs, did some bending and stretching to loosen the muscles in his neck and arms. He felt limber and strong, and optimistic. The sun was high in the sky, the air was cool and brisk in his lungs, with a mountain tang. Even if his thinking was still muddled, his head felt clear. When he turned, Fedorov stood next to the car, yawning and stretching, and asking for coffee. Chapman motioned for him to help himself. Fedorov brought a bottle of vodka from the back of the car and laced the coffee with it. As he drank it off, he surveyed the trees, the granite outcroppings, the mountains and sky with evident pleasure. "No one's followed us up here anyway," he noted.

"Were you watching?" Chapman asked sarcastically.

"When I was awake." He chuckled. "Where are we now?"

"About an hour south of Plattsburg."

Fedorov sat next to him at the roadside log table and said, "There's a motel about ten miles down the road where I'd like you to stop. Take a room, but not in your own name. And don't give the automobile license number."

"What if they ask for identification?"

"They won't."

"Or see the license plates?"

Fedorov poured some coffee into the dirt at his feet, then picked up the mud and plastered it over the numbers on the rear license plate so that even at that close distance they were indecipherable. Then he did the same to the front plate. "Pay them in advance," he called.

"Then what?"

"I'll tell you then."

Angrily Chapman seized the thermos and went back to the car. He switched the ignition on and began to pull away before Fedorov had his legs inside and had not yet closed the car door.

The motel was a semicircle of forty miniature Swiss chalets. Chapman drove up to the largest one in the center, the office, and Fedorov slumped down in the seat. Inside, the desk clerk, an elderly lady heavily powdered and rouged, with purple dyed hair and thick bifocals had a plug in one ear and was watching a television set bolted high on the wall to the right. She handed him the register and Chapman signed the name Alexander Wheelwright, pleased with that, and left the license plate blank, smudging it with ink.

The lady extended a veined hand covered with liver spots in which there was his key with a number of his chalet on it and asked for seventeen dollars. Not once did she take her eyes off the silent moving apparitions on the TV screen. If she were called on to identify him, he was sure she couldn't recognize his face.

Theirs turned out to be the third chalet from the end. Fedorov carried the two battered leather cases and the new plaid canvas suitcase. In the room, he opened one leather bag on the bed and transferred everything from it into the canvas case, except for a toilet kit. That he took with him into the bathroom. When he emerged, clean-shaven and with short sideburns, he looked altogether a different man, his face more like the old Fedorov face Chapman remembered from Moscow, harsher, more decisive, less the Russian intellectual's and more the KGB officer's. His movements were more tightly controlled and precise, his voice more peremptory. "I'll take the canvas bag. When you come back, pick the two leather ones up and take them with you. Bury them, burn them, get rid of them."

He held out his hand. "Your gun, Nathaniel," he requested.

"You ask for a lot of trust, Alek, and you give damn little of it."

"Your risks are smaller and you're naturally richer in trust than I am. You were deprived of a Soviet upbringing."

"Suppose I hand it over"—he took the Walther out of his waistband—"and you gun me down and leave me here?"

"I need you to drive me across the border."

"You could take the car across yourself and leave it there."

"I could, but I have no papers, no license. What happens if the customs stops me at the border?"

"You'll give me your Luger then?"

Fedorov shook his head. "I'm taking it with me."

"If they find that at the border, it's all over. For both of us."

"I must take that chance."

"Then why take my Walther?"

"To minimize the chances of being caught by half."

"And if I take you across and then you kill me?"

"That chance you have to take."

"*Have* to?"

Impatiently, Fedorov growled, "Why are we bickering like this? If you've come this far, go just a little further and trust me a little longer." His eyes were tormented, his lips trembling. Then he controlled himself and said, "If the worst comes to the worst, I guess I can wait until nightfall and walk across the border."

"All right," Chapman agreed and handed the Walther over. Fedorov threw it into the empty leather suitcase. "Get the ammunition box from the glove compartment, please." Chapman brought that back and Fedorov stowed it next to the Walther, closed and strapped the suitcases before handing the keys to Chapman. "You can take the pistol out when you come back to pick up the luggage."

Without another word he led Chapman back to the car, checking twice to make sure that their chalet door was locked. "To town," he commanded.

"Yes sir, Comrade Commissar," Chapman replied, clicking his heels and getting in behind the wheel.

In front of the first barber shop, Fedorov asked him to wait. When he came out, his hair was crew cut, sideburns shorter still and trimmed, and he looked as though he'd just been discharged from the Plattsburg army base. "An improvement, no?" he asked.

"A big change."

"Okay," Fedorov said in English, "now to Dannemora."

Chapman laughed uproariously and began to sing, also in English: "How are things in Dannemora?" and then had to explain, because Fedorov lapsed back into Russian, glancing uneasily around them, and asked if he had gone crazy. Within sight of the prison walls in Dannemora, Fedorov located a photographer's shop. Again he was gone for a time and returned triumphantly exclaiming, "Now to the border!" As Chapman was about to turn back toward Plattsburg, Fedorov brusquely directed him to go through Chateaugay and cross the border there. He wanted to be left in Huntingdon, and said that Chapman could drive back by the Champlain border crossing.

"*Jawohl, Oberleutnant!*" Chapman responded.

"Sorry, Nathaniel, nerves."

About three miles out of Dannemora a small grove of scrub pine grew away from the roadside and Fedorov motioned for him to park. He reached into his overcoat pocket, brought out a plastic bag in which were several canisters of film. "These are the microfilms Wheelwright was after; networks, names of agents, mail drops, safe houses, codes, methods of payment and communication, and contingency sabotage plans for the U.S. and Canada. All the agents in the Soviet networks are here, including the documentary evidence about your friend Andrew Wheelwright. Dossier material, payments into his Swiss numbered account. Those three rolls of film may cost you your life. They almost cost me mine, so before you use them, be sure you know what you're doing."

It was true then, what Wheelwright had said. Alek did have the additional information. And it was true what Fedorov had told him, that he had Wheelwright dead to rights. "You still don't believe me," Fedorov observed mournfully. "Well, I anticipated that." He took a magnifying glass and an oblong white envelope with the letterhead of the Dannemora photography shop on it and laid them both in his lap. From the three canisters he chose one, took the film out of it, and holding it up to the light unrolled it until he found what he was searching for. Then he laid a strip of film across the white envelope, handed Chapman the magnifying glass, and declared, "Look!"

Chapman looked. There were copies of top-secret memoranda from the embassy in Moscow, summaries of coded cables, descriptions of various employees of the embassy and their personality weaknesses, intelligence reports from allies, even one report explaining why it would be desirable to compromise a cultural attaché, one Nathaniel Chapman. But not until he saw two things was he convinced: the first was the KGB notation that the agent code-named Benedikt was Andrew Wheelwright; the second was a finance-section voucher listing payments to agent Benedikt made into a Zurich bank account. Payments went back six years and were in excess of a hundred thousand dollars. "How did you get all this here?" Chapman marveled.

"Smuggled it out of Vnukovo and then, in Europe, before I defected, I mailed the microfilm to myself here."

"To that church?"

"No. To 'friends.' A phone call sent the microfilm to general delivery at the post office in your town, but to another name." He was reluctant to say more.

It all dovetailed more logically than Chapman wanted to see. The man with the muttonchop whiskers at the UN who'd slipped Alek that envelope, the phone calls Alek must have made from town and from the Chinese restaurant in New York, the church in Russian Mill, where Alek probably got false papers, the maps and route to the border, right down to the Swiss chalet motel, were all links in a chain; obviously, others had used that route to escape Them before and would again. And who were those "friends"? Anti-Soviet emigrés helping out of conviction? Criminals, for whom forgery and smuggling were profitable business? Other foreign intelligence services? Chapman didn't know—and he didn't want to.

Fedorov rubbed his naked cheeks and chin as if only newly aware how smooth they were, then ran his hand across his brushlike hair. "For a long time after I arrived here, I thought I wouldn't do anything with these. I brought them out only as insurance, I told myself. I didn't want to hurt or help anyone except myself. I just wanted to be left alone. And then when your people turned me over to Wheelwright for debriefing, I knew I couldn't give them to him or even tell him I had them if I wanted to live. As long as he wasn't sure I had them, he wouldn't be in too much of a hurry to kill me. If I held out long enough, he'd remember we'd been friends and try to use you to pry those loose from me, or at least pry the information loose."

"How did he suspect you had them?"

"I think Galtsev knew. When those Spetsi broke his leg on the ski slopes, he must have told them. I'm not sure, but those bruises weren't the kind you get from falls, but from beating."

"Even Galtsev."

"Yes, even him." He heaved a sigh. "These are the only gift I can give to you and to your country, Nathaniel, for giving me a second chance. I bequeath them to you with fear and trembling. Do with them what you will."

Reluctantly weighing the canisters in his hand as if assaying them, Chapman nodded.

"And now," Fedorov said wearily, "let's cross the border."

At the border crossing a few cars were ahead of them and they had to wait what seemed like an interminable time, but Chapman knew it was no more than ten minutes. It was a weekday and there weren't many border crossings. The customs officer, with only a cursory glance into their car and a few indifferent questions, waved them on into Canada. He didn't even ask for their papers though he did ask if they had them because they'd probably be checked on the way back in. Chapman drove silently toward Huntingdon, the canisters a weight against his thigh. The sun glistened in the trees, a gaggle of swallows splashed merrily in a muddy pool at the roadside, a boy flew a box kite high above a spring wheat field.

When they could see Huntingdon in the distance, Fedorov waved him to the side of the road. He got out, took his canvas suitcase, and waited for Chapman. For a moment, hands on each other's shoulders, they stood at arm's length, and then, Russian-style, they embraced and Fedorov kissed him, a natural kiss and an honest embrace. Tears started in Fedorov's eyes and Chapman felt tears in his own. With an overwhelming sense of loss, he knew they had gone the route as far as they could go together. What he had done seemed to him like what some of his Abolitionist ancestors had done, taking a slave north to freedom, but he knew that was excessive, such historical analogies were misleading. Unwilling to part, they stood until Fedorov put his hand inside his coat and drew out the Luger. With an underhand motion he threw it to Chapman. "Here," he called, "I'm over the border. At last. No more guns. No more of any of that."

Chapman put the Luger in his coat, felt its burden added to the weight of film in his trouser pocket. He got back behind the wheel, turned the key in the ignition, and made a grinding screech because he'd left the motor running. He ground the car back up on the highway, spun it around in a sharp U-turn, and headed back home.

# 16

# *Rendezvous*

Superficially it made sense, yet the underlying meaning eluded him. He went over it again and again as he drove down from Plattsburg, explanations political and economic, sexual and psychoanalytic. None, singly, was sufficient; even all together seemed unsatisfactory. Andrew had been doubled in Moscow: *fact.* Because of Phyliss? Or for reasons far more complex, for which Phyliss's infidelities provided an acceptable pretext? He could remember literally scores of talks with Andrew over the years, bull sessions at Yale, conversations over brandy and coffee, official discussions at the embassy in Moscow, all revealing—through the curtain of Andrew's detached irony and ribald language—disillusionment with America, distaste for ordinary people, disenchantment, even disgust, with democratically elected, incompetent, and corrupt leaders and their ignorant and uncaring constituents. America was too ugly—the lowest common denominator rampant had brought good taste to its knees—too mongrel—the colored, the minorities, the poor, without talent, education, discipline, civility, or background had thrown their weight into the balance to foment chaos—too materialistic—the nation was indulging in an orgy of buying, using up, wasting, wanting—too selfish—the people and their leaders had demonstrated time and again the inability to separate public good and national interest from private profit and personal gain.

Was it because Andrew's unforgiving father, who had run a middling-size Ohio steel mill and named his only son after Andrew Carnegie, had worshiped power? Or because his doting mother had made Andrew's every whim her command? Or that long proud New England heritage going back to the Massachusetts Bay colony? In taking over the mill, a newly acquired family holding, Andrew's father had reluctantly transported that heritage out to Ohio, bringing with him an oasis of New England to the common plain of the Middle West, just as before him his ancestors had moved gradually, with their holdings, from Lynn to Framingham to Worcester and then across the Connecticut border. Some sense of what that Wheelwright family trek meant, Chapman remembered from the one trip Andrew had invited him on from New Haven when they were at Yale. They'd driven up in Andrew's car to his Wheelwright grandfather's house in Litchfield for Thanksgiving.

Even now, in recollection, that house made him uneasy. An enormous old nineteenth-century wooden house of more than twenty rooms, with bright white clapboard and columns on the outside, the interior was full of gloomy rooms dimly lit by fifteen-watt bulbs that shone yellow on portrait after portrait of somber-faced New England ancestors, men in beards and stiff collars, women whose bodies were masked by jabots and whalebone. Litchfield, with all its towering elms still shading the center of the streets. The elms! That was how Andrew knew so much about them. And then he remembered Andrew's sardonic comment as they were driving toward Litchfield, that Goshen lay just beyond. He'd thought it was another smart-aleck Wheelwright remark until years later he found out that a small town of that name actually lay just beyond Litchfield between the two arms of the Shepaug River, yet to this day he was convinced that Andrew had been referring to the Biblical Goshen.

It couldn't be the cash. Even the more than one hundred thousand dollars in KGB disbursements to that Zurich account wouldn't explain Andrew's defection. After all, old man Wheelwright had left his son more than five times that when Andrew turned thirty, and Andrew had often boasted that his father's bankers, who administered his trust accounts, had almost doubled the principal since.

Yet, how different was Andrew's defection from Alek's? Their worlds had disappointed them, personally, professionally, politically, and they had both decided to leave them; but Alek had left his altogether, Andrew only in spirit and allegiance. The whys of Alek's crossing over he understood and sympathized with; the whys of Andrew's baffled him. What took him by surprise was that he felt no anger with Wheelwright for having betrayed him in Moscow, for having fingered him for the KGB, for having been, essentially, the instrument which had moved him out of his career in the Department, though he'd been murderously enraged by Alek's having compromised him and Valya in Kornilov's flat.

Alek had planned his escape and new life cleverly. At the church he'd gotten his passports, more than one, Chapman was certain. At the church he'd also got another Luger. His friend had mailed the microfilms that were his insurance. At the motel he'd shaved off beard and mustache, step one; at the barber, step two, his hair cut and trimmed; step three, the photographer and pictures with his new face for the passports, whichever he chose. Yet no one of them— motel clerk, barber, photographer—could identify Aleksei Mikhailovich Fedorov with the man they had seen. Doubtless Alek had taken care to get both negatives and prints of his passport photos as well. Probably he would choose an English-speaking country for asylum, not only because he spoke the language, but because the kind of freedom to be left alone that he coveted could be afforded only in those

countries. Canada maybe, more likely Australia or New
Zealand. Australia? The poetic justice of returning to Brian
Sunderland's homeland, a life for a life? The hair would be
dyed, the clothing changed—in time, minor plastic surgery
would accomplish changes in his appearance—so that the
new man would, in truth, emerge for a new free life, and
as long as he lived unobtrusively, Alek would be safe.

That no one could positively identify him was amusing
and alarming, yet gave Chapman pause. Had Alek been the
cold-blooded, calculating KGB officer Wheelwright had
depicted, he would have shot him—there'd been ample
opportunity—dumped his car and body in some remote
Canadian lake or bay, and no witness to his departure
would have survived. He was the only survivor, and in not
killing him, Alek had sealed their friendship in yet another
way. In payment, he had to take care that the microfilms
reached Logan Pearsall and that Alek's suitcases and their
contents were disposed of.

Then, Valya was waiting, another sign of Fedorov's
friendship and persistence. And perhaps a lesson to be
learned. You want a new life, Alek's actions said more
plainly than words, seize it. *Seize the day.* Seize every opportunity that comes your way. Not every man's hand will be
turned against you. *Plan. Plot. Persist.* Then, maybe, some
part of the new life will fall into your grasp. Alek had
managed a new beginning against difficulties that dwarfed
his own, so it was possible that he, too, might yet manage.
Why They had let Valya out with Fyodor Vyacheslovich he
didn't know, but in doing so they'd given him the opportunity to seize. He recalled what he had so deliberately
buried of his talk with Valya in that Chinese restaurant, that
they had co-opted her, used her as a "swallow" against the
Moscow diplomatic colony. At the United Nations the scale
of operations was broader, that was all. That must be their
own sufficient purpose. If Fyodor Vyacheslovich was as
good an intelligence officer as Wheelwright maintained, if
he was, indeed, the *rezident* as Alek had told him, then the

Martynovs were a remarkable tandem, and Martynov was undoubtedly his wife's "collar."

Could he remove that "collar," in both senses? He wanted to try, to have the chance at a new life with Valya, because what he had lived to date had been unsatisfactory. Middle age might be grievous but it might also be where he could truly reap his harvest. Moscow was the end of a diplomatic career, two decades finished, but not wasted; it had also been the beginning of Valya, and of a new career as teacher and political scientist. *Things did sometimes work out.* He always had to remind himself of that. Alek had crossed into Canada safely and he had come back over the border without interference, without even having his papers checked. No one had recognized, searched, questioned, or stopped them. He still had the microfilm, the guns, the ammunition. If his last meeting with Valya had been a near-disaster because the sudden sight of her had unnerved him so that he couldn't comprehend what she wanted, he saw now that she needed his forgiveness so that she could shrive herself, even if such forgiveness was not his to bestow.

It was evening when, at Glens Falls, he bought a small corrugated box, some gummed tape and wrapping paper at a stationer's, and boxed and packed the rolls of microfilm. In the car he hunted through his address book, found Pearsall's home address in Georgetown, and addressed the package to him there instead of at the office. At home there would be neither secretaries nor assistants, nor Wheelwright himself, to intercept it. He went searching for a post office, but they were all closed. Having the microfilms with him made him nervous, as if an essential part of his responsibilities had not been fulfilled, as if, until they were in the proper hands, his having helped Alek to cross the border had not been finally justified. Chapman wished he could send the microfilm off instantly, registered mail, but that could only be done from a post office. Besides, mailing it

from Glens Falls—even if he could find a post office—
would be stupid; it would reveal that he'd driven Alek to the
Canadian border. The cover story was that he'd driven only
as far as New York, only to see Valya. Finally, he found a
pharmacy that weighed his package and sold him enough
stamps for special delivery.

Below Catskill, he chose the road along the river and
parked on a lookout point. He took Alek's clothing from
the suitcases, filled the cases with stones and sent them
separately plummeting over the fieldstone parapet. When,
in the fading light, each splashed white into the Hudson
and sank, he considered throwing the Luger and Walther
after them, in the same gesture toward a new life that Alek
had made near Huntingdon, but something held him back.
Most of the clothing was new, some with laundry marks,
and the labels of Washington stores where they'd been
bought; but that was a risk he'd have to take.

In Kingston he was lucky. Outside of a modest white
church stood a small green metal house, like a garden
toolshed, marked for clothing contributions for the poor
and handicapped. Into it Chapman tumbled all Alek's
clothes. When he got back into the car, he was pleased to
see that no one was about.

All that was left was the microfilm to be mailed in Manhattan.

The sweeping arches of the bridge and the vaulting skyline ablaze with lights lifted his heart, but a part of him,
suspicious of exaltation, made him even warier. Near
Grant's Tomb, he locked the Luger and ammunition into
the glove compartment, put the Walther back into his
waistband, then drove on downtown. Who he was afraid of,
what he was securing himself against, he didn't try to answer, but he was certain that it was too soon to throw the
guns away.

Because it was early, he drove past the Russian Tea
Room twice to see if there was any surveillance, but every-

thing looked normal. A few blocks away he parked the car in a lot, took the box of microfilm under his arm, and walked toward the restaurant. Within sight of it, he stood for a full five minutes before he dropped the microfilm into the postbox. There is no way back, he thought. Aleksei Mikhailovich Fedorov had paid his debt to America, and *he* had betrayed his oldest friend. Pearsall would have the networks, the agents, the codes, the contingency sabotage plans, all of it, at the very latest by the following afternoon. Tonight, wherever he was, Alek would sleep easier and so would Genia, if she knew, in faraway Novosibirsk. But what of Andrew, he said to himself. *Andrew, Andrew!* repeated like a dirge.

The brisk walk after made him feel slightly better. He'd driven most of the day, the few hours nap he'd taken at the Swiss chalet motel after he'd come back for Alek's bags had helped, but if he wasn't tired, he was hungry; he hadn't eaten since breakfast.

The Russian Tea Room was filled with the after-theater, after-concert crowd, the small leather booths up front where he wanted to sit all occupied. He said he'd wait and went to the bar, where he drank vodka and watched the other guests. A number were obviously Russian, but of another generation, and their speech had the old-world Tsarist formality and vocabulary. No Khlakov types and no one who seemed strikingly out of place. Shortly before twelve, the handsome woman in embroidered Russian peasant blouse who seated guests showed him to one of the just-vacated booths. He took his drink with him, and in the semi-darkness of the booth, still warm with the heat of other bodies, faced the doorway.

At a minute after midnight Valya walked through the revolving doors. She stood next to the cloakroom, survey-ing the restaurant, searching for him. Her blond hair, high Tatar cheekbones, thin straight nose and flaring nostrils were as elegant as ever, her stance, full of hauteur and uncertainty together, filled him with a yearning to embrace her. When he stood, she saw him and moved eagerly toward him. To avoid an embrace he knew would be too revealing, Chapman took her hand and kissed it, murmuring, "Valentina Andreyevna."

"Nathaniel without-a-patronymic Chapman," Valya replied. Her smile flashed for only a moment. "May I kiss your hand too?" Without waiting for his reply, she drew his hand to her lips and kissed the center of his palm.

Other eyes were on her and, possessively, Chapman put his arm around her waist and led her to the booth. When the waitress came, he ordered champagne and caviar.

"You're rich?" she asked.

"Tonight I'm rich. Champagne and caviar are for love."

"You need help to make love?" Her teasing was light-hearted.

"I don't think so," he replied.

"No moving pictures or tape recorders."

"Definitely not." He smiled then too.

Valya laughed, then looked around the room. "The smells are Russian, but the sounds and sights are American."

"The champagne is French, Cordon Rouge," Chapman announced as the waitress arrived and was puzzled when they both looked at the name and red-slashed label of the bottle and laughed together. "The caviar is Persian beluga, but the food is authentic Russian." They raised their glasses, and over the blond sparkle of the wine Chapman said, "A long time ago, at the university, I read a writer, a Frenchman, who spoke to me as if he were a personal friend. The Duc de Rochefoucauld. Over the centuries. Across the cultures. My toast is a truth he wrote, about others and about us. *Absence lessens moderate passions and intensifies great passions as the wind blows out a candle but blows up a fire.*" Yet as he spoke the line he felt the chill of Wheelwright's presence. The Duc and Niccolo, Andrew had said, were two men to whom he had introduced him. Did that make him responsible for Wheelwright's doubling too?

While they ate and drank, Valya told him what had happened after he left Moscow. "At first They threatened they would tell Fyodor about us and I said, 'Tell him!' They had asked me many times before to be one of their 'swallows' and when I said no they were angry. I knew some of the other girls at the theater played such games for them, for money, for gifts, for being allowed to shop in the special stores, for vacations in Sochi or Yalta. Now they asked again, but this time it was not a request, but a demand. If I said no, they warned me, nothing could keep me out of the Lubianka or the Butyrkii—even worse—they might send me to one of their psychiatric clinics.

"They were very clever. They didn't arrest me, only kept me overnight, then sent me home to 'think it over.' There, Fyodor was waiting. 'Where have you been?' he asked, so politely that immediately I understood that he knew everything. So I told him the truth, about you, about the flat Aleksei Mikhailovich had arranged for us, about the photographs and recordings, about Abrasov and Saribekyan, about what They'd asked me to do. 'It wasn't Fedorov who arranged that apartment for your rendezvous, though we convinced Aleksei Mikhailovich that it was a safe place,' Fyodor told me. 'It was I. And I, too, who arranged to be absent so you could have your assignation with your American at my dacha.' I was stuck dumb. This icy man was not the same one who had taken me to the Lastochka for caviar and champagne"—abruptly she realized that they, too, were drinking champagne and eating caviar and she covered his hand with hers, comfortingly—"he had never betrayed my trust, but now he had connived with Them in cold blood to compromise me."

"Why this time?"

"He knew that with you it was different."

"Was that enough, to turn you over to them?"

"Who can look into someone else's soul and say when it is enough? 'I knew about you and your American almost from the beginning,' he told me, looking at me as if I were an idiot not to have realized that. His eyes were shining, his hands trembling as he poured some brandy for me. Courteous, attentive as always, but I could see that he was excited now, his trousers bulging. I had thought him, known him, to be a man of affection, not of passion, a cool man though not a cold one, but genuine. Now I saw what he was and what he needed. So I understood without his telling me that he was one of Them—but he told me nevertheless.

"He'd been a Chekist from before the war. He was a colonel and hoping to be promoted to general." She paused and swallowed her champagne hard. "Then he told me about his first wife, Paulina, and his daughters. After they'd had the children, his wife became a Chekist herself, a 'swallow,' and Fyodor not only recruited her, he directed her, was her control."

"In such operations?"

"Very unusual for a husband and wife to work like that, Fyodor explained to me, proudly, but They had learned that he was completely trustworthy. After all, he'd come a long way from that peasant hut in Omsk. They could count on him. And those operations had made him and Paulina even happier than before. Each time she returned from an assignment, their lovemaking was sharper, more ardent, their world together more and more entwined. As I would soon see myself."

"They hadn't taken any chances in letting you go home, had they? They had their Trojan Horse within the gates."

"Fyodor told me how good it was to work together, how wonderful his life with Paulina had been, *how glad he was that this had finally happened to us* so that now it could be just as splendid with us. He gave me the brandy and he touched me—*touched me*—as he never had before, as if he were already on fire, as if he wanted to set me aflame. The wetness unbelievably spreading on his trousers."

Chapman busied himself with pouring more champagne, his shaking hands spilling some on the table.

"Stupidly, I refused," she continued. "Him and his 'games,' Them and theirs."

"So you sat?"

"For almost a year, in Vladimir, and in a sawmill in
Mordvinia. I saw my body dying there and I didn't care.
I wanted it only to hurry. But They were very shrewd.
They watched and they knew, and when I cut my wrists
with a piece of glass, they brought me back from Mordvinia and the camp and put me into one of their psychiatric clinics. They fed me and brought my body back
to life, but they told me that I was 'disoriented,' unable
to 'adapt to reality,' and they were going to have to give
me electric shock treatments. And then I panicked."

Chapman took her clenched fists in his hands and
turned them over. The thin white lines on the under-
sides of her wrists were visible.

"I wrote to Fyodor begging him to have me released.
I would do anything he wanted, become his 'little bird'
and Their 'swallow,' anything. And I did. It wasn't very
different from being an actress, only the sets were different, the people real, there was no script and the stage
was the world. It was dangerous, complicated acting,
calling for all my gifts, all my ability to improvise, for
sometimes I had to write the script as I played it. But
there was no audience, no applause, and I missed those.
It was terribly lonely. In that theater, all were actors. I
had to talk to someone, hear an accolade, palms beating, have someone tell me how well I was performing,
so I began to talk to Fyodor. What more natural? He
was my control. And, just as he promised, our lovemaking became better, in fact, began again so intensely that
I was carried away as never before."

His fingers tightened around her wrists, his thumbs
massaged those white scars. "Not even with me?" he
asked.

"This burned with another flame, not gentleness and
affection, not with the desire to be pleased and to
please, but with hatred, revenge, the desire to inflict and
endure pain."

Valya was describing something of what had passed

for feeling between him and Helga, and also the only living current between him and Betsy, so, however reluctantly, he understood what she was saying.

"I still acted on the stage too," Valya continued, "in order to be seen and invited to parties and receptions, but like other lovemaking that kind of acting now seemed inferior, too tame. Yet my directors and colleagues, even some of the other actresses, told me that my stage acting had never been better, more deeply felt and moving, with an ardor they had never sensed in me before." She slipped her wrists from his hands, picked up the champagne, and her teeth sounded against the glass as she drank. "I was successful everywhere, the 'games' I played for Them against foreigners, the playacting at the theater, and at home in bed with Fyodor.

"At the UNO, they expected even more of me. There were many more diplomats here, more information to be gleaned, more people to be compromised and less caution because people feel free here as they do not in Moscow. We were an important asset—a Stalin Prize-winning novelist and his lovely actress wife. Prominent members of the Soviet intelligentsia. Who would think of them as KGB agents?"

"Those who know your country."

"Only those who know it very well and those are few. Most do not, especially from the new countries."

Chapman saw that continuing the discussion was futile. If They had had other intentions in permitting Valya to come to New York with her husband, she was clearly not aware of them. Tinkers to Evers to Chance, all perfectly rehearsed and meshed perhaps, but Valya wasn't a full-fledged member of the team, and wouldn't have been cued in. Yet, so far, despite all the hits and runs and double plays, Alek was for the moment beyond their grasp and had a good chance of being home free.

The waitress came to remove the remains of the *pelmeni* and *kulebiaka* they had eaten, and returned to bring them coffee. They were silent until she had gone, then Chapman took Valya's wrists in his hands once more. She looked down at the scars and whispered, "But the more 'successful' I was, the more I loathed myself. I'd wake up at night in one bed or another, and lift my hands"— she tore her hands away from him and held them in front of her face, then let them fall back into his—"to stare at those scars, wanting to tear them open with my nails and let the blood gush. I had nightmares and depressions, felt I was burning with a fever, and asked myself, 'Why, if it is all so fine, are you so unhappy?'

"Then one day Fyodor's older daughter, Anna, telephoned. She wanted to visit and I told her that her father was in Kiev attending a writers' conference, but it was me she wanted to talk to. She did not visit often—the younger one, Maria, not at all—so I told Anna to come along. The daughters were at the university, Anna studying medicine, Maria literature. They lived in the dormitories though they could have stayed with us in comfort, even in luxury, but though we invited them, they refused. I thought it was because of me, the stepmother, but it was because they hated their father.

"What Anna told me then I should have suspected long before. She knew what I was doing. Her father, she said, had done the very same thing to her mother. At first everything had been fine, her mother was busy and happy being a 'swallow,' but each time she returned from an assignment, Paulina went into deeper depressions. She went to several psychiatrists—They have their own psychiatrists for such matters—and they gave her tranquilizers, sent her on a vacation to Sochi, but nothing helped. It was then Paulina begged Fyodor to 'free' her, to let her out, but he wouldn't. Perhaps he couldn't. She was his 'swallow,' and she would have to fly. So one day, when she couldn't bear it any longer, she took an overdose of sleeping tablets."

"And killed herself?"

Valya nodded. "Then Anna repeated to me a sentence

her mother had spoken to her the day before she died. It was like a sentence of death and it terrified me. Paulina said to her daughter, 'With each triumph, torment, with each success, failure, with each taking, a giving until I am totally bankrupt.' Anna wanted me to remember that sentence; how could I ever forget it? I was so successful—"

"Successful enough for Them to let you out of the country, to let you come here."

Valya bit her lips. "With Fyodor Vyacheslovich as my 'collar,' just as surely as his daughters back home are his 'collar,' though God knows They don't need a collar for him. But they are always insured."

"Against any eventuality?"

"Against all eventualities."

"Even leaving Fyodor Vyacheslovich and marrying me?"

Nervously she drew back, rebuking him, "Don't joke, Nathaniel."

"I'm not joking. Stay here with me, in the United States, away from him and from Them."

Her mouth moved but no words emerged.

"Divorce and defection are what I'm suggesting." He smiled. "Seduction, too. From now on you'll be my bird alone, no one else's 'swallow.'"

"Tonight?" she asked tremulously.

"Now. Right now." He felt the blood beating and lifted her wrist to kiss the pulse.

"Without anything?"

"As you are. You can buy me four scrawny cows for a wedding price later on."

Valya grinned. "Even without my Siberian sable coat?"

"I'll keep you warm. I promise."

# 17

# Under the Elms

Chapman took the long way home, down to the Battery and the Staten Island ferry. His excuse was that it would be easier to see if anyone was following them, but he really wanted to take Valya the five miles across the bay from the foot of Manhattan to St. George because she had never been on the ferry or seen New York harbor. Besides, it felt like a honeymoon thing to do, and he was feeling newly wed. At the rear rail they stood looking back from the moving ferry across the dark waters at the illuminated span and arches of the Brooklyn Bridge and the fiery Manhattan skyline, then at the glowing promise of the Statue of Liberty. "What a mighty right arm! " Valya exclaimed, and Chapman thought of the scars on her wrists. He wondered if Fedorov had ever seen the old lady in the harbor, or known that she'd been built to commemorate the American and French revolutions, and what Alek would have said to *I lift my lamp beside the golden door.* The cool sea air chilled them and they huddled together, arms around each other, while Chapman pointed out the sights, particularly Ellis Island, telling Valya how that had been the funnel through which the torrent of European immigrants had poured into America. Though it was no longer used for immigration purposes, she could take their ferry ride past it as her official entry into the country. Valya turned to kiss him, then recoiled. "You have a gun," she said, pointing.

"I was hoping you'd think it was me."

"I know the difference, both in feeling and location," she replied, unsmiling.

"Flatterer."

"Why, Nathaniel, why?"

"Because," he answered in a faraway voice, "They tried to kill me and to kill Aleksei Mikhailovich."

"*They* truly?"

"Do you know a hoodlum named Khlakov?"

"Lev Mitrofanovich?"

"The same."

"He's a chauffeur at the Mission."

"He's a Spetsburo assassin."

Valya was nonplussed. "That's why he came so often to drive for Fyodor, and why Fyodor always asked for him, especially when we drove out to Killenworth."

The inadvertant pun in the name of the Soviet Mission's Glen Cove estate should have amused him, but it didn't. It reminded him that Fyodor Vyacheslovich was the KGB *rezident,* and that, when Pearsall got those microfilms, his days in the United States would be numbered. Martynov would surely be expelled, sent back to the Soviet Union, and Valya would have been expelled with him. Had he not taken her with him tonight, tomorrow might already have been too late; he would have been the instrument of his own defeat. But now he had his double revenge on Valya's husband, a revenge he could unambiguously enjoy.

"They know where you are, Nathaniel, and that Aleksei Mikhailovich is with you."

"How?"

"Only the devil knows how they know everything."

By now Chapman was certain that they knew where the farm was because Wheelwright had told them. What they did not know—yet—was that Fedorov was gone, or Valya. But, returning to the farm posed a risk and he had a sudden panicky urge to turn tail and run for cover, follow Fedorov to Canada. When he reassured himself, why should they come for him now if they hadn't done so up to now? They still thought Fedorov was safely there with him, and that Wheelwright had him pegged. And Wheelwright thought he had Fedorov pegged for him. In the morning, Chapman realized, he should telephone Wheelwright to inform him that Fedorov was gone, but after mailing the microfilms to Pearsall, he couldn't manage that final, consummate, agent-like hypocrisy.

Going home was a calculated risk, still, though not a great one. Even if they were to run for it, he had to go back to the farm to get money, clothes, passport, other things, but he didn't think they had to run for it. Except for the one incident on the turnpike, They had not risked going beyond their government-imposed twenty-five-mile "permitted sphere," perhaps out of fear that the Bureau or the Agency would be following Them. And Wheelwright would have no cause to suspect anything had changed until tomorrow and then it would be too late—for him.

High above, a dolorous-faced moon circled by an enormous luminous halo edged with a slender rainbow swam in a sea of dark clouds. "It looks like Fyodor's ikon," Valya whispered. And in her eyes it did resemble that Madonna of Tenderness he remembered on the wall of Martynov's dacha. Her wedding gift from him. Was this natural ikon a gift for them, and an omen?

Theirs was the next-to-last car off the ferry slip at St. George and the auto behind them turned south as they went west, so apparently no one was following them. Chapman drove slowly, avoiding the turnpike and parkway once he was across the bridge, sticking to the small local roads, enjoying Valya's warm, perfumed presence next to him. They were not far from the farm when she asked, "Will Aleksei Mikhailovich be awake when we return?"

Chapman couldn't tell her the truth, so he said, "Alek usually waits up for me to have a nightcap with him."

"Like a good wife."

"Or a good friend."

"We must make love, Nathaniel," she murmured, "soon."

"Don't you want to see Aleksei Mikhailovich first?" he teased.

"Later." She touched him. "But us, very soon now."

"Here?" he asked, putting his arm around her and drawing her still closer.

One eye open, she peered at him and chuckled. "In the automobile. I have never made love in an automobile."

"With all your experience, Valya, some things you have missed," he joked, but was instantly sorry because she stiffened against him. "This is young America's mobile boudoir."

"How lucky to grow up in a rich country!"

They drove until Valya said, "Please, Nathaniel, I don't want to have to sit and talk politely to Aleksei Mikhailovich for two hours before . . ."

Chapman wanted to tell her that Aleksei was gone, that the whole house, the privacy and comfort of clean sheets and a quiet bed, of music and wine and unencumbered nakedness awaited them, but he couldn't. The time would come when she would be questioned, and if she did not know about Alek she could tell the truth plainly and convincingly. But her urgency excited him. He knew a glen down a narrow dirt road where on his walks he'd seen the action and evidence that local young people occasionally took advantage of it as a lover's lane. It was no more than a ten-minute drive from where they were, altogether private, and at that time of night almost no likelihood that anyone would be there.

The glen was a veritable thicket, overgrown with shrubs and brambles, and out of it, miraculous as white arms, grew a stand of pale high birch. Chapman turned off the lights and the motor and let the car glide to a halt behind the birches. He took Valya in his arms and tasted her to the palate until she complained, "The gun, the gun."

She moved away to let him take the Walther from his waistband, unlock the glove compartment, and, as he deposited it there, Valya saw Aleksei's gun. "A Luger too! " she exclaimed.

"You know about guns?"

"I've been taught," she confessed.

Chapman closed but did not lock the glove compartment, shutting off its small light. For a while they held hands, then began to caress one another. He explained about the back seat and Valya bedeviled him about being an all-American boy himself, but she followed him out of the front seat though not into the rear one. When he reached for her, she slipped way, laughing quietly. "We must be careful. You've left me without a wardrobe. These are the only clothes I have."

She stood next to the car and undressed, neatly folding all her clothes on to the front seat, then stepped out of her shoes. In the moonlight she was herself a slender birch, more so when her white arms rose into the branches as if in prayer and drew thin brown catkins and toothed green leaves down from the birch twigs to wreathe like laurel in her hair. Momentarily, she seemed to be beseeching the Madonna of Tenderness moon above them, then in the car she descended on him like a cloud of flesh, planting herself on him in a single questing thrust as if connecting her trunk to a taproot from which she grew, moved, then returned and could not separate herself, drawing him up into her, out of himself, her beautiful small breasts swaying away from her body like fruit from a tree, unhurried now and deliberate, rhythmic and inexorable, until in that great arch, her haunches convulsing in his hands, she reared and cried out, "For the love of God, a child, Nathaniel, a child! " then fell on him, spent.

They lay sprawled on the back seat, legs entangled, and she asked to smoke. He took the cigarettes from her purse, lit one, and handed it over. She inhaled, fell back against him, sighing, "That was good."

"Me, or the smoke?"

"The cigarette, of course."

"More where that came from."

"The cock always crows."

She asked if things would be difficult.

"What things?" Chapman wanted to know.

"A Russian wife."

"Not difficult, impossible."

"Don't make fun of me," she commanded. "Do you have enough money? How will it affect your job? Can I find work?"

"Valya, the real problems will be bureaucratic. Getting you political asylum, a visa, and a divorce. Your people will not want to let you go and they will make strenuous efforts to keep you. *They* especially will make trouble, and Fyodor Vyacheslovich too."

"Let them. I'm not afraid."

"I am."

"Why?"

"They're dangerous and determined."

"I'm dangerous and determined too," she declared grimly.

And Chapman knew she was.

He tried to assure her that after the initial troubles, things would go easier for them. He had enough money so they could live moderately well, not lavishly, but not frugally either; and he had the house and farm. If they were pressed, he could always sell off a couple of acres, which every year appreciated in value.

"You don't sell land," was her reproof.

"Peasant! *Kulak!*" he retorted, but explained that he didn't think they'd have to. His research fellowship paid enough for them to live on, it ran for the rest of the year with an option for a second year renewal, and he had a job teaching half-time at the university which, if need be, could be expanded to full-time. But he preferred to finish his book on the Soviet dissidents first.

"Politics again! "

"No, Valya, political science. Theory, not practice. I don't intend to go back into the foreign service and in any event I doubt they'd have me, so a Russian wife is no liability. I'm going to remain a teacher, perhaps a scholar, but no diplomat."

"Not one of Them, and not one of Yours?"

"Neither one nor the other," he replied.

Peaceful and relaxed, Chapman drove slowly off the high road into his *allée* of elms, Valya snug against him. Three generations of Chapmans had walked under those same elms and he wondered if a fourth might still enjoy their shade before the bark beetles and fungi brought them crashing down. Valya was young enough, surely. Clouds had obscured the moon, thickening the shadows beneath the elms, though in the distance, on the rise, he could see the house, silent and dark.

"Look, Nathaniel," Valya noted, "Aleksei Mikhailovich did *not* wait up for you."

"If only we'd known, we could have waited and enjoyed the bed."

"We still can." She laughed. "But now I have been Americanized, and in your automobile."

The visibility was so bad that he flicked the headlights up, and then the car skidded. As he fought to keep the car from smashing against the trees, he thought it was a blowout. Only when he heard the second report and felt the second tire go did he realize they were gunshots. The car stopped a few feet from the elms, parallel to them, and Chapman snapped the headlights off and pushed Valya down on the floor of the car. "Stay down," he ordered. "Someone just shot out our tires." He tried turning the car around to drive back down the *allée*, but the clanking rims and skidding told him that a man could run faster than he could drive. Whoever was out there would surely have a car and would find them much more easily in the car. Best to ditch the car. If they could reach beyond the elms there was cover and darkness. He took both guns and the ammunition from the glove compartment, holding the pin at the side of the compartment down so that the little light would not go on. He pressed the Walther and its ammunition into Valya's hands. "Do you know how to use this?" he asked.

"Yes."

To make sure, he showed her how to work the safety and replace the clip.

"I'll go out on my side, firing. That should draw them to that side, then get out on yours and run for the trees. Keep down. There's a gully just beyond the elms. Jump down into it and work your way back into the shrubbery. Hide there. Don't shoot, and don't show yourself."

"You think there's more than one?" Valya asked.

"The shots were from different guns."

"I'm going out with you," she said. He heard the iron in her voice and knew there was no time to argue.

"All right," he agreed. "Into the back seat."

"Is this the time for such things?"

"What better time?" Chapman responded, and touched her cheek. "Out on the side closest to the trees. We're using the back doors because when you open the front ones the car lights go on."

"I'll follow you." Valya promised and kissed him.

In one heave he was over into the back seat and Valya after him. He opened the door as quietly as he could but the click was loud in the silence. Then, diving out on the road, he rolled over and over into the gulley. "Now," he called back softly. Valya jumped out of the car and in a crouch ran toward him. A burst of automatic weapons fire raked the elms before she threw herself into the gulley. Body to body they lay outstretched. "Are you hurt?" he asked.

"I don't think so."

Another burst from the submachine gun sent a rain of splinters and leaves showering over them. Keeping down,

Chapman drew Valya away from there along the gulley toward a nearby bank of shrubs until from it came Wheelwright's hoarse-voiced English invitation. "This way, Nathaniel, I'll cover you. They've got you surrounded on the other sides." Chapman threw Valya to the bottom of the gulley and covered her body with his own just before Wheelwright fired.

"Nathaniel," Wheelwright's voice called, now in Russian, "we don't want to hurt you. It's Fedorov we're after."

"Alek is in the house," Chapman called back.

"Quit the crap," Wheelwright roared. "The chicken's flown the coop. Where's he gone, Nathaniel?"

"How would I know? I left him in the house when I went up to the city. And I just got back—almost."

"Would you tell me if you did know?"

"Probably not."

"Did Fedorov give you anything to keep for him?"

"Nothing."

"Why don't we talk this over, Nathaniel?"

"If you wanted to talk why did you start shooting?"

Chapman heard them moving out there trying to locate him by his voice and he motioned Valya to follow him along the gulley toward the high road. Wheelwright boomed, "It was a mistake. We thought you were Fedorov."

A mistake! Wheelwright had seen them, called to him, and then shot at him. That was no mistake. And he remembered the filed-down firing pin on the Luger that Wheelwright had given Alek. Friendship.

There were several of Them and probably they'd come in two cars. If they planned an ambush, the logical thing was to have left one car at the base of the *allée* and pulled a second one into the entrance after they had driven in, the stopper in the bottle. Working his way back to the house with Valya made no sense, because They'd been there and surely torn the telephones out. When he raised his head over the edge of the ditch, he saw their car turned horizontally, blocking the *allée*. What he expected. From next to the car, a voice called in Russian, "Valentina Andreyevna. We don't want to hurt you. It's the American we want."

Silently her lips shaped the name Khlakov. Chapman picked up a small stone and threw it against the elms across the *allée* from them. A burst of fire followed the sound. Chapman located the muzzle flash and fired at it, once, twice. With pleasure he heard a grunt of pain and the sound of a body falling. He'd hit someone. Over near the car he saw another shadow come forward and fire a wild burst in their direction.

With Valya he moved back up the gulley toward the house and heard them closing in. He and Valya were hemmed into a space perhaps a hundred yards long and one yard wide. He had a rough fix where Khlakov and the other man were, with the submachine gun, and Wheelwright was in the shrubbery with an automatic. But where were the others? And how many? Now that Wheelwright had revealed himself, Chapman was sure that they would have to kill him. Valya tugged his sleeve. "What are we going to do?"

"Cut across the fields and try to hide until morning."

"They'll kill us with the first light, or when the moon comes out from behind the clouds."

"Valya," a voice called and Chapman felt her fingers clutch his elbow. "Valentina Andreyevna," the voice, louder this time, called again.

"It's Fyodor," she whispered.

"We cannot leave Mr. Chapman alive," the voice went on, calm, logical, unhurried. "But if you come to me, I shall take you back home. It is not necessary for us to kill you."

"Not necessary, but desirable," Valya yelled.

"You have my word, Valya, that we shall do you no harm. You know that I keep my word. She will tell you that, Mr. Chapman, so if you don't want her to die for nothing, send her out to me."

"Let Valentina Andreyevna out, Nathaniel," Wheelwright advised, as if she were being held hostage. "She can't do you any good now."

Unexpectedly then, Chapman remembered the Roche-foucauld maxim that more than any other Wheelwright had quoted: *Perfect courage consists in doing without witnesses what one would be capable of doing before the world at large.* Andrew Wheelwright had reversed that; his valor had consisted in being able to do only in private, in secret, what he could not do publicly before the world, and face it. And the burden of having sent Pearsall the microfilms Alek had given him was miraculously lifted.

"You have five minutes, Mr. Chapman," Fyodor Vya-cheslovich announced, sounding like a timekeeper.

Chapman shaped the word, "Go," without voicing it, but Valya shook her head.

"I beg you," he breathed.

"I was dying before. I'd be dead soon again." She raised her wrists so that the scars glinted.

Without another word Chapman led her along the gulley past where his car had ended up. There was a sharp smell of gasoline before the night exploded. The two cars at either end of the *allée* had turned their headlights on high and were speeding toward each other and flames leaped sputtering down the gulley toward them: They had poured gasoline into it and set it afire. Chapman grabbed Valya's wrist and yanked her out of the gulley, and together they ran across the road toward the protection of the elms on the far side, but at that moment the moon slipped from behind the clouds and its spectral light defined them.

Chapman didn't hear the shot. Her arm went limp and her dead weight threw him to the ground. Frantically he tried to drag her forward with him to the other side of the road, and then he saw that she was dead. On her back, Valya lay with open eyes reflecting the Madonna of Tender-ness moon above them, the slow red stain spreading under her breast.

And then Chapman let go of her wrist and slowly stood up, the gun hanging from his fingers, and waited for them to run him down.